Quiet Time

Katherine Alexandra Harvey

Vagrant Press

Vagrant Press is an imprint of
Nimbus Publishing Limited
3660 Strawberry Hill St, Halifax, NS, B3K 5A9
(902) 455-4286 nimbus.ca

Printed and bound in Canada

Cover image: *Inpatient* © Iness Rychlik
Editor: Whitney Moran
Cover design: Heather Bryan
Typesetting: Rudi Tusek

Epigraph © Camille Rankine from "Emergency Management,"
first published in *The New Yorker*, 2020

NB1608

This is a work of fiction. While certain characters are inspired by persons no longer living, and certain events by events which may have happened, the story is a work of the imagination not to be taken as a literal or documentary representation of its subject.

Nimbus Publishing acknowledges the financial support for its publishing activities from the Government of Canada, the Canada Council for the Arts, and from the Province of Nova Scotia. We are pleased to work in partnership with the Province of Nova Scotia to develop and promote our creative industries for the benefit of all Nova Scotians.

We acknowledge the support of ArtsNL, which last year invested $3.2 million to foster and promote the creation and enjoyment of the arts for the benefit of all Newfoundlanders and Labradorians.

For Jordy and Emma

Some days I want to spit
me out, the whole mess of me,
but mostly I am good
and quiet.

–Camille Rankine

I was born with premature tear ducts, so it was impossible for me to cry. When I woke each morning, my eyes were sealed shut, gooey and filled with pus. My mother would wipe them with a warm cloth so I was able to pry them open and see again. I cannot speak to the moments of blindness, but I remember the absence of something.

I was six months old when the doctor told my parents I would need surgery to open the ducts.

"It will be simple and quick," the doctor stated, matter-of-factly. He had seen this many times, and to him, it was routine. "We just probe the duct to enlarge it."

The doctor couldn't possibly fathom the anxiety my parents felt. Their daughter, the perfect one, the one who had survived, how could she be sick?

We arrived at the hospital on the day circled on the calendar. The walls of the waiting room were painted neon green, covered with images of exotic animals. Zebras, elephants, tigers, lions, and giraffes loomed over rows of interconnected vinyl chairs that linked the expectant children. We were all there for the same reason: we were suffering. Some kids were bald from cancer treatment, others coughed weakly as their parents wiped their runny noses. The corner of the room contained a small plastic table with matching chairs, a bookcase filled with colourful storybooks, and scattered toys as if a child had been ripped away mid-play.

I was sitting quietly in my mother's arms. I had not yet learned to walk or even stand. Had I been free, perhaps I would have crawled around the hospital floor, fitting items into my mouth. My mother gripped me tight.

The nurse, wearing baby-pink scrubs, entered from behind a closed door. "Grace?" she called. Her face was kind, free of lines and wrinkles, as though she were new to the job.

My parents stood, my mother propping me against her left hip, and headed toward the nurse. She held the door open, and I saw an empty hallway ahead. At that moment, lingering on the threshold between sickness and health, my tear ducts opened and I began to cry.

My mother was a superstitious woman. One of my earliest memories was watching her from the back seat of our burgundy station wagon. We had stopped somewhere on our way home. My father climbed out of the driver's seat and disappeared. My brother, William, was strapped in next to me. I reached for his hair, snatching a handful of soft white curls, and tugged. He squealed. I giggled. My mother looked over her shoulder. "Doll, leave your brother alone, please."

She turned around and leaned forward, pulling off her slingbacks and setting her bare feet on the dash. The red nail polish on her toes glistened in the sun as she rotated her ankles.

A loud caw caw caw filled the car. My mother's gaze followed a single crow that had landed next to us in the parking lot. Softly she began a sing-song:

One for sorrow
Two for joy
Three for a wedding
Four for a boy
Five for silver
Six for gold
Seven for a secret, never to be told
Eight for a wish
Nine for a kiss
Ten for a surprise, be careful not to miss

Her delicate hand lingered in the air, and with one eye closed, her index finger drew an X through the bird as it drifted overhead.

"We don't need any more bad luck, children," she intoned, remaining fixed ahead.

I watched as the crow vanished from sight, heading for its nest in a grove of spruce.

Once again, I found myself sitting in that tiny beige room. All these rooms are tiny and colourless. The fluorescent lights buzzed and flickered. A stranger sat opposite me, peering eagerly into my face. Behind him was a small window, a collection of grey industrial buildings beyond it. Minimal furniture occupied the space. We sat on knobbly upholstered chairs separated by a cumbersome cherrywood desk. The smell of stale coffee wafted from a pot, percolating on the edge. A brown so deep it was almost black.

How long has that coffee been sitting there? And who in their right mind would drink it?

The thought made my skin itch. My leg began tapping in an attempt to distract me from a barrage of incoherent thoughts. *Who is this man? Is he married? Why doesn't he have a wedding ring? What's wrong with him? My head hurts. Did I drink any water today? Is it dehydration?*

I pulled the elastic out of my hair, releasing a tight ponytail that was collected at the crown of my head. I pressed my fingers into my scalp, massaging it firmly to alleviate the pressure.

I glanced around the room, focusing on a poster. "If you think you're in hell, keep going." *Is that supposed to be motivational?* I stretched my fingers out, the tendons tightening, and squeezed them into a fist.

Open. Close. Open. Close.

"So, Grace, why are you here?" the man asked.

I answered without hesitation, "Because the psychiatrist at the hospital told me I needed to come."

The man, whose name I had already forgotten, looked at his notepad and scribbled something down. The marker squeaked as it pressed against the paper. My teeth clenched.

The unspoken truth weighed heavily in the room. He knew I had tried to kill myself. It was written on the page in front of him.

A bird landed on the sill outside the window, staring in at me. I stared back. Its eyes, black, vacant, glistening, made the hair on my arms stand on end.

"Well, let's try and figure out why he sent you here then, shall we?"

The smell of putrid coffee filled my nostrils.

I motioned to the pot. "I'm sorry, can we pour that out?"

Dear Sunshine,

I've made a mess of everything. I'm sad and alone and tired of trying, and you're not here. But you never really were, were you?

The doctors say there's something wrong with the way my brain works. They want to analyze my thoughts, study me like a rat in a cage with a cube of cheese at the end of a maze. I told them that maybe, in a previous life, the doctors drilled a hole in my head for the spirits to escape and it never quite healed. They weren't convinced.

They say they're going to make me better. The funny thing is, you were the only one who could have fixed me. But you didn't, did you?

I have to know, why didn't you care? Didn't anyone ever teach you how to love another person? Please, tell me what happened that made you this way. Then maybe I'll be able to understand. I need to understand in order to get better. I need so desperately to get better.

Love,
G

After my mother left for what she claimed would be the final time, I returned home one evening to find her hosting a welcome back party for one of her new, young friends. The house was packed with people who were laughing and shouting over one another. Empty beer bottles and dirty plates were stacked on the counter. A girl was sitting on the couch, cutting up lines of white powder on an oval mirror she had taken down from my wall. Another guy was rolling a joint, busting the weed by hand.

"Grace, come here," my mother beckoned. "I want you to meet someone."

She was elegant and conservative, dressed in black pants and a black blouse that draped off her slender body. Her ankles were exposed, the legs of her pants rolled up. Her feet were bare and flawlessly manicured. I thought of the stinging smell of nail polish remover as, each night, for as long as I could remember, she stripped the red polish from her toes before reapplying a fresh coat.

With arms folded close to her chest, she slowly swayed back and forth, gently shifting her weight from one foot to the other as she often did. She wasn't drinking. I had never seen her drink.

I walked past the painting of a nude woman, her arms bound behind her back, nipples jutting forward, tied to a flaming stake. Her face was soft, her eyes closed, a cigarette dangling between her lips as her head bowed, seemingly about to light her cigarette on the blaze. I crossed the crowded room, making my way between people, dipping and flattening myself to avoid a collision, approaching my mother and the stranger. He was tall, just over six feet, with dark curls piled on top of his head. He had sharp, high cheekbones that protruded just below his eye sockets. His lips were uneven, the bottom much fuller than the top.

"Where's my father?" I whispered to my mother.

"Oh, I don't know." She flicked her wrist dismissively. "In the city with his new girlfriend, I'd imagine." She turned to the stranger.

"This is my daughter, Grace. The one I was telling you about."

The young man reached for my hand and shook it, his emerald eyes lingering on my face. "I'm Jack."

His front teeth were slightly crooked, hugging over one another, the outer edges lifted higher than his canines. His nose seemed ornamental—as if it weren't meant for breathing or smelling at all—with tiny nostrils and meticulously carved cartilage that curved upward. He was wearing a cornflower blue cashmere sweater and holding the roach of a joint between his thumb and forefinger.

"I'll let you two get acquainted," my mother said, as she turned and disappeared through the back door to the patio.

He bent to drop the roach into a half-empty can on the coffee table. It sizzled before dying out. He pointed to the couch, "Join me for a drink?"

Surrounded by a group of unfamiliar people, I sat with Jack as he told me that he and his friend had been on the road for three weeks; they'd driven across the island, taken the ferry, then crossed the border, headed for California.

"Our engine caught fire as we were driving through Arizona." He smirked, taking a long swig from his beer bottle. "We had to call the fire department to put it out."

"No way." I laughed, noticing I was clutching the edge of my sundress. I let go, smoothing it repeatedly. "What did they do?"

"The firemen doused it with some sort of foam," he replied. "We had a pound of weed in the glovebox. Luckily the cops didn't show up. We would have been fucked."

"Was the car okay?"

"No, we had to abandon it and fly home." He sighed. "We never made it all the way."

"That's too bad," I teased. "How are you going to write your Kerouac-inspired memoir now?"

"Well," he paused, intertwining his fingers and pressing them into the back of his head, "maybe you could help me with that. I thought you were the writer."

I titled my head and glanced down, embarrassed for some reason. "I wouldn't say that. Not yet, anyway."

He grinned. I liked the way his front teeth overlapped, his confidence in movement and articulation. The way he smelled: sweet, like almonds, with a hint of spruce.

"How old are you?" he asked, grabbing a bottle of whiskey from the coffee table.

"Seventeen. How old are you?"

"Twenty-three."

I nodded. "Cool."

"Let's do a shot, kid," he said, pouring the booze into two glasses. A red-haired girl stumbled and nearly fell over, cackling as she caught herself against the bookcase.

Jack handed me a glass and I tossed the whiskey down, turning away from him, trying not to gag. "Smooth," I said as I retched.

He chuckled, squinting his bloodshot eyes. "You good?"

"Oh yeah, I'm fine." I laid my shot glass on the Bible my mother used for doodling.

"Hey, don't be so sacrilegious." He nudged me playfully on the shoulder.

"You believe in that stuff?"

"Fuck no. I know God doesn't exist," he declared, his speech slightly slurring. "Science hasn't been able to prove it."

"So you think science is the new religion?" I raised an eyebrow, smirking. "How original."

He allowed his head to fall slightly, shooting me a look. "You're funny. Your mom said you were smart, but what mother doesn't think that about her kid?"

"What's that supposed to mean?"

He shifted, pulling a package of flattened cigarettes from his back pocket, offering it in my direction. "I just wasn't expecting to like you so much, that's all."

At four o'clock in the morning, after everyone had gone home, I went looking for my mother. I found her outside on the balcony in the still night. She was staring intently into the dark woods, smoking a cigarette.

I walked up behind her, standing silently for a few moments gazing up at the sky. The moon was yellow, cratered with grey, nearly full. A few days away from completing its cycle.

"I'm going to marry him," I told her.

I was raised by artists in an isolated town by the ocean, where garbage collection was just a man riding on the back of a pickup truck and the police looked the other way when the trailer park king sold individual cans of beer to minors on the weekends.

Our house was more than a hundred years old. Secured to a dory by rope, it had been floated across the water from another, smaller community. I was told the water rippled as the boat glided through, pulling the house, its furniture and photographs shifting from side to side as it sailed along. Once settled onshore, it was balanced on a row of logs and hauled by horses to its resting place.

I preferred to believe that it was moved by giants. They simply plucked up our two-storey saltbox with their enormous hands and set it gently down on the lawn, like a child playing with her toys.

My parents bought our house when my mother was pregnant. She was twenty-three years old, and beautiful in a way that caused men to fall in love at first sight. Suiters would write poems about her, moaning *Jayde, Jayde, Jayde,* swearing they would die if she didn't return their affections. She was often silent, lost in a daydream. *Sweet Jayde,* they'd say, *come back down to earth.* My father said she exuded a darkness to which he was instantly attracted. They had met at a party. My father saw my mother across a crowded room, later analogizing the encounter to being struck by a bolt of lightning. My mother couldn't remember him being at the party.

My father was a writer, my mother a painter and sculptor.

They had owned a bungalow in the city, but decided to move when my mother became pregnant with me. She spent hours sitting in the living room, her bare legs draped over the arm of a chaise longue, perusing magazines on idyllic small-town living. Their plans were birthed from an old-fashioned notion of romance: two young artists, moving to the country to pursue their careers and raise their family in controlled safety.

My brother, William, was two when they moved. The property needed a lot of work, but that wasn't a problem. My father could do anything.

I was born on the first day of December. Large, fluffy snowflakes drifted peacefully from the sky, clinging to the windowpane of my mother's hospital room. As she clutched me, swaddled in the softness of a blush blanket, she whispered, "Grace, you brought the first snowfall."

Jack sold weed. I used it as an excuse to see him, texting him to buy more before I had even finished my last half-quarter.

Sitting on the oxblood sofa in the living room, I busted some dope with a chipped plastic grinder and poured it into a paper. Specks spilled over the sides, falling onto the table. I brushed them to the floor with the back of my hand. I had meticulously styled my hair, blow-drying it smooth with a round brush, and with much deliberation, decided on a silky black mock-turtleneck dress. I spent an hour carefully lining my eyes, rouging my cheeks, and shaving my legs all the way up to my thighs, just in case.

The front door creaked open and my stomach began to flutter. I busied my freshly manicured hands in an attempt to appear casual. Jack's shoes hit the floor with a thud, and the carpet muted his footsteps as he made his way down the hallway to the living room.

"Hey, kid." Jack smiled, rounding the corner into the room.

"Hey."

"You're quickly becoming my favourite customer." He dropped a Ziploc baggie into my lap, flopping down on the couch next to me.

"That's awkward," I replied, licking the strip on the rolling paper before sealing it. "Because you're not my favourite drug dealer."

He grinned, brushing his fingers through his hair. "Is that so? You must smoke a fuckload of weed."

I placed a joint between my lips, lit it, and took a deep draw, exhaling a cloud of smoke in his direction. "You have no idea." I took another drag before passing it to him; the imprint of my brick-red lipstick remained on the filter. He brought it to his mouth.

"So, I have a plan." I hopped up from the couch. "Let's build a blanket fort and watch a movie."

"How old are you again?" he asked, cocking an eyebrow.

"Shut up." I skipped to my bedroom. "Come on," I called.

"I'm coming."

I grabbed the bottom corner of my comforter, tearing it from the bed. The pillows flew to the floor, knocking against a lamp on my bedside table. Jack reached for it as it swayed in small circles, debating whether it would fall or not, before slowly settling back on its legs.

"Close call," he said.

I shrugged. "I like close calls."

I dragged the blanket toward the couch. My apartment was small, with only a bedroom, an ensuite, and a short hallway that led into the open-concept kitchen and living room. It did, however, have the most lovely backyard—which was rare in the city—so I made the decision to sacrifice spaciousness for the outdoor sanctuary.

As Jack and I began setting up, I remembered building intricate blanket forts with my brother and sister on days when the snow was piled so high it reached the tops of the telephone poles. We'd listen to the radio in the kitchen for the school report, each wrapped in a quilt, only our eyes exposed as the kitchen heaters clicked, smelling of burnt dust. "Closed for the day," the host would announce, and we'd smile inside our cocoons.

"Let's build a fort," William would shout, tossing his blanket to the floor and running upstairs. He was the engineer, Annabelle and I were simply his helpers. The entrance would begin at the top of the staircase and run all the way to the end of the hallway. The sophisticated shelters with multiple rooms were indicative of someone with a mind for compartmentalization, the brain of a problem solver. We filled the darkness with lamps and cushioned it with pillows, collecting them from each room of the house, protective yellow light bathing the dim space. Sometimes, William would carry the tiny television into the fort and we would watch a movie, smushed together.

"After you." Jack lifted the blanket.

I lowered myself onto all fours, the hum of the heaters dulling as I crawled inside. Evening light saturated the burgundy comforter and caused the area to gleam crimson. I could feel Jack close behind me. I settled cross-legged, and Jack did the same. The space was small and intimate, our shoulders slightly touching. I felt safe with Jack, insulated by those recollections of my childhood.

Jack lit another joint, his face illuminated in a glow of orange. The paper and weed crackled as the enclosure filled with grey haze. He licked his lips between each draw.

I stared at him, transfixed. I wanted his lips. My body was both tensed and relaxed, filled with the awareness of his shoulder against mine, hovering between barely touching and touching too hard. I wordlessly willed him not to move.

"Grace?" Jack's head turned and his eyes met mine.

"Yeah?"

"Do you ever wish your parents had stayed together?" he asked. "Made it work, you know? Despite all the bullshit?"

"No," I replied. "I wouldn't wish their relationship on anyone."

He took another draw on the joint, biting his lip. "I'm glad they split."

"That's kind of rude," I laughed. "Why's that?"

He leaned closer. "Because if they hadn't, I never would have met you."

My mother preferred when it was cold. The windows of our home were always open, a hardcover book by Tolstoy or one of the Brontë sisters jammed in place to keep them ajar, even in the winter months. The lace curtains, crisp from the ice that clung to the material's negative space, swayed in the wind. Small piles of snow would collect on the sills and floor, causing me great distress. I would gather it, balling it up and holding it in my hands until it melted. I would warm my fingers, red and throbbing from the cold, by the wood stove.

I was four years old when my mother's belly started to grow. She insisted, more than ever before, on keeping the house cold. As she grew bigger and bigger, the house grew colder and colder. I felt obligated to endure it, to contain my own desire for warmth.

My mother and father sat down with me and explained there was a baby growing in my mother's belly. I was going to have a little sister.

I was terrified she was going to be made of snow and ice like in the fairy tale my father had read me. The woman swallowed a snowflake and became pregnant and, in the end, the infant melted in the heat. I didn't want my sister's life to be filled with coldness, so I did my best to keep the snow away from my mother.

Then, one day, my mother went away. Days passed without any indication as to where she had gone. I kept the windows sealed, watching the snow through the glass. I had no memory of a time before the endless white, and wondered if it would always be this way.

The day my mother finally returned, I heard the car pull in the driveway. I was playing in my room, dressing my dolls in their winter regalia, ensuring everyone in the house was prepared for the arrival of the ice baby.

Downstairs, the door slammed. My parents' hushed voices were barely audible. I jumped up from the floor, barrelling down the stairs.

There Mother stood, a bundle in her arms. Her giant, round belly had disappeared. Her blue eyes appeared flat, with dark circles beneath them. Her dark hair was messy like a bird's nest, as if she hadn't brushed it in days. She was surrounded by bags and strange contraptions. I stepped over a chair with no legs as I moved toward her.

"There's my girl." My father leaned down and grabbed me in his arms. "You hungry, doll?"

I wiggled, shaking my head. He returned me to the floor, and I stood on my tippy-toes to try and see what she was holding. Sunlight reflected off the snow, sending sparkles through the window and onto my mother. The wind howled and the house responded with creaks and moans.

My father made his way to the kitchen. Pots began clanging as he prepared lunch.

"Grace, this is your sister." My mother knelt so I could look at the creature swaddled in a white blanket with pink rabbits. "Her name's Annabelle."

Her eyes were closed, her face squished as if she were already filled with disdain for the world. A quiet gurgle escaped her mouth as it curled into an O. Her brown eyes opened for a second and she looked at me. I reached out to touch her tiny hand, but upon impact withdrew in surprise. It was warm.

For as long as I could remember, I had a debilitating aversion to most fabrics and noises. My parents often joked that I was tactilely and onomatopoeically challenged.

I couldn't handle nylon. Polyester gave me cold shivers. Rayon made my teeth clench. I didn't like hugs or being touched on the back. I once fainted when someone accidentally rubbed two pieces of Styrofoam together in front of me. I had to cover my ears whenever a student made their way to the front of the classroom to sharpen their pencil with the mounted rotary sharpener. If I even thought about the squeak, the soft spot behind my knees went wobbly.

The first night I spent at Jack's place, I couldn't sleep. His striped sheets were made of flannel, and they were knobbed from years of wear. I lay on my back, fully clothed in a cotton gingham pajama set, with my hands on my chest like a corpse, trying not to accidentally touch anything. Jack's face was pressed into the pillow, inches from me.

He twitched, like a koala that suddenly felt it might be falling from a tree, and his arm shot against me. At that moment, he must have remembered I was there. He squeezed my thigh and moved even closer, kicking his leg up and draping it over me. In the process, his foot caught on the leg of my pants. He scraped me with his toenail and then exposed my ankles to the sheets. I could feel crumbs at the bottom of the bed.

Unable to bear it for another second, I shot to my feet. Jack blinked his sleepy eyes open, trying to focus on me in the dark. He cleared his throat, his voice thick. "What's wrong?"

"I can't," I said, tugging at my hair as I paced the small space of his attic room. "I can't sleep here."

Jack propped himself up on his elbow, rubbing his eyes. "Why? What's wrong?"

"The sheets." I continued to pace. "And the crumbs."

Jack laughed. "The crumbs?"

"Don't laugh at me," I whined. "I can't handle it. First the sheets, then the crumbs." I flicked on the light, and Jack shielded his eyes. I pointed. "And your toenail."

Jack was smirking, his pupils constricted, adjusting to the light. "My toenail?"

"Your toenail," I repeated. I felt weak even recounting the incident, but we were both smiling.

Jack pushed the covers off, pausing momentarily in a seated position over the edge of the mattress, and stretched. He then began to pull on his pants that had been in a pile on the floor.

"What are you doing?" I asked.

"Come on, Princess and the Pea." He was on his feet, hugging me to his bare chest. I let my cheek press against his skin. I didn't cringe. "Let's go to your place."

"Father." The word shakily escaped me as I stood in the doorway of my parents' room. "There's a little girl in my room." It was the middle of the night and I had woken with a chill. I opened my eyes to find a little girl, translucent and barely there, adorned in white, sitting at the edge of my bed. Her hair was chestnut brown, twisted into two braids, each tied with a ribbon.

Startled by the sight, I curled myself into a seating position. I blinked ferociously, rubbing my eyes with the backs of my hands.

"Who are you?" I whispered.

"I'm Charlotte," the girl replied.

I clutched the corners of my blanket, yanking them over my head. "Go away."

When I uncovered my head, she was gone. I switched on my lamp. An immediate and harsh light illuminated my lavender room. I hopped up and ran down the hallway to my parents' bedroom.

I knew who she was.

Our neighbour, Mr. Butler, had come to visit one day. We were sitting together on the front lawn, and when my mother went inside to pour him a glass of lemonade, he'd told me the story of the family who'd lived in our house before us.

"Their daughter died of leukemia when she was around your age," he explained, sitting in a deteriorating wooden chair. He was the oldest man I had ever seen. He wore his beige pleated trousers high above his hips, and a baseball cap loosely perched on top of his head.

"What's leukemia?" I asked, stumbling over the word.

"It's a disease. A bad one." He adjusted his thick glasses, his eyes shrunken beneath them.

I was squinting from the sun. The smell of fresh-cut grass wafted through the breeze as I listened to the faint noise of a lawnmower in the distance.

"About a year later, the girl's mother was standing in the doorway and a gust of wind took her." Mr. Butler's hand flew through the air. "She fell and bashed her head on a rock."

I buried my face in my hands.

He paused until I uncovered my face and looked up at him.

"Her husband packed up and left a week later."

My mother returned, carrying a silver serving tray with three glasses of lemonade. She passed one to me and then one to Mr. Butler. "What are we talking about?"

"I was just telling Grace here a little secret." He winked at me and I moved toward my mother, hugging her leg.

Despite the tragedy that had brought Charlotte to my room, I knew she was good. Her energy was calm and playful. Sometimes I would hear her laughing, her light steps creaking up and down the hallway. She only ever came to visit at night.

There were, however, negative forces at work in the house. Sinister memories clutched the mattresses, oozing from the comforters, seeping from the walls, vile and iniquitous. As an adult, I was unable to return. What haunted our house was much more disturbing than any ghost.

I often sat for Jack while he painted me. I could never see my resemblance in his portraits, but as an abstractionist, he said he was capturing my essence.

"Don't move," he instructed. I sat in a faded grey wingback chair by the window, my hair cascading over the headrest, sun streaming on my face. "I can see you perfectly right now."

Staying still wasn't hard for me; neither was being silent. I enjoyed being his object. The way he studied me, analyzing the intricacies of my features. He often spoke of society's obsession with youth and beauty. I think he liked that I was younger than him, and that I appeared even younger than I was. I was like a fantasy. Something he had conjured. He seemed to see painting as a way of preserving the world the way he saw it. The way he saw me. Something that would outlive us both.

Jack approached me, tucking a loose strand of hair behind my ear. He placed his index finger below my chin, tilting my face upward. He was in desperate need of a haircut. His curls tumbled over his forehead and fell into his eyes. Periodically, he would run his fingers through his hair in an attempt to slick it back. The curls would comply for a moment, then fall loose again.

"No, that's not right either." Jack continued to examine me.

I didn't respond. I knew this wasn't intended to be a conversation.

He took both hands and tousled my hair violently. He then extended his thumb, lifted it to his mouth, and, in a series of slow motions, wet it with his tongue. Bringing it down, he let it linger near my mouth before pushing into me, smudging my red lipstick far past the lines of my lips. "That's better, little one."

Returning to his easel, he peered at me. "You'd make such a pretty corpse."

I smiled, my lips pressed together, knowing he meant it as a compliment.

Dear Sunshine,

Remember the day you taught me to paint? You squeezed dabs of colour from tiny tubes onto that block of wood. You told me to go mad. Not to think, just to act. Whatever was meant to come out, would. You didn't care if I wasted supplies or made a mess. You told me it was all important to the process.

We were happy that day. You were happy, filled with equanimous hope. Such a rarity, to see you that way. I wondered why, on that day, you came alive. Was it the paint? The prospect of creation? Or was it the transmission of knowledge, something for which you had passion and promise?

I often remember that day with fondness. It reminds me that it wasn't all bad. We had our moments.

Thank you for that.

Love
G

When my family and I road-tripped across the island in the summertime, my siblings and I were each allowed to choose one outing. Something we would all do together. Annabelle always wanted to find a playground. The biggest, most modern playground in town. She loved swinging on the swings, higher and higher until she couldn't bear it anymore. My father pushed, holding her by the waist and running back and forth, eventually thrusting the swing over his head so she would skyrocket high above the metal bars.

William and I would sit in the grass nearby with my mother as she smoked cigarettes and read books about Antarctic exploration, the men who had been lost or swallowed by ice floes. I studied the minute, almost undetectable transformation in her face as she turned each page. Her dark eyebrows twitching. The space between her nose and the arch of her Cupid's bow narrowing as she pursed her lips together. I still feel a fuzzy shiver when I think of those men who so consumed her.

William liked any outdoor activity—fishing, camping, going to the beach. A typical little boy who wanted to be a man. He would dig in the backyard for worms, filling a container with dirt and shoving them, pink, squirming, and slimy, into their temporary home. We would walk to the water, my father with his fishing pole over his shoulder, tackle box in hand. William would march by his side, carrying his Batman fishing rod in imitation.

I always asked to visit museums and historic houses. I liked to imagine the lives people had lived, their homes protected by those who felt they were sacred. I liked that nothing was out of place. No dirty dishes in the sink, or toys scattered in the parlour. It all seemed so perfect. It was how I wanted my life to be.

I would move quietly through each space, closing my eyes and picturing the little girls who had lived there. They were just like me, only they were born a hundred years ago. I wanted to slide under the velvet ropes that separated me from the untouchable past.

My favourite place was a house built by twin brothers. It had two side-by-side front doors. Once you entered, each frame was a mirror image of the other. Two foyers with shiny, jewel-encrusted chandeliers, two staircases with winding, dark-wooded banisters, two parlours with large bay windows and matching purple velvet sofas, two dining rooms with long oak tables, two kitchens with pot-belly stoves and pantries lined with emptied shelves. I saw the families, a delicate reflection of one another, standing, having their portrait painted, or sitting in the dining room eating their meals simultaneously, each oblivious to the other.

It was like a parallel universe. It gave me hope that if you were making a mistake, someone, somewhere, in the same situation was choosing correctly.

Jack wanted to see where I'd grown up, through my eyes. He had been nagging me for weeks to take him. He thought it would be romantic, returning to the place where we had initially met.

"I don't know," I said.

I was sitting at the kitchen table, hugging my legs into my chest with my chin resting on my knees. My head was throbbing, a dull ache that seemed deep, deep, deep in my brain. I couldn't remember the last time I had woken up without being strung out or hungover. Jack seemed to thrive in this state, bouncing around the kitchen, frying eggs between clearing away half-empty bottles from the night before.

"Come on, little one," he cooed. "It'll be fun."

I glanced out the window at the backyard. Amberish autumn light glistened on the trees as images of the old house flooded my aching head: my siblings running through the halls, my father's office door with its contorted red-faced mask, my mother baking bread, swaying in the kitchen. I saw the little house, sitting vacant on an acre of unmanicured land. I saw the stream that ran parallel to the road, filled with rocks that William, Annabelle, and I would collect and keep as pets because we thought they resembled creatures. I saw the narrow path through the forest that led to the ocean. It had been years since my parents had remarried and moved on. For a second, I longed to see it too.

"Fine." I sipped my coffee. "I'll try to find my key."

It was mild outside so I threw on a jean jacket before locking the apartment and climbing into Jack's car. The skin on my arms felt invaded, as if an army of ants were crawling beneath it. I scratched with a degree of desperation. Letting my nails sink into the soft flesh, I imagined tearing it off piece by piece, exposing my raw, pink, throbbing innards.

Jack noticed my scratching and took my hand, holding it as he drove, smiling intently.

Is he trying to torture me?

The roads were clear and the sun was beating down on trees that were full with brown, red, and orange foliage. The heat made the air in the car stale and heavy, and I found it hard to breathe. Light reflected in my eyes so I opened the visor to shield them. Glancing in the mirror, I made eye contact with myself for a second. Long enough to see something I didn't want to see.

I slammed the visor shut as Jack slowed to take the exit. I laid my head against the window and watched as the landscape changed from desolate highway to farmland. Bundles of hay resembling fluffy marshmallows speckled the sprawling fields. The smell of manure filled the car and I quickly rolled the window up, covering my nose and holding my breath.

"Geez, Grace. Warn me next time, will you?" Jack grinned.

I rolled my eyes. "Gross."

A murder of crows dotted the black wires of the power lines. I counted as we drove. *One, two, three, four, five, six, seven.*

I silently recalled the rhyme my mother had taught me.

One for sorrow
Two for joy
Three for a wedding
Four for a boy
Five for silver
Six for gold
Seven for a secret, never to be told

We drove along the water's edge. A few small boats, not yet stored for the winter, were docked in the harbour. It was all so familiar. The hill we used to climb, where I'd fallen more than once and skinned my knees. The pond where we swam, fearful that eels would coil themselves around our ankles and pull us into the depths. The wharf we'd cast off from, reeling in our lines only to discover we had nabbed another sculpin, before promptly unhooking and returning the bottom-feeder to the sea.

As we approached that final corner, I noticed a cottage overlooking the headland was being torn down. The top half was stripped to its bare bones, only studs and corners remaining, while the first storey was perfectly intact. I remembered how my mother had frequently sent me there to borrow a cup of sugar or a block of butter. I wondered what had happened to the family.

I was jolted back to the present as my old home came into view.

"Right here." I lifted my hand to point, and felt my entire arm go numb.

Inhale. One. Two. Three. Four. Five.

Jack pulled into the driveway.

Exhale. One. Two. Three—

"Whoa," Jack interrupted my silent counting. "Looks like the set of a horror movie. It's so different from what I remember."

The jungle gym was collapsing in on itself, rotten and buckled to the right. The yellow slide had detached and was lying on the ground nearby. The grass on the lawn was wilder and taller than I'd seen before. My father's chainsaw was sitting alongside the barn, covered in rust.

The evergreens in the driveway had grown larger, their limbs scraping the car door as I opened it. I made my way toward the entrance, peering into the window of my father's office as I passed by. The lace curtains were drawn but I could see the outline of a bookcase overflowing with dusty novels.

The orange-red paint on the house was chipped and peeling. A consistent, rhythmic buzzing overhead caught my attention. I looked up and noticed a small papery wasp nest, swirled with greys and browns.

"Careful." I pointed to the nest as Jack approached. "Looks like someone else has moved in."

We arrived at the doorway to find a tattered wooden broom placed diagonally across it.

"Is that your fancy security system?"

"Ha ha, very funny." I took in its damaged bristles. "It lets people know you're not home." I lifted it out of the way, setting it against the house. "So people know not to come by and visit."

"Why would you want people to know you're not home?" Jack swatted at a wasp with one hand as it flew by, digging in the pocket of his bomber jacket with the other. He pulled out a joint, lit it with his Zippo, and inhaled deeply. "Seems like a good way to get robbed."

I shrugged with only one shoulder, unable to get them both to cooperate, before sliding my key into the lock, praying it wouldn't fit. I turned it hesitantly until I heard a quiet click.

An old pickup truck rounded the corner; slowing, the driver craned his neck to see who could possibly be going inside. I lifted my wrist weakly, offering him a slight wave.

"Who's that?" Jack asked, puffing on the joint, his eyes following the moving vehicle.

"No idea."

I pushed the door open and stepped inside.

Everything was exactly as I remembered. The Persian carpet that ran up the stairway was covered in debris. The familiar painting of the nude woman engulfed in fire stared at me. Her erect nipples seemed a fitting response to the temperature in the house. The heat likely hadn't been on in years. I shivered.

"I want to see your room." Jack was already making his way up the stairs. They creaked under his weight.

"It's the one at the end of the hall." I followed him, the air growing denser with each step, my hand dragging along the banister. The yellowed wallpaper was peeling and had begun to curl where it met the ceiling. I stopped to pick at a piece, noticing newspaper glued beneath. The only words I could decipher were "boat ran aground" and the year 1877.

Jack disappeared inside my room.

My throat was dry, my pulse quickening as I rounded the corner, passing my parents' closed bedroom door. I could see them standing behind it. I could hear their controlled yelling as they fought.

Suddenly, Jack screamed. My skin prickled as I sprinted to the end of the hall. "Jack?"

He was sitting on the bed, flipping through a magazine with Mary-Kate and Ashley Olsen on the cover.

"I thought your room would be morbid," he said, smirking. "It's just a typical little girl's room."

The lavender walls. My books, my photographs, my stuffed animal collection. Most everything was perfectly preserved, unsullied by the passing of time. The fireplace mantle that displayed my snow globe collection was covered in shards of glass. The water inside must have frozen over the years, causing them to shatter. I lifted one and twisted the handle to activate the music box. It began, laborious at first, clicking and missing notes before settling into a fluid melody.

"Why did you scream?" I noticed a small slice on my thumb from the broken glass. Blood trickled from the wound so I placed my finger in my mouth to soothe it, comforted by the warm, metallic taste.

"I didn't scream." Jack peered at me, his eyebrows moving together, two indents forming at each brow's edge.

I glanced around the room, noticing a mound of dead houseflies and sowbugs in the corner.

"You okay?" he asked, taking my hand and examining it.

I sat down next to him, feeling increasingly unsteady. "I'm fine."

"You're shaking." He pulled my thumb toward his mouth and wrapped his lips around the gash.

I stared at him blankly.

Letting my hand drop, he moved to hold my face, kissing me gently. I could taste blood again.

I lay back, overwhelmed, my stomach clenched into a ball of tightly knotted parts.

Standing above me, he pulled my tights and panties off. I couldn't move.

He ran his fingers up my dress as the walls and slatted ceiling blended. He undid his belt and removed his pants, stepping out of them one leg at a time.

I lay immobilized.

Grabbing my legs and pulling me to the edge of the bed, he spread my knees apart with his and thrust himself inside me. A sharp, immediate pain shot through my body. I recoiled, but there was nowhere for me to go.

I opened my eyes and looked up. It wasn't Jack. My mouth snapped open and a scream erupted as I shoved him off.

He hit the wall with a thud.

"What the hell?" he snapped, pinning me with an angry look.

I was released. I shot up and grabbed my clothes, heading for the door. "We need to get the fuck out of here."

Annabelle had always been an anxious child. With her long black, whip-straight hair and fair, unblemished skin, she reminded me of the porcelain doll that sat on my grandmother's shelf. The one we were never allowed to play with. When she learned to talk, she began regularly having panic attacks.

Annabelle and I shared a room until we were teenagers. At first, we had a queen-sized bed, but later, having decided it was time for us to be big girls, our parents bought us each our own twin bed. The nighttime was the worst of all, and after the lights were shut off, Annabelle would make me promise she wasn't going to die in her sleep. I'd make the promise, despite my reluctance. I knew I could never be an authority on the matter. But I always got up and pushed our beds together so she would be less afraid.

One afternoon, William and I were playing with his Batman and Robin action figures in the living room. He had carefully removed them from their packaging, to which they were always returned, resealed, and stacked neatly in his dresser drawer. It was tranquil and glittery outside, and light shone through the lace curtains onto the carpet in a kaleidoscopic pattern.

"Come on, Robin," William said, adjusting the arms of his figurine. "Follow me."

I clutched Robin by the waist, making him hop up and down as I moved him along the floor, following Batman. "Let's get the bad guys."

Playtime halted as Annabelle's panicked cries reached us from upstairs. We dropped the toys and ran up the steps, taking them two at a time. The first thing I saw were her pale legs facing out, dangling between the wooden rails of the staircase from the second floor. Then, as I took more stairs, her waist-length French braids and head, trapped between them. She was sobbing and calling for our mother, but she wasn't there, and neither was our father.

William reached for her and held her little face in his hands, squishing her cheeks together. "Anna, you need to try and calm down. We're going to get you out, I promise."

Annabelle was jerking her head violently like a caught animal. I turned away. She looked so desperate, so scared. I couldn't watch.

"Gracie, I need you to go to the kitchen and get some butter," William instructed.

I nodded, ran to the kitchen, and grabbed a block from the fridge. I started unwrapping its grey aluminum as I moved; stumbling, I caught myself on the rail. It had already begun melting in my hand as I passed it to William.

"Anna, I'm going to put some butter on your cheeks, okay? Then you should be able to slide out."

Her dark brown doe eyes were fixed on him as she gave the slightest nod.

"Deep breaths, just like we practiced." They began inhaling in unison as he buttered her cheeks. They exhaled together.

"Pull your head back. On the count of three: one, two, three." William guided her head backwards, but it remained stuck. She wailed and began thrashing again, her cheeks becoming taut and then plump with the railing's pressure. As her screaming intensified, my heartbeat throbbed from my throat to my fingertips.

William dropped the butter on the carpet and sprinted up the stairs, rounding the corner so he was standing behind Annabelle. "Anna, listen. I need you to trust me, okay?"

Droplets of tears were now falling, clinging to her spidery lashes. "Okay."

"Move your head over here." He reached over the railing so she could see as he pointed to the left. "And stay still, like when we play freeze-tag. Can you do that for me?"

She nodded, and I moved to wipe the tears from her cheeks with the back of my sleeve. I smiled, halfheartedly.

William motioned to me with his head, a slight tilt, and I knew. "It's going to be okay," I whispered.

William's leg shot forward and I clamped down on her face, locking it in place. The flat of his foot hit the railing. I shrieked, and so did Annabelle. William's foot raised up again, over and over, kicking furiously until the wood snapped, and our sister was free.

We all hid in William's bedroom until our parents returned later that evening. Our father saw the damage and called us into the kitchen. "What the hell happened to the railing?"

William replied with his head down. "Anna got stuck. We couldn't get her out."

My mother was standing at the kitchen counter with her back to us, cigarette in her mouth, working a mound of red clay that sat on a pile of old newspaper.

"Why didn't you call Mr. Butler? I told you, if there's ever an emergency to call next door. The goddamn number is right here." Our father jabbed at a piece of paper stuck to the fridge, a phone number scribbled in his illegible handwriting.

"She was scared." William's voice was small, barely audible. "I didn't know what to do."

"Do you think money grows on trees? Who's going to pay to fix it, huh? Do you have a secret job I don't know about?"

I stared at the floor, counting the floorboards in my head.

One, two, three, four, five, six, seven, eight, nine, ten, eleven, twelve, thirteen, fourteen, fifteen, sixteen, seventeen, eighteen—

"Go to your rooms, all of you. I don't want to look at you."

My mother didn't even turn around.

"I need attention," I called into the empty hallway.

I was sprawled out on the sofa, wearing nothing but a baby-blue silk chemise. I clutched a half-empty wineglass by its stem, swirling it in small circles. I watched the liquid rise and fall, waiting.

The wind outside was fierce. The trees shook with a veracity that paired well with my unsteady and desperate need for adoration. It felt so much a part of me that, for a moment, I wondered if I was the creator of the wind. "Jack!" I whined.

Jack appeared from the kitchen, carrying a platter of cheeses and cured meats. Placing it on the coffee table, he tilted his head, looking me up and down. "Babygirl."

"I need attention," I repeated, rolling into my side. My hair fell into my eyes but I didn't brush it away.

Moving toward me, he knelt in the space between the coffee table and sofa, tucking the unruly hair behind my ear. "Look at you. My little blue princess."

He ran the tips of his fingers along my bare toes. "Okay, tell me where it hurts."

I let my head hang off the edge of the couch, observing him upside-down, his fingers still on my thigh. "Everywhere."

Jack chewed his bottom lip and when he released it, the pink skin remained white for a second. "Well, we're going to have to do something about that."

He touched my ankle, smiling the way he often did where his teeth were exposed but the corner of his mouth remained slightly lowered. "Here?"

I nodded, pouting.

He kissed my ankle tenderly.

Dragging his fingers to my knee, he glanced at my face, his eyebrows lifted. "Here?"

I bit the inside of my cheeks to keep from smiling. "Mhm."

He kissed each kneecap, his curls brushing against my outer thighs, tickling ever so slightly.

Continuing upward, his fingers rested on my inner thigh. "Here?"

I craned my neck out of its twisted position to see him. "Especially there."

Jack guided his lips to my thigh and gave it little kisses all over. His mouth was wet and warm. His face was strawberry flushed in small, concentrated blotches.

"I'll be right back." He stood, extending his pointer finger before disappearing around the corner. "Don't you dare move," he called, out of sight.

I felt like molasses dripping on the couch, amorphous and sticky.

Jack returned with my wooden hairbrush in his hand. He shifted me into a seated position, sat down behind me, and began brushing my hair in long, fluid strokes.

I was suddenly staggered and deeply touched. Saddened without fully understanding why.

"Jack?"

"Hm?" He stopped brushing and I turned toward him.

I realized the room had gone dark. I reached for the lamp's chain and tugged, illuminating the space. "Did I tell you about my mother?"

He chewed his bottom lip again, then shook his head. "What about her?"

My throat was dry, my lip trembled as I tried to curl it open. I knew what I had to say. But as I dug to find my voice, a forceful gust hit the front door, rattling the knocker, as if someone were trying to get in.

My mother often disappeared. It was her greatest act, like a lady who volunteers to enter the box at a magician's show before being spun round and round until the curtain drops, and everyone's amazed to see that she has vanished.

Early in the morning, I'd hear the disruption of gravel in the driveway as she made her escape. Lying in bed, my stomach gnawing at itself, I would trace the trim on the ceiling with my index finger, straining to listen as the sound of her engine faded, wondering if she would ever come back.

Those days were spent in a quiet, crystalline state. My father would recede into his office and I'd stand outside his door, braiding the long, wiry hairs of the angry-faced mask that was tacked to it, or press against the door, holding my breath. Most often, though, I would wait on the front lawn, sitting on the swing, clutching its bristly ropes with two hands, straining my ears for the sound of a car in the distance.

When she finally returned, just after bedtime, she'd push our half-shut bedroom door open with a gentle greeting and perch herself on the end of my bed. As my eyes followed the ember tip of her cigarette in the darkness, she would tell us about her adventures out in the world, filled with a vibrancy that was almost alien to me. I would learn to cherish these glimpses of her. I loved her best when she was this way.

"I went to an abandoned community," she explained one evening over plates of roast beef and mashed sweet potato, my father still entrenched in his office. My mother's eyes were marvellously blue in the candlelight. They reminded me of a swimming pool, reflecting everything that dared to come close enough to gaze down, searching for the bottom.

"I went inside an old house," Mother announced. "It was filled with all sorts of things. All sorts of treasures." She looked at my sister, who was giddy with excitement, swinging her feet under the table.

"What'd you find?" Annabelle asked, clutching her fork.

"Well, the kitchen table was set with beautiful china dishes. Everything was perfectly placed." She moved her hands around the table, indicating where each item lay, before turning to me. "You would have loved it, doll."

My ears prickled with the mention of her there, thinking of me. That we appreciated the same sorts of things. We were similar, she and I, and that made me exceptional. I thought when she disappeared she forgot all about us.

"It was like the family had been right in the middle of dinner—" She stared down at her untouched plate of food. "Then, poof, they were gone."

I had manically cleaned the entire apartment, disinfected every surface, swept and mopped the floors, washed and folded all the laundry, scrubbed the spot behind the toilet that no one ever dared to touch, and polished the few remaining wineglasses that had not yet been broken.

Jack and I went for a run around the lake, and I smiled and nodded toward each person we passed as Jack manoeuvered heavily a few paces behind me. He lost his breath easily, and we stopped multiple times so he could smoke a crumpled joint he pulled from the inside of his left sneaker.

I fed off the sunshine, and Jack fed off of me. I relished my role, smirking at him. "What's the matter, old man, can't you keep up?"

I was the gatekeeper of warmth.

When we returned to my apartment, we opened a bottle of wine and sat on the plastic patio furniture in the backyard, basking in the glow of the yellowed sun.

"What're you painting now?" I asked, topping up his glass.

He lit a cigarette and exhaled a line of smoke with his head tipped back. "I'm working on a piece about class repression."

"What does it look like?" I wondered how that might be represented in an abstract painting.

"I'm experimenting with darkness and light." He shifted in his chair, shielding his eyes from the sun. His hand created a shadow that spread across the bridge of his nose. "Shapes that don't really fit together. Movement that doesn't go anywhere. Stuff like that."

"Interesting." I glanced around the yard. The budding lilac tree filled the air with a heady cocktail. I felt intoxicated by its sweetness. I leaned against the headrest and sipped my wine.

"So, should we call our guy?" Jack asked after a few moments of silence.

I grinned. "Definitely."

It didn't take long for the dealer to pull into the driveway. Jack climbed into the passenger seat while I sat in the living room, watching through a slit in the curtains. I always worried something might go wrong.

The car door slammed and I heard the faint call of Jack's goodbye.

He barrelled through the door, holding a little baggie of white powder between his thumb and forefinger, shaking it back and forth.

"Who's ready to get fucked up?" he shouted.

I threw myself back onto the couch, launching my feet into the air, kicking wildly. Jack sat down next to me, grabbing my legs and placing them in his lap. He retrieved the scales from the drawer in the coffee table and weighed a dose for each of us.

"I'll get the toilet paper." I hopped up and ran into the bathroom, grabbing a roll from the cupboard. I returned, tossing it at Jack.

"Thanks, baby." He wrapped the white powder in a piece of paper, twisting the top like a tiny present as I settled next to him, extending my hand.

He placed the drugs in my open palm. "Cheers."

As I popped it in my mouth, I willed it to stay intact. Despite my hopes, the toilet paper cracked, and the bitterness of the MDMA hit my tongue. I took a long gulp of beer, swishing it around in my mouth before swallowing.

"Why does mine always break?" I whined.

"Because you, my sweet little girl, are a rookie."

The sun was beginning to set. Jack drew the burgundy curtains, sheltering us from the outside world. I lit two cherry-scented candles to mask the smell of dope and cigarette smoke.

My concept of time had disappeared.

"Do you feel anything?" Jack asked. "I think I'm starting to come up."

It always began with a feeling of mounting anxiousness, then a pleasant warmth in my stomach. It was like I was in a car with a busted muffler that was hydroplaning. I felt compelled to share every word that flashed through my overfiring brain.

I was surrendering to the rapture when the urge to vomit struck. I ran to the kitchen sink, both hands gripping the edge. My shoulders convulsed as my head thrust forward, heaving. My fingers tingled from the cool, clinical feel of the steel.

Wiping my face with my sleeve, I faced Jack. He was tugging at the collar of his Velvet Underground T-shirt, and when he let go, it hung asymmetrically around his neck. I couldn't stop smiling. "Yeah, I think I'm starting to feel something."

I turned the music up even louder, the drums reverberating, building something inside me that I felt could only be alleviated with destruction. I jumped onto the coffee table. Jack followed. Dancing savagely, we thrust our limbs, leaping from the table to the couch to the chair, screaming along to the lyrics. The furniture slid and knocked against the walls as we hurled our bodies around.

The song ended, and in the silence, the energy in the room vanished. The space was dim, the candles burning, a bloodish-red glow emanating from the sofa. A slow song began. Jack extended his hand to me. "May I have this waltz?"

I reached for him and stepped close, wrapping my arms around his neck. He placed his hands on the small of my back, humming in my ear as we swayed. He smelled burnt, like something that had recently caught fire.

"Why don't you ever talk about your father?" I asked, looking up. The blacks of his eyes had swallowed the green parts.

"It's hard for me."

"Well, do you feel like talking about it, with me?"

Jack was silent for a moment. "I guess." He paused; he seemed to be searching for the right words. "Apparently he wasn't a very nice guy. I don't remember him, but my brothers were older, so they do."

He spun me in a circle under his arm, pulling me back in close.

"He was pretty abusive to my mom. He was a mean drunk."

He dipped me low, and held me there.

"Anyway, he got involved with the wrong people and ended up in prison."

He pulled me back upright.

I wanted so desperately for him never to hurt again. I stopped. "Jack, I'm so sorry."

"Thanks." He looked past me. He was sucking on the inside of his cheeks, the concaves and ridges barbarically pronounced. "You know, I've never told anyone that before."

I pressed my cheek against his, feeling the scratch of his stubble. "Well, your secret's safe with me."

Eventually, we flopped on the sofa, but just as we settled, the chemicals peaked again.

I jumped up. "Let's do something to remember this night."

I grabbed the pack of cigarettes from the coffee table, lit one, and passed it to Jack.

"Burn me." I inched toward him. "So we'll always remember."

His smiling eyes darkened as he stood up.

"I want you to mark me." I felt the drumming between my legs now. "I want to be only yours."

"Are you sure?" he asked, taking a long draw on the cigarette and attempting to ash into an empty beer bottle. He missed and it landed on his bare foot.

"So sure." Pushing up my sleeve, I presented him with my forearm.

"Okay, but if it hurts too much, scream 'bananas' and I'll stop."

Laughing, I bent to brush the ash from his foot. "Why 'bananas'?"

"I don't know, it seemed like a good safe word."

The room was breathing, expanding and shrinking in my peripheral vision. I grabbed onto the sofa with one hand. "I'm ready."

I felt the heat as he drew the cigarette close and pressed the tip into my soft skin.

I withstood the pain for a second, then recoiled, squealing and shaking my arm before blowing on the wound. I glanced at Jack, his gaze shifting from my arm to my eyes. The smell was horrible—like rotting beef in a frying pan.

"Fuck, that hurts." I smiled. The throbbing between my legs had somehow connected with this fresh pain. The current travelled, pulsating from my forearm to my pussy.

"Good girl." He stroked my hair, admiring his creation.

I spent most summer days with Annabelle, playing in the unkempt field alongside our house. We'd pretend it was a jungle, amusing ourselves with games of hide-and-seek, Ring-Around-The-Rosie, or make-believe we were contortionists in the circus, practicing cartwheels and bridges until we collapsed, side by side, giggling and exhausted.

One afternoon, while running wild through the meadow, I tripped and gashed my knee on a rock. I was stilled.

My knee thumped with pain as I sat there, staring at the blood, hypnotized. I had never seen anything so beautiful.

"Mother!" Annabelle screamed, running across the lawn toward the house. She disappeared inside, and I continued to watch as the blood doubled, then tripled in size.

My mother came rushing out with Annabelle following close behind. Kneeling beside me, her brow knitted, Mother asked, "Does it hurt, doll?"

I glanced from the wound to my mother and back again. "Not really."

"That's my brave girl." She smiled, wiping the blood with a wet cloth before opening a tube of antiseptic and applying the jelly, all while humming pleasantly to calm me. She peeled open a bandage, covered the cut, and kissed my forehead.

"Mother, what are these green lines?" I asked, pointing at my wrist.

"They're your veins." She traced her finger along my forearm. "They transport blood around your body to keep you healthy and strong."

My eyes followed her finger, mesmerized by what might be inside of me. "Why are they green, if blood is red?"

"It's a little trick our eyes play on us," she explained, crumbling the bandage wrapper in her other hand. "Even though it looks green, it's actually red. It's the way light is reflected."

I tilted my head at her. "Why would we not see something the right way?"

"We don't always see things clearly," my mother whispered. "That's why you have to look closely. You can't always trust what you see."

I brought my nose close to my knee, staring with widened eyes as the dot of blood slowly grew, spreading across the nude Band-Aid, saturating the fabric.

Annabelle stood at a safe distance. Her voice came out softly. "Is Gracie okay?"

"She's going to be fine." My mother stood, repeating, "she's going to be fine."

Lying back in the tall grass, I watched it sway above me and, feeling its pulse, my attraction to blood congealed with the scab on my knee.

I arrived at the psychiatrist's office half an hour early, as instructed. They told me I needed to fill out some forms prior to seeing the doctor.

Standing in the hallway, I could see a woman sitting behind a circular desk. Her head shot up as I pushed through the glass doors.

She smiled. "Hello."

"Hi." I advanced to the desk, resting my elbows on the counter. "I have an appointment with Dr. Brace."

"Grace?"

"Yes."

"Great." The receptionist began thumbing through stacks of paper until she found what she was looking for. She clipped the piece of paper onto a clipboard, attached a pen, and passed it over the counter. "I'll need you to fill this out."

I scanned the form and flipped it over. It was double-sided, containing dozens of questions asking me to rate my various moods on a scale of 1 to 5. Happiness, hopefulness, insomnia, family support, relationship with a significant other, relationship with friends, stress about money, anxiety, depression, suicidal thoughts.

I filled it out, then slid the clipboard back to the receptionist, smiling nervously.

"Have a seat," she gestured. "Dr. Brace will be with you soon."

I stood in the waiting room, unable to sit still. A young woman, covered in tattoos, was seated in the corner, her head down, looking at nothing. I picked up a pamphlet on suicide prevention and skimmed through it, unable to comprehend any of the words.

"Grace?" a voice boomed behind me.

I flinched.

"Sorry, I didn't mean to startle you." He was a tall man, early sixties, with wispy grey hair and a mustache. He wore round glasses and carried an extra twenty pounds in his midsection. "I'm Dr. Brace. You can follow me."

I followed him down the long, narrow hallway, past open and closed office doors. I scratched my jawline vigorously. My shoulders ached, and I could barely hold my head up.

With each step, I thought: *You still have time to run.*

Left foot: Just turn around, Grace.

Right foot: You don't need him.

Left foot: You know exactly what he's going to tell you.

Right foot: You're fucking crazy, he can't help you.

He excused us as we stepped around a woman who was vacuuming the grey carpet.

Left foot: Too late.

I was standing in his office.

Dr. Brace shut the door behind us, quieting the noise of the vacuum and trapping me inside.

"Have a seat," he said, motioning to an off-white armchair in the corner. I'd always imagined a couch.

Wheeling an ergonomic office chair out from behind his desk, he sat facing me, lifted a file folder and a pad of paper, and placed them in his lap.

"How are you, Grace?" He wrote the date in numbers and slashes at the top of his page before lifting his gaze.

"I've been better."

He tilted his pad slightly upward, noticing my eyes on it. "I'm sorry to hear that. I see you've been referred to me by Dr. Jones," he said, peeking at my file. He paused to read over the notes. "She said you've been feeling sad. Finding it hard to get out of bed. Haven't been to work in weeks."

This was something I'd grow to disdain. A medical professional reading to me from my file, using my own words against me.

"I guess so." I ran my fingers through my ponytail, shaking the hairs that stuck between my fingers onto the rug.

He watched the strands of blond hair fall. "What else are you feeling?"

I knew exactly how I felt, but few ways to describe it.

"I feel like I'm disappearing."

"Okay." Dr. Brace straightened his glasses in mild anticipation, as though we were already getting somewhere. "Can you elaborate on that?"

"I feel like I'm not real." There were three light bulbs in the room: two lamps and one overhead. "Like I'm watching my life from afar." Four posters, each featuring some sort of inspirational quote. Each turned my stomach equally. "I'm afraid I'm going to disappear and no one will notice." Three degrees, each stamped with a large red seal and framed in black.

"Are you harming yourself?" he asked. "Cutting? Burning?"

I tried to speak but I couldn't.

He jotted something down on his pad of paper. I could no longer see what he was writing. I just stared at him.

It was chilly in his office, and my nose had started to drip. As I reached for a tissue, I noticed my fists were clenched so tightly that when I released them, my fingernails left half-circle indents on my palms. I pulled a Kleenex from the box on the table beside me and wiped my nose.

"How long have you been cutting?"

"A couple of months," I finally stammered. "I guess."

He turned the pad face down in his lap and placed his hands on top. "It's okay," he reassured me. "I only want to help you. But I need you to be honest with me."

I nodded, crumpled the dirty tissue into a ball and clutched it.

"When was the last time you cut yourself?"

At that point, I wasn't familiar with the way the mental health–care system worked. I didn't know then that you learn to lie or embellish to avoid getting what you need.

"Last night," I whispered.

"Where do you usually cut yourself?"

With my head down, I followed the ecru rug's circular pattern with my eyes. "My wrists."

"Have you ever had to go to the emergency room?"

When I wasn't looking at Dr. Brace, I became more aware of his voice. He used very little inflection, a performative tone that was meant to soothe. It made me uncomfortable. I shifted in the chair, uncrossing and recrossing my legs at the knee.

"Grace?"

I shook my head.

"Can I see your wrists, please?"

No one had seen my wrists in months. I was careful to wear only long-sleeved shirts. Since it was winter, this didn't appear unusual. I was cognizant to never roll them up while washing my hands, letting the fabric dampen and gradually dry against my skin.

Slowly, I pulled back the sleeve to reveal my left wrist. I was naïve; I thought I had to do whatever he said.

Thirteen ridged slashes, one after the other, like lines of cocaine. It was always thirteen. Lucky number thirteen. The cuts were horizontal, starting at the base of my palm and ending just below the crease of my elbow. The whitest and most delicate part of my skin.

I studied his face, hoping for a reaction.

Nothing. He was good.

"Thank you." He regarded the notes in his lap, jotting something down.

My cheeks reddened as the anger surged and the shame built. I yanked my sleeve back to cover my wrist.

"Why do you cut yourself?" he asked, searching my eyes for some sort of tell.

I needed to see my blood to make sure I was real. I liked the way it felt as it trickled down my arm. It was punishment. It was a way to feel something. It was an outlet for my fucked up thoughts. A level of control was required. Never too deep, otherwise you might have to go to the hospital, but just deep enough to feel that release. The warmth of blood soothing the sting of the freshly exposed wound. I would use anything I could get my hands on. A razor blade, a pen, a nail, a needle. I preferred something that made a clean cut. Precision was key. I was always surprised how little it hurt. I hardly felt it.

"I don't know."

Dr. Brace sat in silence, an attempt to intimidate me into saying more. I stared at the exposed parts of the floor, counting the tiles. *Thirty-two.*

The clock on the wall ticked, drawing my attention like a baby crying out for its mother.

"I'm going to prescribe you an antidepressant, something to make you feel a little better."

It wasn't a suggestion. This strange man, whom I had just met, knew what was best for me.

"And let's set up an appointment for you with a psychologist."

MENTAL STATUS EXAMINATION

Grace on a one-to-one presented as a somewhat seductively dressed 18-year-old. Her affect was clearly anxious. Her mood, she described as depressed. When symptoms of depression are reviewed, indeed she describes significant mixed insomnia, tendency to be withdrawn and show little interest. She has significant feelings of tiredness and low energy. She feels that her concentration is poor and she is unable to relax, with excessive worrying or nervousness. She describes classic anxiety symptoms of a panic type with panic attacks occurring approximately once or twice a week. She has been prescribed Ativan to be taken on a permanent basis.

Client did spend a period of time partying when she came to university (i.e. drinking alcohol). She drinks a lot and has not moderated this by her own report. She smokes marijuana daily. She has done so for the last couple of years.

Client denies suicidal ideation or intent. She does, however, cut herself and has done so over the past four or five months. These are relatively superficial and I examined some superficial scarring on her forearms today. She claims she doesn't know why she does this.

DIAGNOSTIC FORMULATION
Axis 1 (Major Mental Illness):

a) Generalized anxiety disorder
b) Major depressive episodes

Axis 2 (Personality Features):
Significant borderline tendencies.

Whenever my siblings and I misbehaved, my parents would threaten to lock us in "the ratty closet."

The closet in my and Annabelle's bedroom was connected to the attic. It had a sanded-down brown door with an iron latch that secured from the outside. It wasn't used for anything other than the storage of old toys we had outgrown, and my mother's sculpting tools. I had never been inside—I'd never even opened it—but I imagined it was inhabited by hideous monsters.

I'd bar the closet before bed, pushing our toy kitchenette against it, and lie awake listening to the sounds of nails scratching and scuttling along the floor above.

One night, after listening to the scratching for hours, I heard a thump and the weight of something shifting, falling, dragging its claws against the walls.

After a few moments of silence, it began pushing against the door. The plastic kitchenette squeaked as the latch creaked. I rose from my bed, moving toward the closet. Annabelle was still sleeping soundly, her soft breathing steady. I knew I had to protect her. I had to kill whatever was in there.

I grabbed a toy pot, my fingertips pulsating. I slid the kitchenette aside as the noise continued. Scratching, thumping, the closet door shifting. I inhaled deeply, my lungs filling, and held on to my breath as I reached for the latch, unhooking it slowly.

I threw open the door, and a creature was in the room. All I could see was a set of glowing eyes. A noise escaped from deep inside me. A sound I didn't even know I was capable of making—high-pitched and deafening. I began swinging. The pot hit the floor, over and over, knocking things in the dark.

Annabelle was awake, shrieking, standing on the bed.

I swung one final time, a hard squish, air escaping, the smell. All the noise stopped.

My parents were in the doorway. They flicked on the overhead light, their faces tired and concerned. "What's going on?"

I looked at the toy pot. It was covered in blood and pink bits. Then I stared down at a flattened rat, its insides spread over the floor, its skinny, furless legs still twitching.

Jack and I would often pack up and leave the city. Without any concrete plans, we'd hop in the car and head west. On the road, detached from the material world, we were most ourselves. The version of us I wanted to be.

With the windows rolled down, the wind whipping through, my hair flew in my face. I struggled to separate it into two even sections before braiding each side and fastening them with a band. "There's a spot my grandparents used to take us when we were kids," I said. "Want to go?"

"Sounds good." Jack lit a cigarette with his Zippo. "Lead the way."

The highway was filled with black circular patches, the destruction from last winter freshly repaved. A combination of fluffy evergreens and branchless stumps lined the road, trimmed back to give drivers adequate warning of moose, should they dart into oncoming traffic. There weren't many other cars on the road, but each time Jack overtook one, swerving into the passing lane, he smirked to himself.

We turned off the highway, heading north. A rectangular green sign indicated there were fifty-six kilometres remaining until our destination. I remembered this drive, the way the view from my window morphed from barren highway to a series of small but lively communities with one sharp turn of the wheel. My grandfather in the driver's seat, peeking at me through the rear-view mirror, only his bright blue eyes visible. When he caught my gaze, he'd smile and reach around the back seat to give my knee a playful squeeze.

I took out my phone and searched for the place. I dialled the number, pressing the phone to my ear as it rang. The man on the other end said they didn't have anyone coming to stay, and it was ours for as long as we wanted. "One night will be fine, thank you," I told him. "We'll see you shortly." I slipped my phone back into my purse. "Okay, we're all set. Now we just need to stop and get supplies."

"We need beer and steaks." Jack flashed me a grin.

"Nothing but the essentials." I reached over and ran my fingers along the back of his neck.

The roads were beginning to mist as we came upon a small grocery store. The sign read *Mary's Groceries.* I couldn't recall ever having seen this place, but the building certainly wasn't new. The clapboarding was weather-worn and faded, and the lettering on the sign was severely chipped.

Jack pulled into the parking lot, turning off the engine and leaning in to give me a quick kiss. "You're so beautiful." My hand still on the back of his neck, I squeezed gently. For a moment, I felt intact and untouchable.

When we entered, the cashier stopped talking to an older man who was propped against the counter, wearing rubber boots and a plaid shirt. They both turned to look at us.

"Hello," she said, nodding her head in greeting.

"Good day," I replied, making my way down one of the aisles.

I collected bags of chips, frozen mini pizzas, and instant coffee while Jack headed to the coolers at the back. Nothing was fresh. No fruits, no vegetables, and definitely no steak. Everything was pickled and frozen, which I should have expected. Preserved foods were essential to communities like these, since the populations were small and it took time for supplies to reach them.

Jack and I met at the cash register. He was carrying two cases of beer, one in each hand, and a package of vacuum-sealed meat. The man in plaid was gone.

"Not from around here?" the cashier asked. She was in her fifties, with frizzy yellow hair that had clearly been box dyed, her grey roots forming a shadow across the middle of her head.

"Nope, from the city," Jack replied, laying the items on the counter and pulling a few bills from his wallet.

"From the city, eh?" She smirked, the gap between her front teeth brown from cigarette smoke. "What brings you folks out here?"

"Just looking to get out of town. This one here is a writer." He laid his hand on my back. "We're always on the move, trying to find inspiration."

I examined the woman as she and Jack conversed. There was something beautiful about the way she hit the buttons on the cash register, removing change from the slots without even glancing down. The fluidity of her motions like that of a classically trained ballerina.

"Well, how about that? " She bagged our items, nodding her head repeatedly. "Always nice to be in the country. Where you staying?"

"A little farmhouse. Not far from here," I replied, reaching for the bags.

She scratched her cheek with her acrylic fingernails, leaving behind a red imprint. "Old Man Caleb's?"

"Yeah, that's the one."

"Be careful." Leaning across the counter, the cashier held herself up on her elbows. She smelled like stale cigarettes and jasmine. "I hear that place is filled with ghosts."

Jack snickered, but I maintained eye contact, searching for a sign she was joking. Then she winked.

"Yeah, we'll be sure to watch out for ghosts," he scoffed, heading for the door.

"Have a wonderful day," she called. "Thanks for shopping with us."

The door dinged as Jack pushed his way through.

We climbed into the car, continuing on. I stared out the window, wondering if the cashier was Mary, or maybe her mother had been Mary and the store was passed down to her. I thought about her life, and if she was happy running the place, the most exciting part of her day conversing with locals. We hadn't been driving for long when a sign that read *Caleb's Retreat* appeared. "Turn here," I said, pointing left down a gravel road.

As we ascended the hill, a two-storey white farmhouse with a picket fence surrounded by pristinely manicured grass came into view. I felt a bead of emotion drop from my throat to my stomach, as though I had swallowed a pebble. It was exactly how I remembered it: idyllic, nostalgic, untainted. A part of the past that had remained pure.

Three brown chickens pecked at the ground, scuttling quickly out of our path as we approached. We parked alongside the house and I hopped out, scurrying after them. "Look," I called to Jack. "How cute are they?"

He eyed me. "Please don't ask me if we can take them home with us. I draw the line at kidnapping poultry."

I jokingly pouted as we unloaded the car, heading to the house.

I pulled the screen door open and checked the doorknob to see if it was unlocked. I knew it would be. People in these towns never locked their doors. There was no danger.

The hallway was papered with vertically striped chartreuse wallpaper, bunches of deep green leaves peppered between the lines. The kitchen was immediately to the left. It was small, with a potbelly stove square in the middle of the room. A mint green gas range sat adjacent to the sink. I placed the bags on the counter, spotting a note taped to the fridge.

Welcome!
Come next door to check in.

"We have to go next door to check in," I called as Jack walked in. "You can stay here if you want. I'll go."

"Okay." He opened the fridge and began unloading the beer bottles. They clinked together as he lined them up. "I'll put the stuff away."

I made my way outside, and as I crossed the lawn, I spun to take it all in. An old burgundy barn with white hearts painted on the doors rested lonely in the field. I remembered my grandfather telling me that people painted hearts on barns to ward off bad spirits. I passed the root cellar that had been dug into the side of a man-made mound with its tiny wooden structure perched on top. There were few trees, mostly crabapple, with underripe fruit not yet in season.

I approached the neighbouring house, which looked nearly identical to the one we were staying in, and rapped on the door.

A tall man wearing overalls appeared. "Come in, child," he said through the screen. His words were drawn out, slow and careful. "No need to knock."

"Hi," I said, stepping inside. The smell of cooking met me. "I think we spoke on the phone. We're checking in. Grace and Jack."

"My God." He examined me, his hands in his pockets. "I haven't seen you since you were a little girl."

I smiled awkwardly. "I know, it's been a while."

"How're your grandparents?" he asked, his grey moustache moving as he spoke.

"Oh, um," I hesitated. "They're dead."

His eyes remained fixed on me. "I'm sorry to hear that."

"Thank you." I shifted my weight from one leg to the other, tugging at the ends of my braids. "We all have to go sometime, though, I guess."

He nodded, and continued nodding for what felt like a little too long. "Well, I know you're here now. You can come pay when you leave." He dug in the pockets of his overalls until, finding what he was looking for, he extended his hand to me. "Here's a key, but the door is always open. You know where I'll be if you need anything."

"Great, thank you," I replied.

"Nice to see you back here, Grace," he said as I turned to leave. "I'm sure you'll see that not much has changed."

I could hear a muffled television in the next room, the pulsating glow spilling through the open door. Someone sat in a recliner, their back to us. I knew they were listening to every word we said.

"It's good to be back." My palms had begun to dampen. I wiped them on the back of my dress before reaching for the door handle.

I rushed through the grass, back toward the house—toward Jack—with a sense of urgency. I thought of my grandparents, how they had loved this place. We would come here every summer, playing board games in the evening, or watching old movies on VHS, then in the mornings, listening to Billy Joel on the radio over pancakes and fried eggs that had been freshly laid.

"Hey," Jack called as I entered the house. "I turned on the barbecue. Want to sit outside?"

"Definitely." I walked into the kitchen and wrapped my arms around him, feeling much more at ease.

The mist lifted, leaving us with a clear, warm, and deeply blue summer evening. It was still, perfectly so, the air heavy and threatening, as if a storm were brewing. I could sense the impending electricity of thunder and lightning. The chickens had returned to their coop, but their occasional clucking and purring was still audible. The moon was low and brilliantly white. It seemed only a high jump away.

Jack and I had settled on the swinging wicker lawn chair just outside the front door, the smell from the charcoal barbecue lingering. I opened two beers, passing one to Jack as I sat in his lap, kissing him on the neck between sips. "I love this place."

His fingers moved along my thigh. "Me too."

We stayed outdoors until it was dark. The still country air invigorated a sense of rebellion in me, as though I were a child again.

"Wanna play tag?" I hopped up and tapped his shoulder. "You're it," I screamed, running full force across the empty field.

"Oh, you're dead!" Jack shot after me, knocking his beer over in the process.

The grass was damp from the mist, moistening my sneakers and bare ankles as I ran in circles. Jack chased me until my lungs hurt. He bounced back and forth, trying to corner me.

My legs were getting weak but I kept pushing until I slipped, falling to the ground with a thud.

Jack stood over me, looking down.

"Okay, okay," I panted. "I surrender."

"Is that so?" He tilted his head. "You surrender yourself to me?"

My heart was thumping in my ears. "I do."

Jack bent and scooped me up, carried me up the stairs, and tossed me onto the bed. As he removed his belt, wrapping one end around my wrists and the other around the iron bed frame, I noticed a crucifix mounted directly above the doorway.

Jack undressed me quickly and, with one eye on my naked body, pulled his own clothes off before climbing on top of me. I watched his face, the delicacy of his features starting to harden, angling severely, the lines running parallel and down. His eyes were domineering, like a mountain cat who had narrowed in on its prey.

The springs squeaked with each thrust, and as the bed frame thudded against the wall, his belt rubbed against my wrists, creating a friction that was starting to tear. Suddenly, he pulled back, striking me hard across the face with his open palm.

Frozen in place, I stared up, my eyes filled with stinging tears. Horrified, Jack scanned my face.

The hot imprint of his hand was branded onto my cheek.

"Grace, I'm so sorry." He climbed off of me, untied my hands, and began stroking my cheek. "I don't know what happened."

I couldn't speak. I wanted to say it was okay, but my tongue was stuck to the roof of my mouth. My gaze returned to the crucifix.

"Baby, say something."

I managed to climb out of bed, walk to the bathroom, and lock it behind me. Sliding to the floor, I sneezed, covering my mouth with the crook of my arm. Sitting upright, I pressed my back hard into the door and sneezed again, spotting a bathmat embroidered with a single crow. Grabbing it, I flung it at the wall with all the force I could.

I glanced out the window at Old Man Caleb's house across the lawn, watching as their lights shut on and off over and over until everything went blue.

Reaching for the sink, I stood and examined my face in the mirror. My cheek throbbed with a magenta hue. I opened my mouth and moved my jaw back and forth, running my fingers along the mark. I didn't think it would bruise, but it stung like hell. Bringing my face close to the mirror, I searched my eyes. Their blueness had deepened, without any light reflecting in them. My black mascara was smeared into the creases below. I had liked being hit. I was excited by it. My quickening breath fogged my reflection as I wondered what was wrong with me. I sure as hell couldn't tell Jack; he'd think I was crazy. Or did he already know?

I let the cold water run before splashing my face to soothe it, drinking a handful, then grabbed the hand towel to wipe my mouth. Catching myself in the mirror, I noticed the towel was embroidered with one crow. "What the actual fuck?" I tossed it down and ripped open the door.

Jack was sitting in the corner like a wounded animal, a cigarette in one hand, his face in the other. He shot up, moving toward me, and hugged me before lifting my chin to look into my eyes. "You know I would never hurt you."

"I know." My face tightened as I broke eye contact. "It's okay."

"I just got carried away." He held onto me tightly. "It will never happen again. I promise."

"Okay." I nodded, slipping free from his arms. "Let's just go to bed, it's been a long day." I walked to the bed, pulled the covers back, and climbed under.

Jack meandered to the opposite side and slid in beside me. He quickly fell asleep, clutching me in desperate remorse.

I lay awake for hours thinking of the flickering lights next door. Jack was breathing in a quiet pattern, twitching ever so slightly, and when I finally drifted off, it was with the visualization of thunder and lightning's veracity.

The next morning, I woke to Jack setting a tray on my stomach. I pulled myself into a seated position.

"Good morning, my angel." He kissed my forehead.

"Good morning." I stared at the tray in my lap. Bacon, eggs, toast, strawberry jam, coffee, and orange juice had been carefully arranged on top of a doily. He'd placed a bouquet of wildflowers on the bed beside me.

"Where did you get all this?" I asked, lifting the coffee to reveal an embroidered crow on the doily.

"The food came from the store. I tried to go back to the place we went yesterday. Mary's, wasn't it?"

"Mhm." I took a bite of toast, crumbs falling onto my nightdress.

"Anyway, strangest thing. I couldn't find it anywhere. I drove around for an hour. It was like it just disappeared." Jack made his way around the bed, straightening the comforter as he spoke. "I ended up finding another spot. It was pretty much exactly the same. So, no harm no foul, I suppose."

I brushed the crumbs off my chest. "That's really weird."

"Yeah. Maybe I just got turned around." He scooped up the flowers and held them out to me, looking adorably proud. "I picked these on my way home."

"You've been a busy boy." I took them, trying to shake the memory of last night. "Thank you. You're officially forgiven," I said, even though I wasn't sure that I meant it. I didn't want to upset him with my emotions. I wanted the discomfort to go away. "Come here." I pulled the blankets back and dragged him under the covers, almost knocking the tray to the floor.

We lay, eating and feeding one another until, intertwined, we drifted back to sleep.

When I woke, Jack was gone and it was quiet in the house. I lifted myself out of bed and walked down the hallway, stopping for a moment to inspect an old black-and-white portrait that hung on the far wall. The man, with his suit and middle-parted hair, startled me. People always seemed so irritated in these portraits. He was quite expressionless; the vertical line of his mouth indicated neither a frown nor a smile. I thought it was strange I hadn't noticed him the night before.

"Jack?" I called.

There was no response.

I began descending the staircase, each step creaking as it bore my weight. Each step bringing the downstairs area further into view.

As I reached the halfway point, I glanced down at my bare feet, feeling as though I'd stepped in something warm and sticky, but there was nothing there. When I lifted my head, the man in the painting was standing at the bottom of the stairs, his face twisted into something unrecognizable, moaning loudly.

I screamed and dropped onto the stairs. Grabbing for the rail, I slid down on my bum. The face continued to weave in on itself, like bread being kneaded, until it settled, fully formed. Caleb was standing there, smiling politely.

"I'm so sorry, dear." He moved toward me, helping me to my feet. "I didn't mean to startle you."

"It's fine. I'm fine." I was trembling; my legs shook as I held my hand to my chest, exhaling through my mouth. "I'm easy to startle."

"Are you sure?" He was wearing the same outfit from the day before. "I just wanted to make sure you kids made out okay."

"Oh, yes." I was still clutching the rail with my sweaty palm. "Let me grab my purse to pay."

"Consider it my treat, in honour of your grandparents." He nodded his head benevolently.

"That's really not necessary."

"I insist." He put his hand on his heart. "Just come back and see us again soon, okay?"

"Okay." I made an effort to smile. "Thank you."

The old man headed for the door. "One last thing, Grace." He stopped, turning once again to face me. "You've always had the ability to see signs. Don't ignore them."

"Excuse me?"

He opened the screen door. "I said, don't forget to sign our guestbook."

"Oh, yeah sure." I watched him leave before hurrying over and slamming the door. My hands continued to shake so I shut my eyes, breathing, counting. Trying to forget. Trying to remember. *One, two, three, four, five. Five, four, three, two, one.*

When I opened my eyes, I noticed the table in the entryway with a coil-bound, golden guestbook sitting on top. I began thumbing through it until I came across my grandfather's writing: *Max, Sophia, William, Grace, and Annabelle.* I felt a pang of grief as the door opened, and I swung around to see Jack. "Thank God," I whispered.

"What?"

"Nothing. Come here and look at this." I reached for him. "It's from my grandparents' last visit with us."

He put his arm around me, took the pen, and signed our names.

As Jack loaded up the car, I took one last look around the property. It was a beautiful day, picturesquely blue and white, and all indication of inclement weather had been completely erased. Sunshine twinkled on the house's windows as the brown chickens pecked away at the grass below.

Jack started the car, and I climbed into the passenger seat.

"Come back soon," the old man called from the lawn.

I held up my hand, waving in appreciation.

Jack glanced around. "Who're you waving at?"

Dear Sunshine,

Did you ever want to get married? We never talked about it.

I always thought weddings were these morbid ceremonies where two people promised one another they would never change their minds. 'Til death do us part, happy or sad, logic be damned. It just never made sense to me.

When I was a little girl, I never dreamt of my wedding day, like most do. I didn't adorn my head with lace curtains, mimicking a veil. I never imagined walking down the aisle, arm in arm with my father. I never saw myself saying "I do." The obligation was always too great.

Maybe it was just me. Maybe I was the unusual one.

What did you want? Did anyone ever ask you that?

Love,
G

I was prescribed bupropion by Dr. Brace. A common side effect is seizures, so I became fixated on the fear that I would have one.

When I was in the seventh grade, I went on my first date with a boy named Steven at the rundown theatre in a nearby town. He was epileptic. He wore an engraved medical bracelet around his wrist so people knew what to do if anything were to happen.

A few days after our date, one of my classmates spread the news she had heard from her mother. The school was alive with gossip before the first period.

One person who didn't know, though, was his best friend, Daniel. He'd showed up late for school that day. I was standing by my locker in the empty hallway when he came up beside me.

"Hey, Grace." He was shorter than me; he hadn't yet gone through a growth spurt like most of the boys in our grade. I hunched, trying to make myself smaller. He must have noticed, his dimples deepening as the corner of his mouth drew up.

When Steven took me on that date, we had doubled with Daniel and his girlfriend, Rebecca. Steven bought me popcorn and candy because I couldn't decide which I wanted. During the movie, he'd reached over and placed his hand on mine, which was lying palm up in my lap. He gently stroked the base of my thumb with his. It was greasy and warm from the popcorn butter, but the gesture was sweet.

"Hey, Daniel." I cleared my throat. I paused, glancing down at the checkered floor in an attempt to steady myself. "I guess you haven't heard."

"Heard what?" he asked, his eyes widening.

"Steven died," I whispered, my voice cracking. "He had a seizure and fell in the shower."

Daniel's face showed absolutely no reaction. He blinked a couple of times.

"He hit his head." I noticed my legs were shaking from bending, so I stood upright, but I continued to shake.

He stared at me, his head tilted up, our height difference now glaringly obvious. "Oh, okay," was all he said, and then he walked away.

The funeral was held in Steven's hometown in a cathedral that sat isolated on a cliff overlooking the ocean with fingers of headland jutting around it. The winds were high and waves crashed on the rocks below a parking lot filled with cars and confused people, dressed in black, clutching their hats and one another, making their way inside.

The church smelled of pine and incense. Multicoloured light leaked onto the altar, streaming through a stained-glass image of the Virgin Mary. I don't think any of us kids fully understood what was happening. I watched as a group of boys made paper airplanes from their memorial pamphlets and let them fly, snickering when they hit the bald spot on the back of an older man's head. One of the boys hissed "bullseye" before high-fiving his friend.

I followed the line of people. I wasn't sure where it was going, but I was trapped in its movement. Wails erupted from the front of the church. The closer I came, the more uneasy I felt.

I reached the front, and the man and woman who stood before me parted ways, revealing an open cherrywood casket lined with red velvet. Steven was lying inside. His eyes were closed, his mouth tightly shut. He looked as though he had been stuffed, like a taxidermized animal that had been hunted and put on display. Wearing a black suit and red tie, with his hands resting on his chest, his skin was so white it emanated blue. The people behind me commented, "He looks so peaceful." He looked nothing like I remembered.

I only glanced at him for a second before my chest heaved sharply and I started sobbing. A woman put her hand on my shoulder and ushered me to a pew filled with my classmates.

The choir sang mournful hymns while Steven's two-year-old niece ran up and down the aisles. Her footsteps and laughter reverberated in the expansive space. Steven's mother and father sat in the first row, quietly crying. The two noises began to meld, their timbres so alike they became indistinguishable from one another.

I stared up at the decrepit three-storey row house. A couple walked by, screaming at one another. "Fuck you, you fucking asshole." The woman's voice was shrill.

"Fuck you," the man yelled back. "Good-for-nothing whore."

"Can't I just wait outside?" I asked, pulling a cigarette from a pack in my pocket.

"You're going to look sketchy if you do that," said Jack.

"Who cares?" I snickered, lighting the cigarette. "No one fucking cares. Everyone's always afraid of looking sketchy."

Jack exhaled and grabbed my arm, digging his fingers into my skin. "Can we not do this right now?"

"Fine." I tossed my cigarette to the ground and pushed past him. I tried the front knob; it was unlocked in anticipation of our arrival.

We entered into a small porch with two doors: one to the left with the letter A, and another straight ahead labelled B.

Jack motioned to the second door. "It's upstairs."

As I opened it and ascended the staircase, the smell of dope hit me. The carpet lining the stairs had a pungent must, as though it hadn't been replaced since the house was built, likely over a hundred years ago.

"Hello?" Jack called.

"Yo, in the living room."

We reached the top of the stairs and followed the sound of the voice. Garbage bags were taped over the windows, and there was nothing hanging on the walls. The dealer sat on a ratty, ash-coloured futon. He had scraggly, greasy hair and was wearing a shirt full of burn holes. A cold sore on his bottom lip leaked clear fluid. The coffee table was lined with empty beer bottles. A box of baggies and scales sat in front of him. I felt I might catch a disease just being in the room.

"What can I do for you today?" he asked.

A cat sprang from the corner like a flying squirrel, caterwauling. I hopped out of its path. "Jesus Christ."

The dealer didn't acknowledge me or his cat. Dealers usually ignored me. I liked it that way. I wasn't interested in interacting with them.

"We're looking for some ecstasy," Jack said.

"I've got some yellow guns," he replied. "They'll blow your head off."

I wondered how many times he'd used that sales pitch.

"Take it easy, Señor Escobar," I muttered under my breath. I wanted to tell him that in the grand scheme of things, he was so insubstantial it was almost heartbreaking. I wanted to yell that he didn't fucking matter. Instead, I ignored his idiotic jokes as Jack unfurled some bills we'd rolled up to snort coke with the night before.

"Thanks, man," Jack said as the dealer handed him a baggie.

"Anytime."

I gave the room one final look before turning toward the hallway, sprinting down the staircase, and whipping open the front door. A sense of relief washed over me. It was humid and my clothes were starting to stick to my back. The evening breeze was refreshing.

"You're a prick," I said as Jack appeared.

"You're fine." He slapped my ass playfully. "Stop being so dramatic."

"Fuck you, and fuck your half-baked Pablo."

We walked quickly without speaking to one another. The less we spoke, the more we could focus on getting home, and the faster we got there, the quicker we could get high.

I unlocked the front door to my apartment. The walls were beige, the standard colour for most rental properties in the city. It was easy enough to paint over as people came and went without much notice.

I ran to the living room and plopped onto the couch. The two chairs alongside the sofa were old and ugly—grey and made of some sort of itchy material. I had purchased them at a thrift shop. It was all I could afford at the time. I never sat in them, only on the oxblood sofa, which I had inherited from my grandmother.

I unlaced one of my shoes. "Jackass," I called, tossing it at Jack as he entered the room.

"Hey." He leapt on top of me and began tickling my ribs. I squealed and thrashed, trying to wiggle free as I yanked the other shoe loose. I kept hold of it, hitting Jack on the head repeatedly.

I managed to drag myself to the other side of the couch as Jack ducked, dodging my blows. His shirt was unbuttoned a little too far, exposing his triangle of chest hair. He was glistening; tiny beads of sweat clung to his nose as he tried to pry the shoe from my outstretched arm.

"Stop," he demanded.

"Make me."

"Stop." He was smiling, and that smile made me forget that anything else existed. It was just me and him. I dropped my shoe.

Panting, I stood up and adjusted my dress, which had twisted itself tightly around my legs in the struggle. I moved to the mirror and reapplied a coat of lipstick, wiping the lines around my Cupid's bow with my index finger. Jack pushed his curls back before reaching into his pocket for the baggie.

"So, you still mad at me?" he asked, selecting four pills from the bag.

I grabbed two from his open palm, popped them in my mouth, and swallowed. "I won't be soon."

We'd planned to attend a party at Jack's friend's place. It was a space-themed funeral, in honour of the Mars rover whose batteries had died.

I had bought sheets of sparkly hot-pink foam paper and was sitting on the floor, busily cutting celestial shapes with a pair of kitchen shears, while Jack sat above me, rubbing my shoulders and chain-smoking. I was in the process of hacking the letters for *Long Live Rover* when I was overcome with sadness. Or maybe it was happiness. It was hard to tell. My head fell forward.

"Baby?" Jack dropped his cigarette in his beer bottle and leaned forward, placing his hands on my face. "What's wrong?"

"I don't know." I looked up at him with wet eyes.

His pupils were huge.

"It's just so sad." I let my head bob back, moving my jaw in circles, grinding my teeth together.

"What is, baby?"

"Everything." I was crying so hard I could barely breathe.

Jack moved to the ground and wrapped his arms around me.

Between sobs, I managed to say the words, "I just loved that little guy so much."

Jack burst out laughing. The noise was like stepping into a warm bath and being submerged in water. "You are so fucking cute." He kissed my cheeks, my forehead, my nose and chin. "And way too high to go anywhere." Guiding my head into his chest, he laughed again. I purposely rubbed my leaking nose against him.

"Gross," he screeched, using his shirt to dry himself. "You're crying and snotting all over me."

My tears turned to uncontrollable laughter and hiccups. I wiped my eyes and nose with my sleeve, and grabbed the baggie of pills from the coffee table. "Well, I guess since we're staying in." I popped two more, chasing it with what was left of my whiskey, before continuing to mash my wet face into Jack's shirt.

"You're sick," he teased as he ducked away, a dark spot of moisture imprinted on the centre of his shirt. He swallowed a couple more pills and hoisted himself back up onto the couch.

I picked up my Polaroid camera and turned it toward Jack. His mossy velvet dress shirt was covered in sparkly planets. His hair was mussed from running his fingers through it repeatedly. Sitting on that oxblood sofa, he was bright and blurry among an endless sea of dullness.

Click. Whoosh.

Jack was watching me in silence, his mouth slightly agape as I floated aimlessly around the living room, grinding my teeth. I was moving in a stop-motion of sporadic jerks.

I approached him and climbed into his lap. He looked completely enamoured. I leaned in to kiss him and our teeth collided. Two rogue satellites barrelling toward one another, crashing and fragmenting. His tongue was dry and rough; all the moisture had been sucked from his mouth. He stood, and I wrapped my legs around him. He stumbled and we fell against the wall, knocking the mirror. It fell hard and fast, shattering as it made impact with the hardwood. He knew I was superstitious. Stopping, he stared at the cracked mirror.

I picked it up carefully, examining the damage. My face reflected in tiny shards. I threw my head back, bearing all my teeth. "Fuck!" I shouted.

"Fuck."

"Fuck!" I turned to him.

"Fuck!" he shouted back.

We screamed "fuck" over and over at the top of our lungs until I dropped to the floor, grabbing the sparkly sticker paper. Ferociously, I cut the letter *F* and stuck it on the bottom of the smashed mirror.

"What are you doing?" Jack asked.

"Shut up." I waved the scissors around. "You're not the only artist around here, you know."

"Be careful, lunatic," he warned.

I howled, cutting the letter *U* swiftly. Then *C*. Then *K*. I returned the mirror to its hook on the wall.

I stood back to study my work. "Now, that's going to be worth a fortune."

I had known James for as long as I could remember. He'd lived around the corner from me in a two-storey canary-yellow house with wooden shingles on the bluff by the ocean. His mother's garden was notorious throughout all the neighbouring communities, earning her the nickname "the flower lady." On days when the torrid sun hit just right, I'd stand in front of her garden for hours, admiring the multitiered flowerbeds, counting and grouping the varies species and colours as the water shimmered and shook just beyond.

Our mothers were friends, so we often dropped by for tea and biscuits in the afternoon. They would sit in the kitchen, sipping from floral teacups while smoking cigarettes, gossiping about the neighbours and their newly renovated kitchens and bathrooms. My mother listened, taking deep drags on her cigarette, as James's mother complained about her job, how underappreciated her skills were there, and how she wished they would just lay her off so she could file for unemployment.

Sitting cross-legged on the floor in the next room, James and I would watch cartoons, half-listening as the threads of their conversations reached us through the open door. I knew my mother couldn't care less about the neighbours' renovations or their financial situations, and in that moment, I realized how deeply bored she must be.

James and I would sit together on the bus to and from school. It was always unbearably loud, kids yelling, taunting one another and whipping paper balls back and forth. We'd slouch down on the grey vinyl seat, pressing our knees into the cushion in front of us, retreating from the madness. When we hit a bump, we'd screech, lifting off. We doodled mythological creatures with felt-tip pens in his notepad or played tic-tac-toe in the condensation on the window. Nobody ever won, but we played anyway.

In the afternoon, the bus would drop us at the corner by my house, the town softened and white, blanketed with snow. James would walk me home, kicking up snowflakes with his boots or leaning to make a snowball with his mittened hands, tossing it as far as he could into the distance. He'd stand on the corner and wave goodbye before continuing to his house.

One day, as we neared my house, James noticed the empty driveway.

"Where's your car?" he asked.

"I'm not sure," I said. But I knew. "I'll call you later."

I walked along the path to my front door and slowly pushed it open. It felt particularly cumbersome, as if it were made of stone. I made my way down the narrow hallway, passing my father's open office door. When I rounded the corner, I found my father sitting at the kitchen table.

"Where's Mother?" I asked.

My father looked at me through cloudy eyes; a deep line imprinted between his thick salt-and-pepper eyebrows. I knew she was gone. He didn't have to say it. But I wanted him to. I needed to hear the words. He just continued to stare and then let out a heavy sigh. Blood gushed to my face, making it hot and blotchy. I turned and ran out of the house, past the front lawn, stumbling through the rough terrain and the woods to James's house. I narrowly avoided colliding with a massive evergreen, my vision blurred by tears.

I arrived at James's house, bending to collect pebbles from his driveway, and hurled one at his window. Nothing. I hurled another. This time, his head appeared as he drew back the curtains, sliding the window up.

I was panting, my heartbeat hammering in my ears.

"She's gone," I shouted. "Again."

I dropped to the ground, hugging my legs into my body. I was sobbing and trembling; I felt like I was going to explode through my skin. James was at my side within seconds, kneeling beside me. He wrapped his arm around my shoulder. "It's going to be okay," he whispered. "She'll come back. She always comes back."

Jack moved in after we'd been together for a few months. With him came all of his art supplies: his tiny tubes of oil paint, his palettes, his rolls of canvas, and one of the smaller easels from his studio. We dragged the oxblood sofa aside so he could set up in front of the large frosted-glass window that faced onto the street. It bothered me that the couch was no longer the focal point in the room, but I didn't say anything to Jack.

When we woke that first morning, I followed him to the living room. Stopping at the coffee table, he retrieved a bud of weed from a glass jar, busting it by hand and sprinkling it into a rolling paper. He placed the joint between his lips, allowing it to dangle there as he stood in front of his easel, tilting his head and heaving great sighs of discontent.

He had been fixated on this particular piece since we met. I gazed at him from my perch across the room. He was wearing jeans but no shirt, and his hands were stained with lemon-yellow paint. Lighting the joint, he took sharp, quick inhales, smoke escaping from his mouth, fanning and lingering in the morning light. The sun reflected off the broken mirror hanging on the wall and I shifted my head to get it out of my eyes.

"Something's missing," he said, slapping down the paintbrush and turning away from his easel. "I can't figure it out."

I pulled my sweatshirt over my knees as I hugged them into my chest, grabbing for my bare toes. The red polish had chipped and needed to be redone. I attempted to conceal them so Jack wouldn't see the imperfection. "How can I help, baby?"

My eyes traced the chaotic yellow lines, speckled with indigo. I never understood his paintings, but that's the way it was with us. He couldn't comprehend the underlying meanings of what I wrote—the poems about my childhood, and the complications of my past—but we admired each other's talents, and supported one another through a mutual understanding that art was vital.

"No, nothing." Jack smiled at me. "Just be here with me."

I sat there all day, drinking coffee and reading poetry by Sylvia Plath. Jack and I spoke very little, enjoying the comfortable silence. The room smelled of dope, cigarettes, and turpentine. My eyes focused on his bare back, pale and smooth, watching as his muscles tensed and relaxed with each stroke of the brush.

Soon it was afternoon, and Jack poured up two glasses of whiskey. He passed me a tumbler and clinked his against mine.

Jack lit a new cigarette using the still-burning end of another and, downing the amber liquid, snatched the painting, letting it fall to the floor. He bent, selecting a blank canvas from his collection piled in the corner, and placed it on his easel. He squeezed a dab of red oil paint onto his palette and, blotting at it with a sponge, he began.

But soon he stopped, setting down the sponge and turning to watch me. His eyes, green and glittery, traced the lines of my lips. He stroked the stubble on his cheek. "You're my muse," he shouted, playfully throwing his head back.

He laid his palette on the coffee table and sprang toward me, scooping me up in his arms. I squealed and dropped my book. He smelled of sweat and sap, sharp like the forest. He kissed my face, my hands, my chest, my mouth, over and over until he lay me back down. He returned to his easel with excitement and began mixing red with white and yellow, adding, "I know exactly what I'm going to paint."

My father, Annabelle, and I were sitting around the kitchen table for supper in silence. William had left home years ago, enlisting in the Navy, and hadn't been back since. My mother had been absent for a month without a word. I was weeks away from graduating, and had been accepted to university in the city. I was counting the days until I would be gone, too.

We were having meatloaf, green peas, and carrots for dinner. My father wasn't much of a cook, and the meatloaf was dry and chewy. I poked at it with my fork. I couldn't eat green peas without gagging. I would place them in my mouth one at a time and swallow without chewing, hoping to avoid the burst of putrid juices.

My father would insist I eat my green peas, despite my obvious distaste for them. When my mother was around, she would say, "It's fine, she doesn't have to eat them."

The phone began to ring.

My father never let us answer the phone during dinner. He said it was rude for someone to call at that hour and interrupt our precious family time. Whatever they wanted could wait until after we ate.

Each shrill ring pierced me. I counted the rings, rubbing my palms together in circles under the table, knowing the answering machine picked up on the fifth.

"It could be Mother," I snapped.

The phone was about to ring for the fifth time when my father crossed the kitchen to pick up the receiver, pressing it against his ear and turning his back to us.

He muttered a few unintelligible words, sighed, and called me over, passing me the receiver.

"Hi, doll." It was my mother.

"Hi."

"Oh, Grace," she continued, "it's so good to hear your voice. How are you?"

"Fine."

"I'm glad. I wanted to ask you something. Will you and Annabelle come and stay with me this weekend?" Her voice at the other end sounded unfamiliar: timid yet liberated.

"Where are you?" I wrapped and unwrapped the phone cord around my finger. I was angry, but I could never admit that to her. She knew I was the weakest child; that's why she had asked to speak to me. I always gave in so easily.

"I'm in the city."

I remained silent. *Why didn't she call, or come back, if she was only in the city, an hour away? How could she leave us here, with him, alone?*

"What do you say? Will you girls come stay with me?"

"Sure," I replied. "I have to go, we're eating dinner."

I placed the receiver back on the hook, returned to the table to retrieve my plate, and walked to the garbage can. I turned to look at my father as I pressed my foot onto the mechanism that opened the top, maintaining eye contact as I scraped the remainder of my peas into the trash.

"What are you doing?" my father demanded.

"I hate green peas," I announced. "And I won't be eating them anymore."

Jack couldn't keep track of his cellphone if his life depended on it. I would find it in the oddest places: jammed between two books on the bookshelf, or under our mattress, or in the toilet tank. I once found it in the freezer, in a baggie filled with half-frozen chicken breasts.

I cultivated the habit of buying him burner phones, which I kept in a drawer in our dresser. Whenever I wasn't able to find the one he had been using, I'd hand him a new one, knowing it was only a matter of time before we did it all again.

Jack was like a child. I had to stay one step ahead of him at all times. I grew to know the spots he frequented: the dive bars, the decks, the gardens and cemeteries. I knew all of his friends and had saved all of their numbers. I stayed on top of where he went and how he had gotten there. I drove him around, or walked with him, carefully counting the hours we were apart, knowing when I needed to check in on him.

One night, he had been gone for too long. It was just after two in the morning, and I hadn't heard from him since ten the night before. I called, letting it ring until I heard his voice, asking me to leave him a message and he'd get back to me as soon as he could. I hung up and dialled again with no reply.

I climbed into the car and began my routine. First, I went to the bar on the corner, asking the boys when they had last seen him.

"Oh, he left a few hours ago," the group assured me. "Figured he'd be home by now."

I thanked them and, downing a glass of bourbon the bartender had placed in front of me, headed out. The barkeep never asked me to pay, and I was uncertain whether it was a gift or if he added it to Jack's tab. I wondered how big that tab was right now.

I drove to the deck downtown. It was grungy and loud, littered with cigarette butts that had been stomped into the wood, the dried tobacco leaves spread everywhere. No one had seen Jack since that afternoon. I smoked a cigarette, trying my best to block out the scream-singing of some local punk band.

When I arrived at the city garden, it was empty and damp. The flower beds were designed with symmetry in mind, peppered with tulips and roses, with ivy and pothos clinging to the rock face walls. The benches were vacant, shimmering with droplets that reflected the yellow street lights. I wiped a space with my sleeve and sat, doing a bump of cocaine with my car key before continuing on toward the graveyard.

The witching-hour air was bitingly bitter. I walked along the paved path, the whistling of wind and my heels clicking created the only noise in the vicinity. I examined the headstones, covered with moss and barely legible wording that had been flattened by time. I stopped in front of a small headstone that was encased in a rectangle of wood. I ran my fingers along the tomb, making out the date: 1876–1877.

I was on edge, spooked and half-cut, driven by my desperation to find Jack. It was always stronger than any of my other emotions. It was carnal, compulsory, illogical. My eyes scanned every nook and cranny as I periodically peeked over my shoulder to ensure no one was following me.

Then I heard a groan. I knew that groan. I followed it until I found Jack, lying between two headstones, wearing his navy-blue cashmere coat and pleated brown trousers. His hair was damp, his forehead gashed, his hair caked with dried blood. I ran toward him and dropped to my knees, shaking him furiously. "Jack?!"

He writhed on the ground and continued to moan. I repeated his name, shaking him.

Then, as if nothing had happened, he opened his eyes, green and dewy. "Grace?"

"Yes, baby." I smiled, forgetting the entire night in that moment. My anger and desperation melted, and I was filled with relief and warmth. "It's me. I need you to get up."

"Gracie, tell me a story."

"Okay, but I need you to get up first." I tried yanking him to his feet, but he just flopped.

He groaned and chuckled, chanting, "Story, story, story."

I immediately remembered one of the nursery rhymes that William would recite whenever I had misbehaved as a child. Knowing that Jack wouldn't comply until I told him something, I began:

Jack and Jill went up the hill
To fetch a pail of water
Jack fell down and broke his crown
And Jill came tumbling after.
Up Jack got
And home did trot,
As fast as he could caper;
Went to bed
To mend his head
With vinegar and brown paper.
Jill came in
And she did grin
To see his paper plaster;
Mother, vex'd,
Did whip her next
For causing Jack's disaster

Jack's forehead creased, the lines of dried blood separated and lifted from his skin. He repeated "Jack's disaster, Jack's disaster, Jack's disaster" until I got him onto his feet, out of the cemetery, and into the passenger seat.

I was sixteen, sitting on the front step waiting for my best friend, Hannah, to pick me up. It was a relatively warm evening for May and the wind wasn't blowing, so I didn't bother with a jacket. Culminations of grey clouds lingered, unmoving, obscuring the moon. The tire swing tied to the oak tree in my front yard was fixed in place.

Through the quiet, I could hear her car approaching. The muffler of her father's beat-up old Chevy sputtered and roared in warning. I watched as she pulled onto the shoulder, then I crossed the lawn, swung the door open, and lowered myself into the passenger seat.

"Hey." I reached for my seat-belt buckle, clicking it in place.

Hannah's left hand was draped over the steering wheel, pastel green nail polish chipped to bits, her nails bitten down to the skin. "It's the perfect night, isn't it?"

"Yeah, it's eerie."

There weren't many things to do in our small town, so we made our own fun. We headed down the coast.

"Do you think we'll see her?" Hannah asked, cocking an eyebrow.

I smiled, hesitantly. "I don't know. But if we do, I'm going to lose it."

Darkness was descending as we followed the shoreline to the clearing by the pond. The water was calm and black, reaching for the shadowy headland across the harbour. I stared out the window, wondering what gathered below the surface. My grandfather told me never to play near the water at night. He said that was when the terrifying creatures of the underworld searched for souls to drag down.

"I heard that if you see her, she grabs you by the hair and pulls you into the lake." I reached over and yanked Hannah's hair as hard as I could.

"Stop! Stop!" she squealed, giggling. The car swerved into the other lane as her head bobbed. "Grace, let go. If I crash this car, Dad will kill me."

I released her hair, and we continued to laugh like hyenas. When my laughter died down, Hannah would start again, then I would, too. My face felt tight, as though someone were stretching my skin back. For a second, I thought I may burst into tears, but then I chuckled again.

I wiped my eyes as Hannah slowed the car and came to a complete stop in the middle of the road. She turned off the ignition. When the engine died, it was utterly silent. I focused on my breath, irregular in anticipation.

"Ready?" she asked, her fingers on the headlight switch.

"Ready."

She slowly flashed the lights, illuminating the strait of empty road and evergreens ahead. We counted along.

Click. "One."

Click. "Two."

Click. "Three."

Hannah turned toward me; her blond hair shone red, reflecting the brake lights. "This is where she drowned her kids, right?"

As I went to answer, I realized I was holding my breath, avoiding the rear-view mirror with my head down. I could hear a dull pulsation in my ears. I exhaled. "I think so."

I raised my eyes without lifting my head, peeking into the rear-view mirror. A young woman, bloated and bluish-grey, with chapped lips and cracked skin, was sitting in the back seat. Her long black hair was dripping wet, and her brown eyes were fixed on me. She smiled slowly, her lips pressed together as though they were glued shut.

I screamed and my hands shot up, reaching for the door handle. I threw the door open and jumped out, peering in through the window. I glanced over my shoulder at the lake, then up and down the road, straining my eyes for any movement in the distance.

Hannah shot out of the car and ran around to my side. She hopped up and down in place, "What? What? What?"

"Did you see her?" I shrieked, lowering my head through the open door.

"No, are you serious? Where?" Hannah bent to peer into the back seat, brushing against my back.

I jumped, spinning around, "Don't touch me. Jesus Christ."

"Sorry, sorry."

"It was the woman. She was behind you." I checked the back seat again. "Get back in the car. Get in the car." I climbed in, swiftly slamming and locking the door. I put my face in my hands and shut my eyes, tugging at the skin on my cheeks.

"Are you sure it was her?" Hannah was back in the driver's seat, scrambling to start the engine.

"Yes, I'm fucking sure."

"What did she look like?" she asked, both hands on the wheel.

"She was wet. Her hair and eyes were dark. Then she just smiled at me. It was the creepiest thing I've ever seen."

Hannah was silent for a moment. "I can't believe you saw her." She glanced at me through the corners of her eyes. "I don't think anyone has ever actually seen her before."

My eyes remained fixed on the road, waiting for the woman to reappear. I checked the back again. It was empty. I turned and reached, running my fingers over the seat. It was dry.

The clouds had cleared and the halved moon was high in the sky as we followed the shoreline home. The radio played softly as we drove. I watched the water, wondering what would cause a mother to drown her own baby.

Eventually, Hannah pulled onto the shoulder. The windows of my house were already dark. I reached for the door handle and noticed my hands were shaking.

"Are you okay?" she asked, her eyes wide.

"Yeah." I nodded. "I'm fine."

"Are you sure? You're kind of scaring me."

"I said I'm fine," I snapped, pushing open the door. "I'll see you tomorrow."

"Okay."

I leapt from my seat and ran the short distance to my house as though I were being chased. I threw open the door, slipped inside, and secured the deadbolt, peeking through the window one last time.

I ran up the stairs two at a time, drifting past the various portraits of naked women that lined the wall. I could feel the murderous mother behind me in the darkness, her brown eyes locked on my head. I stopped outside my parents' bedroom door—their lights already out—and considered knocking. I could hear my father snoring on the other side of the door, so I continued to my room, holding myself at the elbows.

I crawled into bed and pulled the covers to my neck. Every time I closed my eyes, I saw the drowned woman. Her sunken cheekbones and large brown eyes with clumped, wet eyelashes blinking slowly. Staring. Silent.

The longer I lay awake, the more sorry I felt for her. She was trapped. A victim, too, after all.

After my mother escaped, she began spending time with twenty-year-olds. Annabelle and I went to stay with her in the city. She was living in her sister's house, the one who had remarried after her first husband left her. Whenever they visited, my aunt's new beau would hold my face in his calloused hands, pinch my cheeks, and stare at me a bit too long.

Father dropped us at the end of the cul-de-sac, avoiding a run-in with my mother. The snow had stopped earlier that morning but a decent amount had accumulated, salted and browned from vehicle excretion and city pollutants. Annabelle and I lugged our bags down the road through the slush. My mother was perched on the concrete step, wearing nothing but a knee-length ice-blue blouse, smoking a long cigarette. "My darlings," she called, waving her free hand.

She was eager for us to meet her new friends. Once we were settled, without much explanation, she took us to a gathering in a poorly lit basement apartment. There was weed paraphernalia everywhere: Bob Marley and Snoop Dogg posters hung on the walls, three bongs sat in the middle of the coffee table, which was also littered with pipes, busters, rolling papers, lighters, and baggies of dope. I could have sworn that even the walls were a muted green.

I sat on the dingy sofa and considered whether these weird almost-adults with their unruly haircuts, worn-out clothing, and unclipped fingernails were worse than the monsters I was afraid of as a child. At least with the monsters, my fear was never confirmed. These people were very real, chatting around me, laughing, messing up my life.

I watched my mother press her lips to the bong. The water gurgled as she held a lighter to the bowl and inhaled, then exhaled a cloud of smoke that seemed much too large to have fit in her lungs.

"Girls," my mother announced as she stood. "Samuel and I are going to run to the store." The guy she was with nodded at me, smiling in a way that was trying too hard to be empathetic. Like that moron had a fucking clue about anything.

"Okay," I replied.

I noticed fat pouches ripple along Samuel's thick neck as he turned to exit the room. I wanted to pinch them until he screamed.

"We won't be long," my mother called.

Annabelle, who had been sitting mutely, leaned in and whispered in my ear, "Grace, I'm scared."

Two guys remained, sitting on the couch across the coffee table: one fat, one thin. They both had patchy beards. I can only assume this was because they were too lazy to shave.

"So, you guys are Jayde's daughters, right?"

I narrowed my eyes in their direction, trying to discern which one had spoken. The guy spoke again, "Which one of you is Grace, and which one is Annabelle?" It was the skinny one. Despite his scrawniness, his voice was deep and carried well, like a man who had been performing on stage his entire life.

"Yeah," I replied. "I'm Grace. This is Annabelle."

He squinted at us. "How old are you guys—like, eighteen?"

"I'm seventeen." I pointed at Annabelle. "And she's thirteen."

"Holy shit." His eyes widened as his eyebrows shot up.

"It's fine, people assume we're older all the time." I glanced at Annabelle. "We're pretty mature. I suppose you have to be when your mother is like that, you know?"

The fat one, who was clutching the bong, snickered as he leaned forward and grabbed a pinch of weed. He sprinkled it into the bowl and motioned toward me. "Want a hit?"

"I think I'm good." I shifted toward my sister, who was becoming increasingly uncomfortable. "It already feels inappropriate enough here without us smoking weed with some twentysomething strangers."

The skinny guy and the fat guy laughed in unison. "Suit yourself."

The fat one took a hit, coughing loudly for what seemed like a long time. I started to wonder if he was going to hack up a lung in front of my petrified sister.

When he recovered, he ran his fingers through his wiry beard, sinking deeper into the sofa. "You know she's fucking Samuel, right?"

"What?"

He shrugged. "You're going to find out sooner or later. I figured I'd be the first to tell you."

My eyes clouded over, sticky from the smoke. I blinked rapidly but could still barely see. "What the fuck is wrong with you?" I realized my fists were clenched; releasing them, I grabbed Annabelle's hand and floundered for the door.

As we surfaced, the freezing night air stung my overheated cheeks and filled my lungs. I coughed, its fresh crispness shocking my system.

We sat down on the curb. I was still clutching my sister's hand; it was clammy, so I let it fall, rubbing my palms along my pants to dry the sweat.

The streets were lined with cars, likely left behind by people in a drunken stupor headed downtown. Flecks of snow casually fell from the sky, collecting on Annabelle's black hair. She started to shiver, our coats remained inside. I unbuttoned my cardigan and peeled it off, wrapping it around her shoulders. When she turned her face toward me, smiling in appreciation, I noticed a speckling of snowflakes had landed on her eyelashes, and as she blinked, they glittered under the street lamps.

I smiled back before reaching over and pulling her in close. Rubbing her arms to keep warm, I scanned the distance for our mother, praying she would appear.

Annabelle's timid voice finally broke the silence. "Do you think he was telling the truth?"

I lowered my gaze to the sidewalk, unable to look back into those hopeful eyes. "Of course not."

I always knew there had been a daughter before me. She was named Sophia after my mother's mother, and was born in the springtime. I came the following winter. My parents rarely spoke of her unless pried and prodded. She was buried in a cemetery on the outskirts of town, near the garbage dump. I don't remember ever visiting her grave as a child, although my parents assured me that we did.

One afternoon, tucked away in the drawer of my mother's bedside table, I found an old photograph of Sophia and me lying in a crib together. We looked incredibly similar: both heads covered in blond fuzz, large dark blue eyes peering up at the camera. We were dressed in matching onesies covered in little bears. If she hadn't been nearly twice my size, we might have been twins.

I brought the photograph to my mother who was mixing cookie dough in the kitchen. "Will you tell me about her?" I asked, my arm extended.

"Grace." She wiped her hand on her apron and took the photo from me, stuffing it into the pocket of her cotton pants. "Mommy told you, she doesn't like talking about this."

"Please," I pouted. "Just this once and I'll never ask again."

She sighed, glancing out the window for a moment. She lowered her voice. "Okay. You can ask three questions."

Smitten, I began. "What was she like?"

"Well, she was a very sweet little baby. Her laugh made everyone around her laugh, too." My mother smiled, looking past me. "The two of you were always giggling together, speaking a secret baby language."

"So we were friends?"

"Oh yes, best friends." She cracked an egg on the counter and raised it, letting it fall into the metal mixing bowl. "Okay, hurry up, last question."

"What happened to her?"

My mother inhaled, peeking over her shoulder toward the door. "It was an accident."

"What do you mean?" I tucked my hair behind my ears.

"Sometimes accidents happen," she explained, picking up the wooden spoon and resuming her mixing. "And it's no one's fault."

My father entered the room and my mother flinched, ever so slightly.

"What are we whispering about?" he asked, grabbing an apple from the ceramic bowl on the kitchen table. He tossed it into the air and caught it with the opposite hand.

"I'm just teaching Gracie my secret cookie recipe." She winked at me, and my father nodded in approval before exiting the room, taking a bite from his apple.

Standing at the kitchen island, I thumbed through a frayed copy of *The Joy of Cooking*. William was coming for dinner and I'd promised him our mother's chicken cacciatore. Annabelle had left home when she was old enough to do so, vowing she would never return to the island so long as she lived. Even in death, she said, she wouldn't be brought back here, and at sixteen wrote a fake will that she made me sign, promising I would keep her corpse away from this family. I hadn't seen her since.

I poured myself a glass of wine and began to sift through the produce: mushrooms, garlic, carrots, bell peppers, onions, parsley, and basil. I brought the latter to my nose, inhaling deeply, the same motion I had seen my mother make a hundred times.

Jack was in the living room, working on a painting using only shades of red.

I had spent the afternoon cleaning the entire house around him, scrubbing the floors, polishing the wineglasses, digging through the drawer of silverware for our matching forks and knives, and folding cloth napkins into little hats.

William and Jack hadn't met. William had only just returned from his most recent deployment.

I cubed the vegetables between smoking cigarettes and snorting lines of coke. I opened a can of crushed tomatoes and dumped everything into the cast iron pot, plopping the raw chicken thighs into the liquid before sprinkling dried oregano and red pepper flakes over the top. I jammed it into the oven, shook off the oven mitts, and railed another line

By the time William arrived, I was on fast-forward.

I heard the knocking—three succinct raps—and ran to the door, threw it open, and leapt into his arms. "Will!"

His curly hair was buzzed down; only a coating of blond stubble remained. He was freckled and pink-cheeked from the cold, wearing a sapphire button-down and carrying a bottle of red wine under his arm.

Jack was straightening up, sealing tubes of paint, as we entered the living room.

"William, this is Jack," I announced, motioning from one to the other. "Jack, William. William, Jack."

Jack wiped his hand on his shirt before extending it to William. "Nice to meet you, man."

"Likewise."

They shook.

"Who's hungry?" I shouted, smelling something burning.

I darted into the kitchen, whipped open the oven, and grabbed the pot with a dishtowel. It spewed steam and smoke, and as the towel slipped, the soft pads of my fingers made contact with the pan. Cursing loudly, I dashed to the sink, running my fingers under cold water as William made his way into the kitchen. "Are you okay?"

"I'm fine." I turned, my fingers still under the faucet. "Just a little burn."

Jack came up behind me, took my hand, and examined the marks that were already shiny and puffed out, a blister forming.

"I think dinner is burned," I laughed, shutting off the tap.

"Dinner and you." Jack smirked, kissing the wound.

We ordered pizza and drank wine until it ran out. Jack had an early meeting at his gallery, so when we switched to whiskey he excused himself and went to bed, leaving William and me standing in the kitchen.

We began cleaning in silence, loading the dishwasher with the precision of two people working on a factory line. As we established a rhythm—William passing me an item, me rinsing it before placing it in the dishwasher—we started adding little spins and twists between each movement.

When we got to the cutlery, William began tossing pieces to me from across the table, some hitting the floor with a clank, others I caught, poking me in the hand. We were feeling no pain, laughing hysterically. William grabbed me, twirling me in circles until I was dizzy and had to brace myself against the counter.

As our laughter faded, he wrapped his arms around me and hugged me close. We stayed in that embrace for a few moments, and I felt calmer than I had in a long time.

"I missed you," he said.

"I missed you, too."

William let go, making his way to the other side of the island as I soaked the pan that contained our burnt meal.

"Sorry about dinner." I scraped at the black crust with a spatula. "I know you were excited about it."

"Oh, I don't care about that." William shook his head. "I'm just happy to see you."

Abandoning the pot, I sprayed the counters with disinfectant and wiped everything down. I returned the spices to their designated place on the rack and dramatically dusted myself off.

William was watching me, his head tilted. He licked his lips and I could tell he was trying to find the right words.

"What?" I topped up my glass with whiskey, then moved toward William to top his up too.

His eyes followed the liquid as it poured into his glass. "Are you happy, Gracie?"

"Of course." I smiled, taking a long sip and shrugging my shoulders. "As happy as someone like us can be."

Bent over the island, William used the tip of a cut-off straw to snort one of the lines I had divided up. Propping himself up by his elbows, he continued to examine me. "You don't seem happy."

"Well, I am," I assured him. "Are you happy?"

He rubbed his nose with the back of his wrist. "I'm trying to be."

I twisted my mouth to the side empathetically. He did the same, mirroring me.

"So." I looked away. "What do you think of Jack?"

"He's alright."

I chuckled. "What's wrong with him?"

"Nothing. He's fine, really. He's just not, you know." He paused, chewing the insides of his cheeks, still clutching the straw tip. "You're the most special person in the world, Grace. And you deserve to be with someone who can see that. Someone who understands you."

I swallowed, flicking my eyes away from him. William was so much of what I remembered. He was so much of me. Being there with him, it was easy to feel it all. It hurt me to think of what we'd been through. That I hadn't protected him better. I stared at his hand, the stub where his pinky used to be, pressed into the countertop.

"All I want is for you to be happy."

In the beginning, I loved everything about doing coke. I loved when my dealer showed up. I loved the secrecy of slipping bills into his hand and getting that baggie in return. Something I wanted more than anything. My anxiety would dissipate as soon as I wrapped my fingers around that beautiful little baggie. I would head for the nearest bathroom. I didn't care about anything else. I loved crushing it up with the back of my credit card. I loved pouring a pile of that shiny white powder onto the toilet tank, and the ritual of cutting up lines, making them perfect. I loved rolling up that bill and devouring the line, snorting it into my nose with one controlled motion. I loved the way it smelled—like gasoline and decaying bugs. I loved the way it dripped down the back of my throat, prompting my tongue to tingle and go numb.

The first few lines were what I lived for. I'd apply a fresh coat of lipstick, hitch my skirt up a little higher, and undo an extra button on my shirt. When I emerged from the bathroom, I was myself again. Confident. Sexy. High. It was how I wanted people to see me. It was who I wanted to be. I was quicker with my wit, sharper with my comebacks. Mostly, I loved coke because I knew who I was when I was doing it. I knew everything about that girl. She was sure of herself. Everyone loved her. Men and women wanted her. And she always got what she wanted.

But after those first few lines, the want became need. I was no longer in control of myself. I didn't know what I was saying, where I was going. I was shaky, spilling all my secrets, talking simply because it felt good. I just wanted that next bump. It was all that mattered. I had to maintain the feeling. I didn't want it to ever go away. Fiending, wild-eyed, scanning the room. Who has coke? Do you have any coke? Where can I get more coke?

I became sloppier. The ritual was no longer important. I just needed it. Now. I didn't even try to conceal it. Snorting key bumps under my coat. White powder caked in my nose. I didn't care about anything. I just needed it now.

I would pace around the room as the sun came up. Some guy passed out nearby. I wanted out of my skin, out of my body. Out. Out. Out. It wasn't fun anymore. This isn't fun anymore. Cutting up lines not because I wanted to, but because I couldn't stop. The self-loathing would come. When the coke ran out, the self-loathing would come. Lying in bed, crying and praying to God to please let me sleep. Please kill me. Please God, just let me die. Let me die tonight so this will be over. I can't take it anymore. Please. Let me die. Please.

That part I didn't love so much.

Dr. Brace wanted to see me on a semi-regular basis, but he also wanted me to see a psychologist. On his recommendation, I went to see Dr. Rowe. She was a small, mousy thirtysomething with blond hair and eyebrows that had been overtweezed to the point of no return.

"You can call me Joanna," she said, in an obvious effort to make us appear more like equals.

"And you can call me Grace," I replied. Noticing my shoulders were drawn up, I let them fall.

She was watching my movements, her skinny eyebrows squiggling with sympathy. "How are you feeling?"

I ran the flats of my palms over the velvety fabric of the armrests. "I'll be honest with you, I've been better."

"Why do you say that?"

"Well, Joanna, it's been a tough year." I lowered my gaze to the white tiling of the floor. "First, I killed my baby. The one thing I was supposed to protect. Then Jack left me. He found someone else." My voice came out louder than I had anticipated. "So as you can imagine, it's getting pretty dark inside my head."

She took notes as my disdain for her built, my disdain for this entire fucked-up system. For what I had done, and for what I had allowed to be done to me.

"When you say you 'killed your baby,' what exactly do you mean?"

The rage was pressing against my skin, heating me, grinding against my organs. "Does it matter?" I snapped.

Psychologists, psychiatrists, social workers: they each have a unique approach, but they all want the same thing. A psychologist will work to recondition you, attempting to break your bad behaviours, retraining you to think in a healthy manner. Psychiatrists, those mad scientists looking to level the chemical imbalances in your brain, will throw pharmaceuticals at you, turning you into a pill-popper. As if I needed any help with that. Social workers work for the good of society. They want to fix you, and integrate you back into a world that is made newly whole and cured as a unit. But they all want you to talk about *everything*: your past, your childhood, your parents, your grandparents, your future. What do you think? How do you feel? What's on your mind? Where do we go from here?

"Well, yes, it does." Joanna shifted forward in her chair. "I think you are placing blame on yourself for something that wasn't your fault at all."

The fleshy tips of my pointer fingers circled the nail beds of my thumbs, a habit I had picked up to calm myself. I said nothing in reply.

"I think you would benefit from cognitive behavioural therapy." She was clearly an academic, dressed in plain clothes and wearing no makeup. It was obvious she had more important things to do than agonize over her appearance. "It's a form of therapy where we focus on your negative thoughts and try to replace them with more positive, healthy thoughts."

I rolled my eyes without meaning to. I hoped she hadn't seen. I wondered if she was a lesbian. I thought about how easy it would be to fuck her right then and there, bending her over her desk and slipping my fingers between her thighs.

Joanna eyed me curiously. "How does that sound?"

My left arm began to tingle. I tried bending each of my fingers one at a time to ensure they still worked. *Pinky, ring finger, middle finger, index finger, thumb. Repeat.* My leg was shaking; the heel of my shoe tapped against the hardwood floor over and over.

Tap-tap-tap-tap-tap.

"Fine," I said, quietly. "That sounds fine."

"Okay, you can book your next appointment on the way out." Joanna motioned to the door with her pen and shut the file in her lap, indicating our time was up. "Thanks for coming in today, Grace. I'm looking forward to working with you."

"Yeah, me too."

I exited the room, made my way down the narrow, windowless hallway, and rushed past the receptionist. Pushing open the door, I let the cold winter air hit me. The noise of the city was violent—car horns honking, traffic lights beeping, strangers strolling and conversing, busy with their lives, completely unaware, unconscious. My shadow appeared in front of me, giant and lanky, like a cartoon villain. I turned away from it. It made me feel fictitious, a figment of someone's depraved imagination.

I never went back, but that night I masturbated to the image of my face buried between Joanna's legs.

July 25

I saw Grace on one occasion for intake. Session focused on anxiety and family concerns. G did not attend her last scheduled session in December and did not reschedule. This file is therefore considered closed.

Jack was AB negative and I was type O negative. The holy grail of blood. Coming down one morning, we decided we should donate. It seemed the logical thing to do after a bender of self-indulgent debauchery.

"Are you sure you're okay to drive?" I asked, lifting my hand to shield my eyes from the sun.

Jack opened the passenger door for me. "Don't be silly."

It smelled of summer: floral, grassy, still, and dry. My skin was buzzing. We hadn't slept at all. I stared out the window as we drove, watching the trees blink by. The world was blurred and unbearably loud. Mufflers growled and garbage trucks grinded and beeped.

My ears were blocked, so I plugged my nose and swallowed.

Jack killed the engine. "You ready, my little bloodlover?"

My ears popped as I shifted my jaw from left to right. "Yeah."

We climbed out of the car, entering the sterile building and making our way to reception.

A woman sat behind the desk, wearing thick-rimmed black glasses. Her hair was pulled tightly into a ponytail. "Hello, do you have an appointment?"

"No." Jack approached the desk, resting his elbows on it. "Do we need one?"

"You do not. First time donating?" She blinked at us.

"No," we said in unison.

"Alrighty, I'll need you both to fill out these forms." She slid two pieces of paper across the counter using her index finger, as if she were discreetly offering us a pay increase.

The form consisted of a series of yes/no questions. Jack and I began circling our responses, lying where necessary without hesitation.

Are you exhibiting flu-like symptoms?
Do you have diabetes?
Have you had dental work in the past three days?

Have you ever tested positive for HIV/AIDS?
Have you travelled outside the country in the past year?
Have you used cocaine in the last year?
Have you had sex with a man who in the last year had sex with another man?
Have you been in contact with or exchanged bodily fluids with a monkey?

Snickering, I slid my finished sheet back to the woman.

I watched as Jack answered the last few questions. "Didn't you just have sex with that monkey last week?" I tapped my long, manicured fingernail on the desk, soothed by its clacking. "I thought you guys made a cute couple." I turned to the receptionist and smiled charmingly.

"She's kidding." Jack handed over the form.

The receptionist was unamused. "Have a seat in the waiting area. They'll call your names when they're ready."

Jack and I settled on the padded grey chairs. The majority of people in the room were young, in their thirties and forties. A red-haired man in a blue suit sat across from us, reading a magazine. He reminded me of William for some reason. Maybe it was the freckles, or the way his brow was furrowed. I missed him; he had been offshore for the past few months.

Most people were alone, so there wasn't much chatter aside from the receptionist's hushed voice as she answered the ringing phone.

I rested my head on Jack's shoulder and shut my eyes, thinking of blood, of bodies, and of magic.

I straightened and scooted over, leaving an empty seat between us.

"Wanna see a trick?" I asked, pulling a deck of cards out of my purse.

"Sure." Jack grinned.

I cut the deck. A woman wearing an orange sweater covered in pictures of cats shot me a look, as if to say this is not a place to play. I maintained eye contact as I shuffled until she backed down.

"Pick a card, any card," I said in my best announcer's voice.

Carefully, Jack selected one, eyeing me to make sure I wasn't peeking. I separated the deck into three piles on the chair between us.

"Place your card on top of one of the piles, please, sir."

He placed it on the middle stack. I began counting, laying them into more piles. Then, I reassembled the deck.

"Is this your card?" I asked, fully aware that it was not.

"No." His eyebrow cocked, assuming I had messed up.

"Oh, shoot. Can you tell me your card?"

"It was the queen of hearts."

"Okay. I'm going to spell it out for you."

"Q." I flipped a card, placing it face-up.

"U." A second card.

"E." A third card. All the while counting in my head.

I turned the cards until I reached the last letter: "S." Flipping the final card, there it was: the queen of hearts.

"Aw, cute," he said.

"Jack?" The nurse called from the doorway.

Jack stood and I followed, sliding the deck into my purse and grabbing his arm. The red-haired man glanced up from his magazine, smiling at me. I smiled sweetly.

"Can we go in together?" Jack asked.

"Sure," the nurse agreed, turning for us to follow.

She pulled back a curtain, revealing chairs and empty blood bags hanging from hooks attached to moveable poles.

Jack and I sat side by side as the nurse pressed her index and middle finger into my forearm, trying to locate a vein.

"Can you make a fist for me, please?" she asked.

"Sure." I clenched my fingers into my palm. "My veins are small, people usually have trouble finding them."

The nurse cleansed the area with an antiseptic wipe, the clinical scent hitting my nostrils. I watched closely as the needle pierced my skin. A slight pinch, a sharp inhale, and that was it.

I've always loved needles. Even as a kid at school, when it came time for us to have our shots, while all the other children cried and feared the nurse, I excitedly offered to go first, staring as the metal tip entered me. I felt a sense of exhilaration, letting a stranger inside my body.

"This will take about ten minutes," she explained.

Jack took out his phone, passing me an earbud, and pressing the other into his ear. We listened to The Cranberries as the clear bags that hung overhead slowly turned red, our free hands joined. I thought about growing old with Jack, and how I might have to watch him die, lying in a hospital bed hooked up to machinery, his skin sagging, his eyes clearing in preparation for the transition. A lump formed in my throat and I swallowed, blinking rapidly to keep the tears from falling.

After the needle came out, as we ate our cookies and drank our juice, I examined the bags of syrupy blood. No matter how long I stared, I couldn't differentiate mine from Jack's.

Dear Sunshine,

It's a boy.

Love,
G

In high school, my English teacher favoured me. He wasn't a particularly attractive man—his features were slightly too close together, his nose pointy, his mouth a small wet hole—but he possessed a certain charisma and eloquence. He called himself a writer, despite being unpublished, boasting he could have been as great as Hemingway, if only he'd had the time to write. Saintly sacrificing his own career for the children, he felt it was his duty to share his gift. A true martyr, really.

He was a friend of my father, and had been for as long as I could remember. A frequent dinner guest in our home, he and my father would drink bourbon from glistening tumblers and argue loudly about the nuances of Raymond Carver in the darkness of the kitchen.

I was on the cheerleading squad and my English teacher was the team supervisor, so he was usually at practice on the weekends. I always hoped he would show up, and took comfort in the fact that he was watching me. I saw him as a protective father figure and felt a sense of safety in the way he seemed to care about me.

I found myself seeking his approval in all that I did, and began asking him to read my poems after class. Unlike my father, he was encouraging of my pursuit to be a writer.

One day, I knocked on his open door.

"Come in, Miss Grace." My English teacher glanced up from his papers, waving me in. All of the desks were empty, lined in straight rows and evenly spaced. The quiet classroom felt strange.

He was seated at a large wooden desk at the front, grading papers, his reading glasses perched on the tip of his nose. "What can I do for you?"

"I wrote a new poem." I crossed the empty room, my notebook extended, and pulled a chair alongside him. "I wanted you to read it."

"I'd love to." He eyed me and reached for the notebook, then placed it on his desk and scanned the page. His hands clutched the edges, crinkling the paper slightly.

The air smelled of chalk dust and coffee; a half-empty mug was balanced on a copy of *To Kill A Mockingbird.* I glimpsed around the room, reading a Jane Austen quote that was scrawled across the chalkboard: "*Seldom, very seldom, does complete truth belong to any human disclosure; seldom can it happen that something is not a little disguised or a little mistaken.*"

When my English teacher finished, he peeked at me over his glasses. "That's lovely. Really good work."

"Thank you." I smiled, feeling victorious. "Is it long enough?"

"It could use some more visuals. Keep working on it, it's almost there." He pointed to the page, and I noticed a small paper cut on his finger. "You misspelled 'language' though."

"Oh?" I leaned forward, reaching for my notebook, momentarily creating a crevice between my breasts and shirt. My English teacher glanced down into the space, quickly raising his eyes to meet mine as he became aware of where he was looking. "I want you to write 'language' ten times for me."

I leaned back slightly. "Now?"

Flipping to a blank page, he slid it toward me. "Yes, now."

I picked up a pencil. Pressing the tip onto the paper, I wrote in cursive:

Language
Language
Language
Language
Language
Language
Language
Language
Language
Language

"Good work," he said, examining the words. "Now you'll never misspell it again."

I nodded.

"You know that you're very talented, don't you, Grace?"

"You think so?" I tugged at my blouse.

"I do." Leaning forward, he placed his hand on my knee. "You're going to be very successful."

I shot up abruptly, my chair sliding backwards.

"Thank you." I fumbled for my book. "I should go."

My English teacher lowered his gaze, straightening a pen on his desk so it was perpendicular to the stack of paper. "Okay, keep up the great work. Will I see you at practice this weekend?"

"Of course." I was halfway gone. "See you."

My eyes burned as I exited the classroom, a sob welling like a wave retreating, preparing to crash forward. Hurrying down the empty corridor, I accidentally passed my locker; turning around, I fumbled with the lock before pulling out my bookbag. I tore through my notebook, locating the page lined with *language*—I ripped it from the coil and crumpled it before stuffing my notebook into my bag. I swung it onto my back, buttoned my shirt all the way up to my neck, and tossed the ball of paper into a trashcan.

"What do you do, Grace?" an overweight man in an ill-fitting striped button-up asked. Pockets of fat peeked through the gaping holes along the button line. He stuffed a triangular sandwich into his mouth and spit crumbs in my direction as he spoke.

I glanced to the door as a woman with intricately lined eyes and a sharp bobbed haircut entered. We were at the home of one of Jack's colleagues for the annual party hosted by the Arts Bureau that aimed to connect artists with philanthropists. I always dreaded these events. They were filled with self-important people bragging about their menial accomplishments, sucking up to rich people, blabbering about why their particular type of genius was deserving of funding. It made me feel like a whore.

Jack said it was important we attend because he needed their money. He called them *funders*. I called them *fuckers*.

"It's all part of the show, babe," Jack reminded me before we went in. He lit a joint, took a puff, and handed it to me. "You need to play the part if you want the life."

I remembered when I was a child, and William and I would venture through the stream up the road from our home. Making our way to the top, hopping from rock to rock with soaking wet feet, we would sit there for hours listening to the water gush, splashing on the rocks, shrieking with laughter.

"What do you want to be when you grow up, Gracie?" William asked.

"I don't know," I replied, letting the cold water flow over my bare feet, tickling and cooling my toes. "I just know I don't want to be an artist." At a young age, I'd learned that their lives were difficult. I saw my parents struggle and fight about money constantly. I saw the narcissistic people they surrounded themselves with, often drunk and spewing their own praises.

The stranger cleared his throat, and I was returned to the present moment.

"Sorry. What was the question?"

"What do you do?" he repeated, more intently.

"Oh, I'm in school right now."

"Ah, university, the golden years. The years of nourishing the eager, young, malleable mind." He gazed to the distance, perhaps remembering a time when his shirt actually fit him. "What I wouldn't do to go back."

I smiled before chugging the rest of my drink.

"What are you studying?"

"Joint major. Folklore and literature."

"Hm," the man leaned in eagerly. "What is folklore?"

I inhaled in preparation for my rehearsed response. "Folklorists are like historians, except they study the stories of everyday people. The ones who didn't make it into the history books."

"Interesting. I love history," the man replied, picking something from his teeth with this thumbnail. "What's your favourite part of folklore?"

He pulled a wet blob from his teeth and sucked it from his thumb.

I tried to hide my disgust, swallowing a nearly audible retch. "My area of specialization is supernatural folklore and superstitions. Ghost stories, urban legends, faerie lore, that sort of thing."

"That sounds fascinating."

I had drunk too many glasses of wine and was starting to feel lightheaded. I hadn't seen Jack in ages, and this sweaty man was getting on my last nerve.

"Will you excuse me?" I scanned the room for the exit. "I need some fresh air."

"Of course." He stepped aside.

I pushed my way through the crowd to the back door, grabbing two shots of whiskey and sliding the patio door open using my shoulder. I stepped outside, downed one of the shots, and balanced both glasses on the rail. I dug in my purse for a cigarette.

"Ah-ha, there you are." I pulled one from the pack and placed it in my mouth, sparking the lighter. I held the cigarette with my teeth and pulled a plastic baggie from my bra, dumping a line of powder onto the back of my hand. I brought my hand to my nose and snorted it up with one swift inhale.

The backyard was lit with floodlights, and beautifully landscaped with a nod to Parisian decor. Shrubbery was strategically planted on the outskirts of flowerbeds, all to draw attention to the focal point: a giant frog-shaped fountain with extended frog legs, as if it were about to launch into the air, water spouting from its mouth. I laughed at how ridiculous it all was, snatched the second whiskey shot from its perch, and tossed it back.

Through the still evening air I heard Jack's voice, but I couldn't see him. I took a long draw on my cigarette and licked the remaining coke from the back of my hand.

The patio wrapped all the way around the house, so I followed it. My high heels clacked on the wood as I headed for Jack. I carefully avoided the slats as I passed the window. Glancing at the group of people sipping from champagne flutes, standing too close together, flicking their heads back, their jaws unhinged, I thought, *Idiots.* I stepped forward without looking and my heel landed between the slat. I hollered and stumbled forward as the heads inside turned toward me. I straightened and waved. "I'm fine." Yanking my leg to unstick my shoe, I continued on, rounding the corner.

There was Jack, standing alone with a woman. She had short red hair and was wearing a low-cut black cocktail dress.

Jack caught sight of me and froze for a second. "Hey, baby." He extended his hand, pulling me in by the shoulder. "I've been looking for you."

"Oh, really?" I shrugged loose from his grip, glaring at the woman. "That's funny. I was just inside speaking of academia with a most lovely gentleman."

They both stared at me, then at the empty shot glass in my hand.

I tried to remember the man's name. "Bob. Brian. Bill. Phil. Anyway, big guy. It was a real treat. What a gas, indeedy do." I took a sloppy draw on my cigarette, and blew smoke up and down and to the left and the right. The redhead fanned the air in front of her face.

"That's great." Confused, Jack turned and motioned to the woman. "This is Jessica. Jessica, this is Grace."

I extended my hand flatly, inviting her to kiss it. "Charmed, I'm sure."

She took my fingers and shook them awkwardly.

Jack stepped alongside her and mouthed "money" to me, in an obvious attempt to get me to behave. I shook my head at him and examined Jessica's face. Her eyes were large and brown, shiny and reflective, like those of a well-trained border collie.

"It's so nice to meet you, Grace," she said. "Jack has told me so much about you."

"And it's so nice to meet you, Jessica." I let my head bounce from side to side as I repeated her name: *Jesss-ick-ahhh.*

Jack cleared his throat and I continued, "May I say, you are just lovely. You look like you'd make a great wife. Just great. Curled up on a Sunday morning with the newspaper. Freaking beautiful."

Jessica glanced at Jack, who shrugged. "That's so sweet." She smiled, revealing her humongous teeth. "You, uh, look like you'd make a good wife, too."

"And what large teeth you have," I announced, stumbling forward, tossing my hands in the air and letting my empty glass fly free. It landed in the grass. "Oopsie daisy."

Jack grabbed my arm and squeezed it tightly. "Are you high?" he whispered through clenched teeth.

"No, darling, I'm not high," I replied at an audible level, rolling my eyes. A waiter passed carrying a tray of drinks. I waved, "Yoo-hoo, garçon, over here."

The waiter stopped and I snatched one.

Jack's eyes narrowed. "Sweetie, I think you've had enough."

"I'll know when I've had enough, trust me." I took a large gulp. "Don't be such a bassoon."

Jessica sipped her glass of wine and stared past me.

I burst into laughter. "Did I say bassoon?" I couldn't stop. I was roaring. "I meant bassoon."

"I'm sorry," Jack apologized, his eyes meeting Jessica's. "I'm going to take her home."

"That's probably a good idea." She looked me up and down before leaning in and kissing him on the cheek. "I'll talk to you soon."

"Yeah, talk soon." Jack was still clutching my arm, as though I were a child who had misbehaved. We turned and began walking toward the balcony.

"The better to eat you with, my dear," I shouted as Jack dragged me out of sight.

My father spent days locked away in his office, so my mother was left to entertain us. She would often pack my siblings and me into the car and we'd drive to nearby towns. We'd go to the supermarket or the drugstore, or the movie store to pick a video to rent. She'd give each of us a quarter, and we'd push and shove as we ran for the machines that dispensed handfuls of candy. Our palms became sticky as we clutched our treats, momentarily distracted, allowing our mother a few moments of quiet reprieve.

On one of these trips, William and I were bickering. Annabelle was just a baby, strapped into her car seat.

William pinched my arm.

"Mother," I screamed. "William pinched me."

"Stop it," my mother sighed.

I leaned over and grabbed the skin on his leg, pinching it as hard as I could between my thumb and forefinger, leaving behind a red imprint.

William shouted, "Mother, Grace pinched me."

"I'm warning you two." My mother regarded us in the rear-view mirror. "Stop that now."

William stuck his tongue out at me.

I stuck my tongue out back.

"You're adopted," William whispered.

"Mother, William said I was adopted."

"She stuck her tongue out at me."

"You did it first."

"That's it." My mother slammed on the brakes. My body jolted forward, my seat belt catching me. She turned around and shouted, "Get out of the car, both of you."

"No," we whined in unison.

"Now."

"But Mother."

"Now!" she screamed.

Reluctantly, we opened the door and climbed out onto the shoulder of the road. We stood in silence, expecting her to tell us to get back in. "Close the door," she called. William pushed it shut, giving it an extra kick with his sneakered foot, huffing loudly.

The wheels spun on the gravel, kicking up a cloud of dust before the car pulled away. I began coughing as we watched it grow smaller and smaller, eventually disappearing completely over the hill.

William reached for my hand and squeezed it gently. His little face was pink and twisted with anger. Neither of us said a word.

Finally, he broke the silence. "Don't worry, Gracie, it will be fun to live outdoors. More fun than being in that dumbhead house."

I stared at the road: nothing coming or going.

"We can eat bugs and sleep under trees if it rains."

"But I don't wanna eat bugs," I whimpered.

He poked my cheek. "You used to eat bugs all the time."

I smiled, wiping my runny nose with the back of my sleeve. "That was when I was a baby."

William always joked when he was nervous. We had taught ourselves to laugh when we really wanted to cry.

We stood there, waiting, scanning the distance for the car to return. My stomach hurt as I kept smiling, trying not to cry. My mother had dropped us on the side of the road before, but she had never driven out of sight.

William grabbed a stick and sat cross-legged in the gravel, tracing a circle with its tip. I sat next to him, my eyes following the lines he created.

I counted the seconds as high as I could, until I didn't know what came next.

Then, as if nothing had happened, the station wagon appeared. A dot on the horizon, growing bigger and bigger until it was upon us. My mother stopped the car, and we crossed the street and climbed in. I sat in the middle seat, between my siblings, and remained quiet. The gnawing feeling in my stomach—the one that I have grown all too familiar with—wouldn't subside, even as we pulled into the driveway of our home.

That was the day I realized I didn't know what my mother was capable of.

The blueish-white sunlight of early morning poured through the open window. I listened as a blue jay rustled in the tree outside, preparing his nest. Jack was stroking my hair and staring past me. "What's on your agenda for today?" he asked.

"I have class at noon, then work later."

I had been hired at a second-hand bookstore downtown. My evenings were consumed with sifting through dusty books, stocking shelves, and reading the classics. Jack said it was the perfect job for me.

"How about you?"

"I've got to go to the gallery." He paused. "I have a meeting with a potential buyer. Someone I met at that party, actually."

"Oh?"

"Yeah. You met her, remember? Jessica?"

I felt my shoulders tense. "Yeah, I remember."

Jack kicked the sheets off before standing. I reached forward, grabbing the edge and automatically smoothing them out before covering myself. I stared as he rummaged through the closet, selecting a green corduroy shirt. He pulled it on, one arm at a time, and began buttoning it.

I kicked my feet beneath the sheets and sighed in an attempt to get his attention. Jack continued to button, his head down. "What will you do after the meeting?" I asked, though I knew he would head to the dive bar around the corner. Either disappointed with the outcome of the meeting or celebrating a successful day, he'd sit at the bar with the regular daytime drunks, telling jokes and buying them drinks.

Jack was no good with money. I managed our finances for that reason. He disliked the business side of his work, saying it was tacky to have to deal with selling. He was always looking to outsource that part of his job, wanting someone to find clients for him and deal with the transactions. Then all he would have to do was paint.

"We'll see," he said, stepping into a pair of blue jeans and slipping on a frayed leather belt.

I put on my baby voice. "Hey, Jack?"

"Yes, darling."

"Why do you love me?"

Pausing for a moment, he turned to face me. He sat on the bed and reached out, holding my chin in his hand. "Well, I love you because you're absolutely beautiful. You're brilliant, you're funny as hell. You're dark, but you're also light. You make me want to be a better person." Letting my face go, he wrapped his arms around me and pulled me close. "Oh, and you have a killer ass."

I laughed. "Good to know you're not superficial."

Jack carefully watched me before kissing my forehead and climbing out of bed.

I lay back and listened to the clanging of dishes as he made breakfast, then drifted back to sleep.

In a field filled with nothing but red roses, I walked and walked until I came across a little girl. She was small at first, only the size of a toddler. I ran toward her, concerned that she was alone. I didn't recognize her; the reds all blended into a hodgepodge of petals and swirls. As I got closer, the girl began to grow, her brown eyes expanding until they were two giant boulders blocking my path. Her mouth parted into a smile, all teeth, like the keys of a grand piano. Her hair was made of rose petals and fluttered down, joining with the ground under my feet. She was now a giant, and she stood, staring, her teeth growing larger and larger and sharper and sharper. She opened her mouth and swallowed me whole. Everything went black just as the loud bang of the front door startled me awake.

Jessica.

"What the fuck?" I rubbed the sleep from my eyes and stretched my legs, groaning from the release. I stood, straightened the pillows, and tugged at the edges of the blanket, adjusting the left side slightly, and then the right side, then the left side again. Satisfied, I walked to the bathroom to take a shower, spotting a tiny yellow sticky note on the mirror:

She didn't want to be loved
She wanted to be idolized

Jack liked to gag me and tie me up. Jamming a pair of panties into my mouth, he'd loop his belt around my ankles and wrists, or use one of my scarves to hog-tie me as I lay on my stomach. Sometimes he'd bring rope home from his studio and tie intricate knots around my hips and breasts. Securing me to the bedpost or the closet door, legs and arms spread wide open, he'd leave me there for undetermined periods of time, waiting for him.

It reminded me of a game Hannah and I invented when we were ten. We called it "monster."

One afternoon when Hannah and I were sitting in my bedroom, she asked if I wanted to play. I stuck my head out and listened down the hallway before closing my bedroom door and securing the lock.

"Do you want to be the monster?" I asked excitedly. "Or will I?"

"I'll be the monster."

"Okay." I smiled, sucking my lips in until they disappeared. I liked it best when she was the monster.

I lay down on the bed and raised my hands above my head, waiting motionless.

Hannah stood, looming over me, and tied my hands with a skipping rope. Once around the left hand, once around the right hand, then around both hands twice. She walked to the other side of the room. "Where's my prisoner?" she snarled.

I didn't say a word, but let out a small giggle.

She lowered herself down on all fours and started crawling toward the bed. One limb at a time, she climbed onto the mattress, twisting and growling.

She mounted me, straddling my body, her bare knees buckled on each side of my torso. Inching her face closer and closer, her long yellow hair cascaded alongside my face as if our heads were in a tent together. I could feel the warmth of her breath. She began kissing me. First on my cheeks and forehead, then she began gently pecking me on the lips. Pushing her wet tongue into my mouth, she let her hand trail down my stomach. My shirt had ridden up and my back was exposed, itchy against the crocheted blanket. Hannah slipped her hand under the waistband of my pants.

I was afraid that if I moved she would stop, so I ignored my desire to scratch. I held my breath and kissed her back. The white hairs on her legs softly brushed against my pale sides. My entire body felt flushed, as if I were a melting Popsicle. A ticking sensation, like the arm of a clock, began in my private area.

Suddenly, there was a knock on the door.

Hannah hopped off of me and I quickly sat up, my wrists still tied.

"What?" I called, attempting to sound normal, but it came out high-pitched. I cleared my throat.

"Supper's almost ready," my mother called through the closed door. "Hannah, will you be joining us?"

"No, thank you," she replied. "I should get home."

Hannah stood, back on to me, adjusting her dress. I could see that her hair had tangled and I wanted to tell her, but nothing came out. Neither of us said anything. Without looking back, she hurried out of my room, shutting the door behind her.

Still bound, I began to pull at the knots with my back teeth.

Jack called and asked me to meet him in the park. I had been up late the previous evening, finishing a term paper on psychopomps. School was closing in on winter break. I was exhausted and beginning to feel the effects of the changing season, which left me a little melancholic and despondent. I needed to see him.

Jack hadn't been home for a few days; busy with work, he was sleeping at his studio. He was beginning to make a name for himself, selling a lot of pieces and having difficulty keeping up with the demand. I was happy for him, but at the same time something monstrous inside, something I barely wanted to acknowledge, resented him for his success.

I felt untethered without his presence to ground me, like I was too deep in darkness. I walked the short distance from our house.

It hadn't snowed yet, but the temperature hovered near freezing. As I moved, I tugged the collar of my mohair coat into my neck. The grass was crisp and patchy, and each step felt like I was breaking glass. A group of kids kicked a soccer ball back and forth, colourfully bundled in hats, mittens, and scarves. I stopped for a moment to watch, hoping to absorb some of their carefree glee.

A lanky man in his late sixties stood nearby, propped against the trunk of a tree. He waved in my direction. I looked around to see if he was waving at someone behind me, but there was no one else. I smiled politely and nodded in greeting, then continued on. Scanning the park, I spotted Jack through the dying trees, sitting amid a cluster of people. They were drinking beer from cans, perched on a tattered blanket, the kind that someone's grandmother had likely passed down to them when they moved out of their parents' house.

"Hey, baby." Jack waved, beckoned me to join them. I sat next to him and glanced around at the group. They were all wearing black. Vintage cashmere coats, scarves, leather gloves, tartan hats. All black.

"Who died?" I whispered to Jack.

He smirked and kissed me on the cheek as my gaze landed on Jessica's face. My throat clenched and let go. I hadn't seen her since the party.

"Hey, Grace." She was wearing a black beret, her silky red hair peeking out beneath. "Jessica, remember?"

"Of course." I forced a smile. "Nice to see you."

"We were just talking about how Jack has the best hair." She giggled, reaching up and running her fingers through his dark brown curls.

I began scratching my neck, and thought of how I had given him his last haircut.

Jack eyed her before pulling away.

He reached to put his arm around me and I recoiled. My eyes met Jessica's, and she grinned. Those giant teeth. They seemed whiter in the light of day.

"I think I'm going to run to the store." I stood up, my knees shaky. I steadied them, turning to Jack without making eye contact. "Do you need anything?"

He peeked down at the half-case next to him. "Um, no, I'm good."

"Anyone else?" I asked the group.

The unfamiliar heads shook from left to right in their sea of blackness.

I walked at a clip toward the road. The group of kids who had been kicking the soccer ball now sat motionless and silent. Their heads rotated in unison as I approached. I felt as if I were in some sort of twilight zone.

It was cold, insufferably so. My breath turned to vapour as it met the air. Fishing in my pocket for my pack of cigarettes, I tripped, catching myself before I fell.

Jack was chasing me. I could hear him staggering behind me. I'd recognize his tread anywhere. Moving as fast as I could, I hoped to outmanoeuvre him, but he caught up, grabbing me by the arm and knocking my cigarettes to the ground. His mouth was turned down at the corners. "What's going on?"

"Seriously?" I bent to retrieve the package. Standing, I pulled a cigarette loose with my teeth.

"Why are you being so weird?" Jack raised his gloved hand to meet the tip of my cigarette, lighting it with a flick of his Zippo.

I inhaled, attempting to silence the throbbing between my legs. It always aroused me when he lit my cigarette.

"I was up all night. You didn't come home, again." I was whisper-yelling so as not to draw any more attention. "Then I came to meet you—which you begged me to, by the way—and have to watch some bitch run her fingers through your hair."

"Oh please, don't be dramatic." He reached for the cigarette and took a long draw before placing it back in my mouth.

I was melting into placidity, so easily malleable. Jack had this effect on me. He could soften me with a few simple gestures. I wondered why I was even mad as I scratched my neck again, digging my nails in hard and fast, up and down, feeling the warmth and wetness of blood.

"Babe, stop scratching." Jack grabbed my hand, holding it in his. "You're bleeding."

"No, I'm not." I was stubborn, clutching the ire, questioning myself, questioning everything. I jerked my hand away, staring at it. Blood was caked beneath my nails.

I glanced past Jack, spotting the lanky man once again—the one who had waved at me. He was standing nearby, clutching a penny-farthing bicycle. Our eyes met.

"I'm sorry about Jessica," Jack said, softly. "She's just high on a power trip or something."

"Don't be sorry." I took a draw on my cigarette before flicking it. Turning away, I began walking straight through a garden plot filled with flowers in various forms of decay. I heard a crunch and stopped, standing on one foot, balancing to see the bottom of my boot. A withered rose was jammed into the groves of my sole. I looked over my shoulder.

Everything had vanished.

I was cracking into smaller pieces, each morsel stringing, viscously adhered to my foundation. It reminded me of when I was a child, playing on the merry-go-round at the park by our house. Annabelle and William sat beside me as I clung to the metal bars. Glancing at my knuckles, I noticed the yellow and red paint was chipped underneath, revealing black iron speckled with rust.

The park was quiet and empty. It had been raining all morning. The swing set and teeter-totters were vacant and dewy beneath clearing grey skies, and as the heavy clouds shifted, the sun revealed itself. The grass glistened with beads of moisture as my father hunched over, an old blue baseball cap fitted on his head, his feet firmly planted on the ground. His jeans were worn at the knees, and the neck of his burnt orange T-shirt stretched from my mother's inability to properly do laundry. Each time we spun around, he grabbed the metal, pushing us with all the force he could muster, nearly falling over with each thrust. Annabelle's long black hair flew backwards as she clutched the rail, her arms and legs wrapped around it. She was terrified. William let his head fall back, laughing and squealing, shouting, "Faster, faster, faster." The sheer velocity at which we moved should have catapulted us from the merry-go-round, but physics kept us from falling.

I was spiralling out of control. Barely holding on as I swung in desperate circles. My wrists were breaking, my neck was snapping. It wasn't a game anymore.

I called Dr. Brace and requested an emergency session. My head was filled with murky water. I couldn't concentrate, focus my eyes, or sit still.

"I'm scared," I whispered, circling the kitchen table over and over and over, the phone cradled in my neck.

"Come in right away," he said calmly.

I didn't feel safe to drive. I could barely see what was directly in front of me. Objects were indistinct and nebulous; everything seemed to lack definition. I called for a cab.

When it arrived, it smelled of stale tobacco and vomit. There were tiny black-rimmed cigarette burns in the leather seats. I ran my fingers over them.

"Where to?" the driver asked, peering at me through the rear-view mirror. He was middle-aged, with a shiny bald spot on the crown of his salt-and-peppered head.

"The Crisis Centre on Pleasant Ave."

He nodded, and we rode in silence.

My movements seemed inconsequential and like they were happening in slow motion. My senses were heightened to the point of nausea. It seemed as though the world was made up of only lengthy shadows. For a moment, I couldn't see any light. Unable to stomach looking out the window, I stared straight at the meter as the price went up by five cents every few seconds. I shut my eyes for a moment.

"Here we are."

Startled, I opened my eyes as the driver turned to look at me. I forgot where I was. I forgot everything. His eyes were strikingly blue, clouded and crystallized with age. I tossed a couple bills over the seat and pushed open the door. "Keep the change."

Standing outside the rusty-red and brown brick building, I let my head fall back, counting the windows. I kept losing track, forgetting what came next, and beginning again. The taxi driver honked his horn, jolting me back.

I headed for the main door and tugged the handle. It was locked. I pressed the buzzer three times, waited a few seconds, then buzzed again. A robotic voice came through the intercom: "Yes. Do you have an appointment?" This made me smile a demented, tight-lipped grin. *How crazy do they think I am? They really need to protect themselves from me by a locked door and intercom?*

"Yes," I replied, giving the door a second and third yank before it clicked open.

I nodded at the intercom woman as I passed the front desk, barrelling down the hallway. I turned my head from left to right, counting and humming. *One, two, three, four; closed door, closed door, closed door, closed door.* I reached the familiar precipice of Dr. Brace's office and entered without knocking.

He was sitting in his chair but, startled by my entrance, was quickly on his feet. "Grace, what's going on?"

"I can't sleep." I paced back and forth in the narrow space. I couldn't look at him. I imagined sinking my nails into my skin, smashing my head against the wall over and over until blood poured from my orifices and I lay motionless on the ground. My thoughts were moving so quickly I visualized them, like wires of unharvested electricity circuiting through.

"Would you like to sit?" He motioned to the chair.

"I can't sit. I can't stop. I need to keep moving, otherwise my thoughts might take me. They might take me away and I don't know if I'll come back this time. I don't know if I can make it back down."

He grabbed his notepad. "Can you explain what you mean a little more?"

I just screamed.

Dr. Brace picked up the phone, dialling quickly a number he had memorized. He spoke into the receiver as I disappeared. I wasn't in the room anymore. I wasn't anywhere.

I counted with speed and ease, muttering in a hushed tone, as if everything in the room were numbered. The chair was made of one hundred and ninety-three beige polka dots. The desk had nine drawers, eighteen knobs. My eyes traced the moulding on the ceiling over and over until I became dizzy and had to sit down.

I closed my eyes for a moment, and when I opened them, a police officer and social worker were standing before me. I examined the two men, deciding they were a strange combination. The officer was abnormally tall and had a baby-smooth face. He must have shaved that morning. The social worker was shorter, leaner, and had a head of thick, jet-black hair. His lips were the colour of Red Delicious apples, full and juicy. I wanted to bite them. I wanted to sink my teeth into the soft, red flesh and suck the nectar from them. I wanted him to push me to the ground and yell at me: "You're acting crazy, snap out of it."

Dr. Brace was peering down at me. "Grace, you're going to go with these gentlemen to get the help you need, okay?"

I stood and held out my hands. "Okay."

"Oh, we won't be cuffing you. You're not under arrest." The officer rubbed his baby-smooth chin. "You just come with us, Grace."

We exited the building and I climbed into the back seat of the police cruiser. The flashing lights, red and blue, were carnivalesque. They danced on the constable's face playfully. There were no sirens, only lights. I don't remember anything they said, but the indentations on the social worker's face were deep with concern.

They escorted me to the entrance of the Psychiatric Assessment Unit and rang the buzzer.

A lanky security guard dressed in a blue uniform with a gold name tag arrived to retrieve me. The fluorescent lights reflected off his tag, obstructing the engraved name beneath. He held the door open for me. I was his responsibility now.

I suddenly had the urge to hug the police officer, so I turned and wrapped my arms around him. "Thank you, Father," I whispered. He remained stiff as I squeezed him, one hand on his holster.

I let go, leaving the other two men behind, and followed the guard through a series of locked entrances, his electronic pass opening each door with a loud beep.

The walls were lined with Tyvek, the raw beams exposed.

"They doing renovations?"

"Yes," the guard replied. "It's been going on for a while."

I dragged my hands along the Tyvek, which made a faint crinkle, as I headed toward the buzzing light in the distance.

The guard was used to dealing with crazies. You could always tell. He didn't recoil when I spoke to him. He wasn't afraid of me.

He led me to the front desk. Dr. Brace had clearly called ahead and warned them of my arrival.

"Grace?" The receptionist spoke through the rectangular slit of a plastic partition.

In the light of the waiting room, I was now able to see the guard's tag. Burned in a bold, black font, it read, *JACK*.

I squinted at it, drawing my eyebrows close together. I began to shake. "Jack?"

"Yes?" He looked from his tag to me, and back again.

"Jack. It's me, Grace," I screamed, jabbing myself in the chest with my pointer finger. "Grace. Remember? Grace." I kept screaming as the guard retreated through a door and disappeared down the corridor.

The receptionist hurried around her desk and restrained me as another woman appeared, injecting me in the arm with a syringe.

When I came to, I was lying in a little white room. I felt as though I was in a crib, confined by the narrow walls. Crammed next to me was the woman who had injected me, sitting in a scratched-up vinyl chair. Her hair was grey and feathery, cut in a short, boyish way. She wore blue scrubs and white, lace-less sneakers. Directly above me was a window with iron bars. It was dark outside. There were no curtains and no bedsheets. No way of escaping.

"Hello, Grace." The woman's tone was familiar, as if she knew me. Maybe she did. I had dealt with so many health-care professionals over the years it was hard to remember. "How are you feeling?"

"A bit better." My voice came out weakly, strained from all the screaming.

"Can I get you anything?" She uncrossed her arms, glancing at the clipboard in her lap. "Some water, maybe?"

"I'm fine."

Pursing her lips, the lines around her mouth deepened. She looked like a marionette. "Grace, I'm going to ask you some questions and I need you to answer as honestly as possible. Okay?"

"Sure." I pressed my cheek into the striped pillow with no cover.

"How old are you?"

"Twenty-three."

She jotted my responses onto the page in red ink. "Are you currently taking any medication?"

"No." I shook my head and tugged at the skin on my neck.

"Do you have any history of self-harm?"

I paused. I was wearing a hospital gown. *What have I gotten myself into? Did this woman undress me? She must have already seen the marks.* "Mhm."

Through the thin walls, I heard the scuttle of a woman entering the room adjacent to mine. She was crying hysterically. "I wrapped all my pill bottles in Bubble Wrap," the woman explained through dramatic sobs. "I don't want to kill myself."

"What an idiot," I muttered.

Venturing outside for the first time in months, Jack and I walked from our apartment to the park. It was springtime once again, and the weight of winter was starting to lift. People were emerging from hibernation to face the grey and foggy months they knew were ahead; all of us on the island were accustomed to this pattern. The earth was coming alive, smelling of dampness and rebirth, and it filled me with a sense of hope. It reminded me of a beautiful bruise oxidizing: green, yellow, blue, and then purple.

"We should take a trip this summer," Jack suggested.

I felt a flutter in my chest. I couldn't help but smile. "Where should we go?"

"You always talk about New York. Why don't we go there?"

As I considered the possibilities, I heard a youthful, sing-song voice. I glanced toward the precipice of the park where I saw, sitting cross-legged beneath a tree, a little girl in a summer dress with short brown pigtails. She was singing. Encircled by yellow dandelions, she snatched one from the earth and placed her thumb beneath the flower's head. With an effortless flick, the top popped clean off and landed on the grass nearby. She continued her ritual. I listened, closely, straining to hear her tiny voice.

Mama had a baby and her head popped off.

Mama had a baby and her head popped off.

Mama had a baby and her head popped oooooooffffffffff.

I felt liquid climbing up my throat. Just as I turned away, vomit spewed from my mouth. Jack grabbed my hair, holding it away from my face with one hand and stroking my back with the other. "Are you okay?" he asked.

I wiped my mouth with my sleeve. "Yeah, I'm fine."

Jack had this look in his eye.

When I was eight, my grandfather insisted I accompany him on his annual trip to snare rabbits. My father used to go with him when he was a boy, so when I told my parents I didn't want to, they said it would be good for me to experience new things. Things that they had already experienced.

"Will you come too?" I asked my father, as he sat in the living room. I was dressed in my one-piece purple snowsuit, hat, mittens, scarf, and boots. I could barely bend my arms.

Glancing up from his novel, he studied my face. "No, your grandfather and I don't get along so well anymore." He shifted his gaze to the window, his fingers clutching the edges of his book. "You should go wait for him outside."

I hesitated, watching my father as he continued to stare out at the trees, wondering if he would say anything else.

He remained silent.

"Okay." I turned, heading for the door.

Snowflakes were whipping and whirling in a tornado-like pattern as my grandfather's black pickup truck floated into sight. He pulled into the driveway, killing the engine before climbing out.

"Hello, doll," he called.

I walked toward him slowly. I hardly knew this man. He was tall and thin, with a carefully trimmed white beard and hair that was slicked back, resting just beneath his ears. He wore a red-and-black flannel jacket, jeans, and darkly tinted aviators. He walked around the truck and as he crouched to hug me, I saw my reflection in his sunglasses.

"Hello, Grandfather."

He opened the door and helped me onto the passenger seat. My legs dangled, unable to reach the floor.

My grandfather climbed into the driver's seat, and as he shut the door, he passed me a contraption. "Hold onto this for Grandpa."

Reluctantly, I reached for it, placing it between my knees. It resembled the noose I'd seen once in a movie my parents said I wasn't allowed to watch but had watched anyway. "What is it?"

"It's a snare." He looked over his shoulder as he backed out of the driveway. "To catch rabbits."

I examined the snare. It was just a stick with an attached wire. Tugging its end, I watched as the silvery loop tightened and loosened.

We drove in silence to my grandparents' cabin, the wipers flicking at full speed as snow flew at us, my grandfather hunched forward, clutching the steering wheel. I stared out the windshield. The dash was covered in a layer of dust that lifted off as soon as the heaters kicked in. It felt like we were hurtling through outer space.

When we arrived at the threshold, my grandfather put the truck in park before climbing out to open the wooden gate. I examined the cabin, which was built from misshapen logs that had been painted light blue. The driveway was completely untouched and white. It looked like something from a fairy tale; a witch's dwelling in the woods that a group of kids had happened upon in misfortune.

My grandfather returned, climbing into the driver's seat once again, leaving his seat belt unbuckled as we drove through. The truck beeped repeatedly in warning as I glanced in the rear-view mirror, noting the disturbance we were causing to the peaceful, resting snow. An ugly wreckage of tire marks and dripping oil.

My grandfather led me down a path into the woods. I didn't know what to do with the snare, so I carried it as we walked, clutching it tightly. I wanted to drop it and pretend it was an accident. I didn't want any part of this.

The evergreens were blanketed with snow, their limbs drooping from the weight. We walked, and I counted the trees.

I'd gotten to sixty-six by the time my grandfather stopped. "This is a good spot. Give me that." He motioned to the snare, and I handed it to him. He scanned the distance before bending, raising the snare, and driving it into the snow with a sharp blow.

I dropped to my bum then flopped back, windshield-wiping my arms and legs.

"Look at me," I announced. "I'm an angel."

"Grace, this isn't playtime. Get up."

I stood, embarrassed for having been reprimanded. Staring at the ground, I thought of the rabbit, wondering if it would be a mother or a father.

"Let's go back and wait." Grandfather began walking, and I hurried to catch up without saying anything.

I counted the trees again, wondering if the rabbit's babies would die because of us.

Sixty-eight.

When we arrived at the cabin, my grandfather pushed the door open and I followed, scanning the small interior quickly. I had never been inside before. It consisted of one open room. There was a sagging periwinkle sofa in the middle, upholstered in a fabric that resembled corduroy, a small table with two chairs against the only window, and an unmade cot against the wall. A stove, a sink, and an ancient-looking refrigerator were bunched in the opposite corner.

My grandfather grabbed the kettle from the stovetop and filled it from the sink's tap. "Do you want some hot chocolate?"

"Okay." I nodded before adding, "Please."

He turned the burner on and retrieved two mugs from the cupboard. Hesitantly, I sat on the sofa and waited.

It was freezing in the cabin, and my breath took shape as it left my mouth. I rubbed my hands together before lifting them to my mouth and blowing on them.

The kettle began whistling louder and louder until my grandfather grabbed it and flicked the burner off. He filled two mugs, stirring the mixture before pulling a silver flask from his breast pocket. Adding a generous amount of the amber liquid to his own cup, he walked over and passed me the other. "Do you like marshmallows?"

I looked inside the cup, the white marshmallows bobbing on the brown surface, the steam warming my face.

"That's a stupid question," my grandfather snickered. "Of course you do. All kids like marshmallows."

I didn't.

Sitting next to me, he took large gulps from his mug. His smell was unfamiliar to me, mixing with the scent of chocolate. I peered down into my cup and, using my thumb, pushed the marshmallows into the liquid, pretending they were little creatures I was drowning. "Help me, help me," I said quietly from the side of my mouth, in a cartoon-like way.

My grandfather took my hand as we walked the trail, retracing our path through the snow. I tried to distract myself by stepping only in my grandfather's footprints. He was a big man, with big feet, and my footprint didn't even fill half of his. I struggled to keep up and fumbled. My grandfather caught me and hauled me upright by the arm. "Pay attention to where you're going," he scolded. "You need to be vigilant."

"Sorry," I muttered.

As we walked, I prayed the snare would be empty.

"We got one," my grandfather whispered.

I could hear the creature struggling, scurrying and thumping. I swallowed the lump in my throat as he picked up his pace, dragging me along.

We arrived, and there it was, a white rabbit, grunting and squeaking like a tiny piglet, the wire noose wrapped tightly around its neck. It was about the size of our family cat. I remembered learning in science class that rabbits changed colour in the winter so they could hide. This was supposed to protect them from predators.

The rabbit was in shock. Petrified, it stared at me, and I stared back. Its nose twitched and I shrieked.

My grandfather snatched the rabbit by the ears, peering into its face for a moment. Then he dug in his pocket, pulling his knife from its sheath.

"Grandfather, don't."

"This is how the world works, Grace." He lowered his knife and cut the rabbit's throat. Blood poured out, the snow reddening and melting in a lopsided circle at my grandfather's feet. As the bleeding slowed, it beaded on the rabbit's fur before slowly trickling onto the ground, drop by drop. "Kill or be killed."

When we returned home, my grandfather presented his kill to my mother. She dissected the rabbit on the kitchen counter. I remember the blood, the bits of pink flesh, and the chunks of fur.

Mother boiled its parts in a stockpot on the stove, which caused the entire house to smell of death. She filled jars with liquid and placed the remains inside, like some sick science experiment. The bottles sat on the shelf in our kitchen for weeks. Every time I saw them, I visualized the rabbit's shiny black eyes, remembering the way it had looked at me.

It was the exact look Jack gave me that day.

Dear Sunshine,

I've been counting silver trays. The first, when I was a baby; the last, that day in the hospital when you never showed up. Me, lying on that table. So many in between.

They have been present my entire life. Sanitary and sterile, lined with needles and knives, tools to poke and prod. Dangerous objects that are supposed to somehow heal you.

They say I've been saved one too many times.

How many silver trays have you seen?

Love,
G

My great-grandmother had the gift of second sight. She was the seventh daughter of a seventh daughter. On the island, the seventh daughter of a seventh daughter was known to possess certain magical abilities. She was a hundred and one years old, and lived alone in an entirely beige two-bedroom apartment. My great-grandfather had died the year before I was born. I knew two things about him: he rarely smiled, and he had a prosthetic leg.

I went to visit my great-grandmother one afternoon when Jack was at his studio. I removed my shoes as I entered the apartment, feeling the plush carpet on my bare toes. The television's volume was cranked and the thermostat was set to cremate.

My great-grandmother was sitting in her rocking chair facing the television, a small pile of candy bars on the table beside her. I kissed her on the cheek and sat opposite her on the couch. "How are you?"

The wrinkles in her face were like craters, her hair thinned to the point of transparency. She was so little, she couldn't have weighed more than ninety pounds. Pointing the remote at the television, she clicked the button over and over to minimize the volume. "I'm going to die in four days."

It stung, the thought of losing her. "Why do you say that?"

"I dreamt it last night," she explained, reaching for a candy bar. "My dreams always come true, you know this."

"Well I really hope this one doesn't," I said, my voice small.

She peeled the wrapper from the candy bar and bit into it, chewing carefully and swallowing. "I don't want you to be sad, though." She smiled knowingly. "Someone new will be coming into your life."

I smiled back, despite the queasiness I felt in my stomach.

Four days later, I was awakened by the oak grandfather clock. The coils wound and spun, then it chimed loudly. Startled, I sat up in bed.

Jack wasn't home yet. The clock had never worked, it was simply decorative.

I looked to the door, and my great-grandmother was standing in the entryway. She was glowing, beautiful, smiling and hazy, as if she were a dream. As she stared, a wave of peacefulness rippled through me. Then, she vanished.

I returned to sleep, feeling the warmth of maternal protection.

The next morning, as I sat in the living room drinking coffee and thumbing through an old magazine, the telephone rang. I lifted the receiver to my ear. "Hello?"

"Doll?" It was my mother.

"Yes?"

"I've got some bad news." She paused, letting out a sigh. "Nanny died last night in her sleep."

I turned the page of my magazine. "I know. You didn't have to call."

When I was seven years old, my parents enrolled me in Sunday school.

I spent Sunday afternoons in the dusty basement of the Catholic church with a gaggle of shrunken, ancient nuns and the mothers of other children. We coloured images of Mary, Joseph, and the baby Jesus using cracked crayons with frayed paper, sang hymns, and listened to stories about what made people good and what made them bad.

One afternoon, I was sitting by myself at a table, colouring a picture of Jesus on the cross. I clutched the nub of a red crayon, scribbling well outside the lines of His body. In my mind, He was covered in blood. Sipping from the straw of an apple juice box, I hummed to myself.

Sister Laracy, a ninety-year-old nun, hobbled toward me, dragged a chair alongside, and struggled to sit before collapsing into the chair with a thump.

"How are you, Grace?"

"I'm good, Sister," I replied without looking up. "How are you?"

"I'm well, child."

My legs didn't reach the ground, so I allowed them to swing back and forth as I worked on my colouring sheet.

"Have your parents mentioned anything about their plans to get married?" she asked.

"No, Mother says she doesn't want to get married."

"I see."

I glanced at Sister Laracy. Her eyes didn't quite focus, her pupils were full of little spots. Returning my gaze to the sheet on the plastic table, I admired all the red, wondering if she could see.

"You know, having children out of wedlock is considered a sin in the eyes of God."

"Yes, I know." I remembered the priest explaining all the sins in church. *Honour thy mother and father; Thou shalt not steal; Thou shalt not murder; Thou shalt not covet thy neighbour's goods.* A long list of things you weren't allowed to do.

"Grace, look at me please."

I raised my eyes to meet her face, feeling my cheeks redden in embarrassment. I guess she could see, after all.

"You know, fornication outside of wedlock is a sin." She pointed her crooked, arthritic finger at me. She inhaled deeply, her chest expanding. "'Let marriage be held in honour among all, and let the marriage bed be undefiled. God will judge the sexually immoral and adulterous.' Do you know what that means?"

I shook my head. Some juice dripped down my lip but I didn't lick it off.

"It means those who sin will be punished in the afterlife. It may be too late for your parents, but you can still be saved." She began her struggle to get up, grabbing ahold of the table and pulling herself to her feet. "Don't make the same mistakes as them."

Jack and I drove in silence, his hand on the back of my head, gently massaging my hair. The rosary beads that hung from the rear-view mirror swayed back and forth. We pulled into the parking lot of the pharmacy, narrowly avoiding a collision with a sunken-eyed, scrawny teenager who sprinted away as though freshly escaped from some mental asylum.

"Methadone clinic," Jack reminded me.

Inside, the fluorescent lights hit my eyes and I could feel a tension headache beginning in my temples, so I pressed my fingertips into them, digging in. It hurt in a good way. The colours, the people, the bright lights, the choices, it was all too much. White flashes began creeping in.

Jack could always tell when a panic attack was coming. He grabbed my hand. "It's fine, little one. This will just take a second."

We made our way through the store, excusing ourselves as people stepped out of the way. Soap, shampoo, razors, toothbrushes, condoms, lubricants. We arrived in the family-planning aisle, both of us staring dumbly ahead. First Response, Clearblue, e.p.t.

"This one has two in it," Jack said, pointing. "Let's get it, in case one's a dud."

"Alright," I said, grabbing the box and heading for the cash.

The curly-haired cashier was hardly tall enough to see over the counter. She struggled to scan the item as she open-mouth chewed a stick of gum. "$20.68, please."

Jack pulled some bills from his wallet as she bagged the box, blowing a bubble with her pink gum. The bubble popped and shrunk. She sucked it back into her mouth, handing him change and a brown paper bag folded over on top. "Have a nice day."

"You too."

As we made our way to the car, another methadone-clinic teen, this one with a teardrop tattoo on his face, asked if we had any change.

Jack gave me the paper bag so he could dig in his pocket. He located a couple of coins and passed them to the kid.

We drove to the apartment in silence. I counted the traffic lights. *Nineteen.*

Jack wanted me to take the test right away. I sat on the sofa and opened the box, reading the instructions in their entirety as he shifted canvasses around, holding them up to the light and examining them. Once, twice, and a third time. My eyes scanned the words—four, five, six times. I balled up the paper and stuffed it back in the box.

"It says you should take it first thing in the morning."

"Okay." He was separating the pieces into three piles. "So you'll take it when you get up tomorrow?"

I nodded.

I wanted to savour this time. I didn't want anything to be certain just yet.

I woke up at five o'clock and had to pee. I carefully removed Jack's arm from around my shoulder and climbed out of bed, making my way to the bathroom. It was still dark outside, so I switched on the light and grabbed the pregnancy test from the cupboard below the sink. I opened the box and turned it upside down, allowing the plastic-encased contraption to slide into my hand. I used my teeth to tear it open, digging in the box for the crumpled instructions:

Place directly below the stream of urine for five seconds.

It sounded easy enough. I pulled down my underwear and sat on the toilet, placing the pregnancy test between my legs, and started to pee. It was harder to manoeuvre than I'd thought.

"Fuck," I muttered as I peed on my hand.

The instructions said the results would take a couple of minutes. I put the cover back on the testing strip and laid it flat on the counter. I lathered my hands with soap and rinsed them in the sink, wiping them with an indigo hand towel that hung nearby. The smell was overwhelming, so I paced back and forth in the bathroom, trying not to throw up, reciting the words that I had long ago memorized from the framed poem on our wall.

One day at a time,—this is enough.
Do not look back and grieve over the past, for it is gone;
and do not be troubled about the future, for it has not yet come.
Live in the present, and make it so beautiful it will be
worth remembering.

Heart racing can't feel left arm can't feel left leg shake leg make sure it's working left arm so heavy lift it lift it above head vein in neck throbbing check pulse head so heavy can't hold anymore down lay down Ativan where the fuck look up down grounding exercise five things see television coffee table water drink water mouth so dry can't swallow swallowing you're fine you're fine tongue numb smile is smile normal stroke panic attack five things mirror book four things hear cars driving clock ticking fan whirling buzz television three things smell coffee peaches cleaner two things taste mint bile the last thing oh fuck chest tight heart attack breathe deep breath one breathe deep breath two breathe deep breath three breath deep breathe four deep breath breathe five breathe breathe breathe you're fine you're fine no you're not you're fucking not fine.

Pulling my legs close, I balled myself up on the sofa in the living room and clutched the pregnancy test. A dim yellow light crept through the window, landing on Jack's easel. I traced it to the street lamp across the pavement that was still illuminated. The early morning stillness was disturbed only by Jack's incessant pacing. The rest of the world was sleeping.

"What do you want to do?" he asked, standing over me. He was shirtless, his arms folded across his bare chest. His jeans dangled, barely clinging to his protruding hip bones.

"What do you mean, exactly?" I asked, allowing my legs to fall and placing my bare feet on the cold hardwood floor.

He paused, squinting his eyes tight before speaking. "Grace, we're so young. You're still in university. You want to be a writer. I'm a painter."

"So?" The word came out sharp and my head shot forward. I felt savagely protective.

"So, how are we going to support a baby right now?"

I knew what he was insinuating, and I resented him for it. I had no desire to be reasonable. "I hope you're not implying what I think you're implying."

"It's not a big deal. People get abortions all the time."

"You fucking asshole." I pushed myself off the couch, past Jack and into the kitchen. I grabbed a bottle of cleaner from below the sink and started spraying the counter.

The smell of bleach reminded me of the public swimming pool we used to frequent when I was a child. On days when my mother was too depressed to get out of bed, my father would dress us in our bathing suits and smear us with sunscreen. We'd walk the short distance to the pool, my father carrying Annabelle in one arm, a *New Yorker* tote bag filled with towels, books, and juice boxes in the other. Between dips in the water, we'd play a game of soccer. My father was the goalie, and the three of us would take turns trying to score.

Convinced my mother hated me, I'd stand outside her bedroom, trying to muster the courage to enter. After a few minutes, I'd push the creaky wooden door open. "Mother?"

The room was dark, a slit of light spilled through the curtain's edge. My mother would be on her side, back to the door. "Mother? We're going to the pool. Do you want to come?"

She'd moan, and without so much as looking at me, say, "No, doll, Mommy isn't feeling well. Shut the door."

As I pulled the door closed, I remained in place, listening to her groggily singing:

You are my sunshine, my only sunshine
You make me happy when skies are gray
You'll never know dear, how much I love you
Please don't take my sunshine away

Jack appeared, leaning against the doorway. "It's the logical thing to do, baby."

"The *logical* thing to do is to kill our child?" I took a cloth and began wiping in furious circles, my voice shaking. "You know my mother was twenty-one when she had William."

"Yes, I know. But you don't have to relive your parents' lives."

I slammed the bottle down. "How dare you."

"I'm sorry. I didn't mean that." His voice was soft and unwavering. "I just don't think it's the right time for us."

"It's never going to be the right time, Jack." I stopped wiping, and turned to look into his eyes. "I'm keeping it. With or without you."

He sighed, stepped toward me, and put his arms around my waist. "Okay."

I had my mother's eyes. Iridescent; a deep ocean blue when my thoughts clung to darkness, lightening only when it lifted.

When I was a little girl, I wanted to be my mother. I often sat at her maplewood vanity. Gazing into one of the three mirrors, I would take her black eyeliner and draw dark circles around my eyes in imitation of her. I would smear her brownish-red lipstick on my lips, overlining them dramatically and smacking them together, pouting and blowing kisses. I would apply coats and coats of mascara until it formed thick clumps that resembled spider legs. I would brush out my naturally curly hair, sweeping it to the side before standing on her bed, mimicking her gestures, smiling and chit-chatting with an imaginary audience.

Melancholy came with her eyes. It would appear in me seemingly out of the blue, looming with destructive silence. For my mother, when it arrived she was confined to her bed, lying in the quiet darkness all day and night. I took a slightly more destructive approach—active in the world, spreading the pain.

I inherited my father's nose. A small button nose with an upward curve. With this nose, I could smell. I could smell sweet lilacs and grass in the summertime, and the heat of Jack's skin after a day at the beach. I could smell the saltwater clouds that lingered before a storm, and the scent of whiskey on Jack's breath, just like my father's, and my grandfather's before him. I could smell the half-empty beer that had staled, left out on the kitchen table from the night before.

When I became pregnant, I could smell everything more clearly than ever, and as I pursued redolence, I wondered what Jack and I would unwittingly pass on to our baby.

Surrounded by sterility, I sat on the examination table in the doctor's office. The paper crinkled beneath me as I shifted my weight, attempting to alleviate the itch of the blue hospital gown. Jack stood nearby, dressed in a black T-shirt and jeans. There was no paint on his clothes or on his hands. I wondered why; it seemed he had been spending all his time at the studio lately.

The shine of the stirrups caught my eye, and I began biting the skin from the sides of my nails. Jack reached over and guided my hand into my lap. "Don't do that."

The action reminded me of my first boyfriend, Ethan, and how he hated when I chewed my nails.

I was fifteen, and Ethan asked me to his house one afternoon. I didn't particularly like him, but I said yes because all the other girls were getting into relationships and I wanted to fit in. I had always struggled with intimacy. The idea of opening myself up to someone was foreign. I believed vulnerability to be a weakness punishable with abandonment.

Ethan lived nearby, so I walked to his house and snuck in through the back door, entering into the unfinished basement. My bare feet treaded lightly on the concrete floor, collecting dirt and sawdust as I followed him to his bedroom.

"My feet are freezing," I said, flopping on the bed and dropping my legs in his lap. He began rubbing them with both hands in an attempt to create friction as particles of dirt fell onto the comforter.

"Are your parents home?" I asked.

"No, I think they went to the store." Ethan was handsome, with tanned skin and blond hair. He played hockey, went to church every Sunday, and did well in school. My parents liked that he read fiction for pleasure, and responded politely when asked a question.

"Why'd I sneak in then?" I nudged him with my foot, playfully.

He bit his lip, one corner of his mouth rising. "I thought you just liked doing that."

Picking up a book from his bedside table—something by Charles Bukowski— I began flipping through. I knew he wanted to have sex, he had been hinting at it for weeks. I didn't want to get a reputation for being easy, so I was making him wait. But I was bored, and I had never been good at waiting.

"Hey." I peered at him over the spine of the book. "Wanna have sex?"

He lifted his eyes from my feet. "Seriously?"

I nodded and dropped the novel. "Do you have a condom?"

"I think so."

He slid from the bed, bent down, and lifted the corner of a blue mat, revealing a loose floorboard that he jiggled free before retrieving a box of condoms.

I rolled onto my stomach and laughed. "Clever."

Ethan kissed me for a few minutes, jamming his tongue into my mouth without any rhythm, before unzipping his fly to reveal his erection. It was the first time I had seen a penis. I thought it was gross, like a big bald head aggressively staring at me. He spent a few seconds trying to manoeuvre the condom. "Sorry," he said awkwardly as he managed it.

"It's fine." Savouring the moment, I took him in, knowing this was meant to be important. I silenced the nun's voice in my head, her omen about sex before marriage. I told myself I was about to metamorphize. No longer a little girl. I made my own choices. I was about to get fucked.

Grabbing me by the legs, Ethan dragged me to the edge of his bed. Still standing, he hiked up my dress, removed my panties, then pushed himself inside me. I remember the pain—sharp and piercing, like my flesh was being torn. By instinct, my body withdrew, but he yanked me back.

Staring at the ceiling, I wondered what this would mean for us. He groaned with pleasure as I lay there, quiet. Was I supposed to love him? What did love even feel like?

It didn't last long, maybe thirty seconds and he was done. He flopped on the bed, panting.

I rose, and a small bloodstain remained on the sheets. Snatching my panties from the floor, I balled them up in my hand, stuffing them into the pocket of my dress.

"I have to go," I decided, my stomach clenching and retracting like a deflating balloon.

"Why?" Ethan asked, lying flat on his back, his thick blond eyebrows furrowed.

"My parents will wonder where I am."

"Can't you stay?" He pulled the condom off and, from where he laid, tossed it in the direction of the garbage, missing by an inch. It hit the concrete ground with a wet splatter. His penis had shrunk and was flopped onto his leg, looking even grosser than when it was hard.

I tried not to show my repulsion, smiling sweetly. "I'll call you later. I promise."

"Okay." He puckered his lips and blew me a kiss.

After that, he became increasingly obsessed with me. He told me he loved me constantly, walking me to and from class, carrying my books in one arm, the other tightly clung around my shoulder. I didn't feel the same, but I revelled in the power imbalance.

A few weeks later, I told Ethan I didn't want to be his girlfriend anymore. As I turned to leave, he grabbed my arm, his eyes filled with tears. "If you leave, I don't know what I'll do." He breathed heavily, his chest heaving. "I'll kill myself."

As I walked out, I couldn't help but smile. It was thrilling.

Ethan didn't kill himself, and when he showed up at school the next day, he told everyone I was a slut. The boys on the hockey team starting messaging me at night, asking for photos of my tits. They said I made their cocks hard, and I grinned behind the screen, realizing how easy it was.

Last I heard, Ethan had married at twenty-four in our hometown church and has two kids, both girls.

"Sorry to keep you waiting," Dr. Jones announced as she entered the office, closing the door behind her.

I had already peed in a plastic cup. The doctor asked us to come receive the results in person. I knew I was pregnant; I didn't need to hear it from her. My boobs were so tender I couldn't even wear a bra. Everything tasted like metal: shiny, chemical, and grey. I just didn't know how far along I was. I had a hazy memory of when the conception might have occurred. We'd been drunk off our asses, high on something, and didn't use a condom. Jack said it was fine because I was on the pill. The problem was that I was so fucked up most days, I couldn't remember if I had taken it or not. I didn't tell Jack that.

"How're you both doing today?" Dr. Jones asked.

I let Jack answer. "We're fine, thanks."

"Good, good. Let's get right to it," she said, reading from the folder in her hands. "We have your results: you are, in fact, pregnant." She glanced up at us for some reaction.

"Wow." Jack leaned into the examination table and ran his hand over his face. "Uh, okay. Wow. Do we know how far along?"

Dr. Jones's finger moved over the page as she scanned it. "It says here about six weeks, but these things aren't exact..."

Her voice faded out as I muttered to myself, "God help me."

Jack's mouth was moving, but all I could hear was a high-pitched ringing that perforated my head and left me breathless. It rang louder and louder and louder, burrowing its way through me.

I had already fucked everything up.

There is a scientific explanation for panic attacks. The body enters a state known as fight-or-flight. It is an evolutionary response developed for life-threatening situations. A part of the brain called the hypothalamus activates two systems: the sympathetic nervous system, through our nerve pathways, and the adrenal-cortical system, through the bloodstream.

The sympathetic nervous system sends a message to the adrenal medulla to release adrenaline and noradrenaline into the bloodstream. The release of these stress hormones causes various changes in the body, such as increased heart rate, dilated pupils, elevated blood pressure, and tense muscles. All senses are heightened.

Meanwhile, the hypothalamus releases the corticotropin-releasing hormone into the pituitary gland, which activates the adrenal-cortical system. The pituitary gland secretes adrenocorticotropic, which then makes its way through the bloodstream to the adrenal cortex, where it releases roughly thirty other hormones that, together, prepare our body to deal with a threat.

This response was once meant to prepare us to either physically fight danger or flee from it. The amount of stimuli we now experience on a daily basis has confused our fight-or-flight response, but the instinct remains.

My body was attempting to warn me; it knew something that my mind had not yet realized.

Jack's paintings were selling. His work had become quite sought-after almost overnight, following a national interview that had run in the newspaper. It was something one of his dealers had arranged and I knew little about until the article ran.

He had stopped selling dope, and we decided I would drop all my classes at the university and continue to work part-time at the bookstore downtown until the baby came. I called in sick one day, consumed with morning sickness, unable to keep anything down. All I wanted was blueberries.

"Will you go to the store and get some blueberries?" I asked Jack as I stood in the kitchen doorway. He was sitting at the table, painting, surrounded by open tubes of paint and wooden-handled paintbrushes. He was using a plate as a palette. "I'm going back to bed."

"Of course," he replied without looking up.

The artificial cherry blossom smell of the dish soap, left open by the sink, was turning my stomach. I walked over and dramatically pressed the seal shut with the palm of my hand. I sighed loudly, staring at the back of Jack's head. I wanted to smack him. "Can you keep the fucking lid closed on the dish soap? It's making me crazy."

Jack was silent as I left the kitchen. I climbed back into bed and pulled the covers over my head, waiting for him to make a move. I retched, but nothing came up. I swallowed and retched again. My throat felt like it was filled with cuts, raw and inflamed from all the vomiting. Rage was surging in synchronicity with the nausea, intensifying with each passing second. I clutched the bedsheets between my fists and squeezed. "Jack?" I called.

"Yeah," he snapped, the chair legs scraping against the kitchen floor as he stood. "I'm going."

When Jack returned from the store, I found the blueberries weren't the same as the ones I'd had when I was a child. They were much larger than the wild ones we had foraged, and pale and tasteless in comparison.

Sitting at the table, I told Jack how each August my family would hike deep into the headlands of our hometown to pick blueberries and partridgeberries.

"Everyone needs to fill one bucket before we go home," my father instructed, passing each of us an empty ice cream container.

"Why can't we just buy berries at the supermarket?" I whined.

"Because I said so," my father replied.

Walking along the gravel path toward the headlands, I was careful not to venture too close to the edge. The landscape was vibrantly green, peppered with wildflowers of orange, white, and yellow. I plucked a dandelion and held it close to my mouth, and with one large exhale the fluffy white seeds dispersed, gliding gently through the air like feathers.

The land dipped and hollowed in unexpected places, and I stumbled into a groove at one point, rolling my ankle before catching myself. Piles of flat rocks in asymmetrical squares—foundations of former houses—lay throughout the open space, overgrown and forgotten.

I picked a partridgeberry and squeezed it between my thumb and forefinger, watching as the deep red juice trickled down my hand like blood.

My grandmother had told me stories about the faeries. "They're fallen angels that were kicked out of heaven by God," she explained as I sat on her knee.

"Why were they kicked out?"

"Because they were too bad for heaven, but not bad enough for hell," she said. "So they are stuck on earth, and they play tricks on humans to entertain themselves."

My grandmother warned me that the faeries would lead you astray when you were picking berries. They sang beautiful melodies to entrance you, and you would become hypnotized by it. Carrying bread was supposed to protect you from the faeries because it was blessed in the name of the Father, Son, and Holy Spirit by the bakers.

In the community where my grandmother grew up, a baby went missing from his stroller. The entire town converged to try and find him. They organized search parties and sent people into the forest to systematically scour the land.

After searching all day without any luck, the parents returned home to find a deformed creature lying in the baby's stroller. The faeries had taken their baby, and replaced it with a changeling.

The mother peeled pages from the newspaper, crumpling them into a ball in her hand while the father went outside to collect kindling from their shack. When he returned, he lit a fire, and they impatiently watched as the orange-blue flames doubled and tripled in size. The mother plucked the creature from her baby's stroller and held it with outstretched arms, as far from her person as possible, approaching the fire. She released the creature from her grip, dropping it in. Engulfed in flames, the changeling began to burn, screeching and crying. Sizzling, demonic smoke-shapes floated overhead as it crumbled to black ash. Then, from the ashes, their son appeared: naked, giggling, newly pure.

I lay on my back with my sweater pulled up, exposing my swollen belly. Staring at the fluorescent lights in the ceiling, I examined the dots in the speckled white tiling as the technician smeared a clear, gooey substance on my stomach. I wondered what my baby thought of the world so far: whether they liked their home, whether they felt safe inside me. The coldness of the gel caused me to inhale sharply and recoil.

"Sorry," the technician apologized. "I should have warned you."

My head throbbed as if someone were consistently rapping on my forehead with their knuckles. I imagined my baby asking who was knocking.

"I'm sorry?" she asked, tilting her head slightly.

"Oh." *Did I say something out loud?* "Nothing."

The smell of the gel was unbearable, sweet and sickly, like cherry Coca-Cola. I began to cough, covering my mouth with my sleeve.

I hadn't told Jack about the appointment. He was at his studio, so it wasn't hard to sneak away. I needed to be alone. Just me and my baby. I knew I would never be able to ask the questions I needed to ask in front of Jack. Better to ignore everything and pretend it's okay, that was his method.

The screen to my left displayed a black-and-white alien. A little head, perfectly round in profile, the tip of a nose curved upward, just like mine. I could see my baby's brain and skeleton; the sheer bones of its legs and toes. I stared at the image, grasping for emotion, but I couldn't connect.

"There's the baby," the technician announced, smiling. "Do you want to know the sex?"

Jack didn't want to know, but I already did.

Two days prior, in an attempt to walk off a panic attack, I was pacing the streets, staring at the sky, watching the clouds take shape. The outline of a teddy bear, fluffy and soft, comforting in its circular symmetry, swiftly began to stretch and narrow until, coiling, it transformed into a serpent. I lowered my gaze to the sidewalk once again, hurrying onward. My knees ached with each step forward, bearing the force of percussion between my feet and the concrete. Unaccustomed to the additional weight I now carried in my midsection, I was forced to walk in a new and foreign way, pulling my centre of gravity backward. My feet went forward first, my upper body followed. I was constantly afraid of toppling over like a bowling pin that had just been struck.

The houses along the way were large and decadent with peaked roofs, bay windows, and decorative detailing that reminded me of the icing on a gingerbread house. As I walked farther down the street, the houses became more dilapidated. Shutters hung loose from windows, paint was chipped and peeling, and lawns were overgrown with wildflowers, weeds, and tall grass.

I saw a man in the distance, headed toward me. I looked left and right, up and down the street. I waited for a car to pass before crossing. When I reached the other side I turned my head, and just above where I had been standing, four crows were perched, evenly spaced, on the black telephone wire. One began cawing, and the others responded, echoing.

Four for a boy.

Lying on the examination table, I nodded. "Yes, I'd like to know the sex."

"I was hoping you would." The technician pointed to the screen. "Do you see that?

I couldn't see anything but static. Pushing myself up closer to the screen using my elbows, I squinted. "I don't know what I'm supposed to be seeing."

"That, there." She used her finger to circle an area on the screen. "That's a penis. Congratulations, it's a boy."

Dear Sunshine,

You told me that your grandfather mined for gold. The one who died long before we were born. What happened to him? It was always such a taboo topic. But then again, we never talked about much, did we?

I saw the pictures of him and the other men. Black-and-white photographs in the mines, hard hats with flashlights and cigarettes dangling between their lips, faces blackened with soot.

You said he was a pirate, always searching for buried treasure. He'd loot shipwrecks and row to smaller islands off the coast of our own, digging in the dirt. Six feet down.

Did he ever find what he was looking for?

Did you?

Love,
G

Jack and I always fought when he wanted to spend time with someone else. I felt abandoned and worthless whenever he wasn't with me. I thought that was normal.

One evening, I was sitting in the living room reading from a collection of Anne Sexton's poetry when I heard Jack call from the kitchen, "Babygirl, I'm going to the bar with some friends."

"Which friends?" I closed the book and yanked my dress down over my knees, hugging my legs into my chest.

"Some painters. You don't know them."

"I wanted to hang out with you tonight," I whined.

"I'm sorry, little one."

He had been going out a lot, and I was spending the majority of my time at home alone.

I stood up and wandered into the kitchen. "I feel like I haven't seen you at all lately, between all the late nights at the studio and days at the pub."

"That's not true." Jack's speech was slurred. He was sipping something amber from a glass. I traced my eyes along the counter, trying to find the source. An empty bottle of bourbon sat uncorked next to the sink. "We spend all our time together."

"Sleeping together doesn't count as spending time together." I peered at him with my best wounded look, trying to appeal to the part of him I used to be able to manipulate so easily.

"I'm sorry." He downed the remainder of his glass, placing it in the sink. "We can hang out tomorrow."

"That's what you always say. "My skin was prickling, my ears began to burn. "Tomorrow there will be some other excuse." I held onto the table. I was losing my grip.

"Why are you trying to start a fight right now?"

Outside, rain was coming down in heavy blasts. I watched the offbeat drips through the window, clinging to the rain gutters before falling to the ground. The neighbours' wind chimes clinked together, jingling as if they were trying to score the scene. I hoisted myself up on the table and hiked up my dress, spreading my legs wide.

Jack shifted his focus between my legs. "You naughty little girl."

I bit my lip. "If you stay, you can do whatever you want to me."

He moved toward me, placing a hand on each of my knees. He shut my legs and kissed me. "I have to go. It's work."

I felt as if I'd been branded with a hot poker. I shoved him away and he stumbled backward.

"If you leave, don't bother coming back."

He didn't say anything as he headed for the door.

"Jack?" I called desperately, holding back tears.

"What?" he snapped, flicking his hood over his head.

"Don't go out the front door."

"Why the fuck not?"

"You came in the back door," I whispered, pointing in its direction. "It's bad luck to leave through a different door than the one you—"

The door slammed. The floorboards vibrated under my feet. A whoosh of wind. He was already gone.

When my father and my mother fought, Annabelle, William, and I would run away. We would pack our backpacks with snacks and clothes and descend into the woods, the three of us, hand in hand.

We lived beside a forest that was three acres wide. William had built us a clubhouse in an old spruce tree. He was the only one who knew where it was; whenever I tried to find it on my own, I would get lost. We would follow a trail, cross a makeshift wooden bridge over a small stream, and turn the corner at a fallen-down tree, its roots brutally exposed to the earth, a twisted tornado of pedigree.

"Gracie? Anna?" William called, turning back to look at us, his golden blond curls shimmering in the sunlight. "You have to hop from rock to rock. The ground is hot lava."

"Okay," I replied, hopping carefully with my arms extended straight like the wings of an airplane.

When I lifted my head, I saw that William was standing perfectly still. He held his hand up, indicating for us to stop, and I tried to peek around him. "Nobody move," he whispered.

There, among the trees off the path, stood a moose as tall as my bedroom ceiling, balancing on skinny stilt legs. It didn't have any antlers. It was mostly brown but its back was speckled with white spots. Its ears, perfectly erect, suddenly shifted back, and William shouted, "Run!"

I snatched Annabelle's hand and bolted, dragging her through the trees, pushing branches and twigs from our path, nearly on William's heels. Adrenaline coursed through my body, and I felt no pain as I pushed myself as fast as I could, my heartbeat drumming in my ears.

When we arrived at the clubhouse, William screamed, "Get up, quick."

My body trembled as I lifted Annabelle, giving her bottom a shove. She began scurrying up the flat pieces of wood that William had nailed onto the tree, spaced perfectly for our little legs to make it all the way to the top. "Hurry!" I called before following, my limbs weakening as I clung to the bark.

Halfway up, my foot missed a step and my shoe slipped off. I turned, watching it fall and hit the ground with a thud. William was behind me and grabbed my foot, guiding it back onto the step. "Don't look down. Go. Go." He nudged me upward.

One at a time, we arrived on our perch. We huddled together as we tried to catch our breath, scanning the dangerous forest from up high. I placed my head on William's shoulder, glancing at my shoeless foot.

He was our protector, until he couldn't protect us anymore.

Blinking my eyes open, I tried to sit up, but there was a pressure on my chest, gluing me to the mattress. My arms and legs were like blocks of concrete. I opened my mouth, but my tongue remained fixed to my bottom teeth and a quiet gurgle escaped. The more I struggled, the less my body responded.

I was paralyzed.

Unable to turn my head, I saw from the corner of my eye the flutter of a figure lingering in the doorway. It floated toward the bed. I wiggled as much as I could, using my shoulders to create momentum, beginning a slow, rocking motion from side to side.

The figure was now beside my bed. It was human-like, but lacked some of the features that make humans distinguishable. It was tall—so tall it almost reached the ceiling—with no nose, no mouth, grey holes for eyes, and arms that turned into hands that were attached to fingers, but it had no legs. I desperately tried to call for Jack, but only a whistle of air escaped. The weight on my chest was suffocating.

The figure raised one of its fingers, bringing it closer until it was resting on my stomach. My body was rocking harder and harder, a silent scream lodged in my throat. The figure pushed. I could feel the wet warmth of tears in the corners of my eyes as the figure pressed deeper and deeper and deeper. I knew what it wanted; it wanted to hurt my baby. I could feel my son's pain inside me, begging for me to protect him.

Rocking even more violently, I hurled myself with all the force of my weight one final time, rolling off the bed and onto the floor, landing with a loud thump.

I had been freed.

Sitting upright I scanned the room, but the figure was gone. A throbbing pain in my stomach was all that remained.

I heard Jack shuffle from the couch in the living room. He moved swiftly down the hallway and entered our bedroom, crouching to help me up. Fully dressed in jeans, shirt, and socks, his face showed no indication that he had been asleep. There was no yellow crust in his eyes, no puffiness to his cheeks or lips. His hair was neat, the curls undisturbed.

"Are you okay?" Jack grabbed my forearm, clutching tightly as he guided me to a standing position.

"Where were you?"

"I got home late so I slept on the couch."

"That makes no sense." I shook my arm free from his grasp. He knew I hated when he slept on the couch. "Why would you sleep on the couch instead of with your pregnant girlfriend?"

"I'm sorry. I didn't want to wake you," he explained. "Are you okay? Should we take you to the doctor to make sure the baby is okay?"

"I'm fine." I exhaled, moving toward the kitchen. Jack followed. The room smelled of Jack, musky and like fallen pine needles, but there was something I couldn't quite place. A faint element of coconut or something creamy and white.

"Are you hungry?" he asked.

"No." I stood on my tippytoes to open the cupboard, shifting through boxes of dried pasta and cans of beans. "I just want coffee. I've got a splitting headache."

"Sit down, I'll make it for you." Jack pulled a wooden chair out from the table, motioning for me to sit.

Reluctantly, I looked at him before taking a seat. "Where were you last night?" The wildflowers in the vase on the table had dried up, their colours nearly faded. I began picking at the petals, letting them fall. The sun was beginning to come up, and the window facing the backyard was lit like cotton candy that had been left out in the rain.

Jack grabbed the mustard-coloured kettle and held it beneath the tap. "I told you, I went to that gallery opening. The one uptown."

I shook my head. "You never told me that."

Jack set the kettle on the stove and turned the burner on max. He walked to the fridge and grabbed a carton of eggs from the top shelf.

I clasped my hands together and laid my chin on top of them, waiting for a response.

Jack bent to retrieve the cast iron pan from the cupboard and placed it on the burner. He set it to medium heat and cracked two eggs.

My head was ticking like a metronome. I could sense the extra heartbeat inside me. "Jack, did you hear me?"

"Sweetie, what did we talk about?"

A swell of steam was beginning to shoot out of the small hole at the tip of the kettle. It whistled ever so slightly.

"Don't patronize me."

"I'm not. You know your pregnancy brain has been bad lately." The eggs were beginning to sizzle and spit oil into the air. Jack grabbed a spatula and flipped them as the temperature of the kettle continued to climb.

"Are you seriously gaslighting me right now?"

"I'm not doing anything, Grace."

The kettle began screaming.

"Jesus Christ," I shouted. "Shut that fucking thing up."

Jack shoved the kettle from the burner. It hit the counter with a bang.

The noise slowly dulled.

"Happy?" He laid both hands on the counter, relaxing his weight into the granite, and sighed.

I stood, approached him and wrapped my arms around his waist. "I'm sorry."

Jack shrugged, shifting from my arms. "It's okay." He poured the boiling water into the French press.

I picked up the spatula from the counter and began poking at the eggs. "Jack?"

"Yeah?"

"Do you believe in omens?"

"You know I don't." He passed me a cup, his eyes on the coffee, avoiding mine.

I paused before taking it, blowing gently on the liquid's surface.

"Grace?"

My English teacher approached as I bent to add my health textbook to my bag. Standing upright, I shut my locker door and fastened the lock. I turned and waited, pulling the straps of my bookbag over my shoulders and clinging to them with my fingers. My English teacher was wearing brown trousers that were pleated down the leg and a black cardigan sweater. His short grey hair seemed wet, but as he got closer, I realized it was some sort of product. Taking small, calculated steps to avoid colliding with a group of students who were coming toward him at an angle, his cologne reached me before he did.

"I was just talking to your father," he said, removing his hands from his pockets. "He asked if I could give you a lift home."

"Alright." I studied him, chewing on the insides of my cheeks. "Did he say why?"

He shrugged. "He just said he had something to do."

"Okay."

"You ready?" he asked, raising his eyebrows.

I clutched my bookbag straps tighter, running my fingertips along the smooth edges. "Yeah, I'm ready."

"Alright, let's get a move on."

I knew my English teacher was going to want to come in. He had been unusually quiet on the drive; he seemed deep in thought, picking at the cuticles of his nails and using his knees to steer. When he pulled into the driveway, he immediately killed the engine. "I'm going to have to use the john, if you don't mind."

"Sure." I opened the car door and hopped out, grabbing my bookbag from the floor. It hit a branch on the tree in the driveway as I tossed it over my shoulder, startling me slightly. My English teacher walked behind me, and I could feel his eyes on my bare legs.

I opened the front door, calling out to see if anyone was home, but there was no response. Dropping my bag by the door, I kicked off my sneakers, headed for the kitchen, and poured myself a glass of water from the tap. My English teacher continued down the hallway to the washroom. He was familiar with the house, due to his many evenings here with my father.

I hopped up onto the counter, swinging my legs as I sipped the icy water. Our water supply came from the well that my father had dug, and it tasted like nothing else: clean, crisp, untainted, and brutally cold. I heard the toilet flush and the door close, and my teacher's steps as he made his way toward the kitchen.

"Want a glass?" I asked from my perch on the counter.

"Sure, I'll get it." He grabbed a cup from the cupboard, where all our dishes were on display behind a glass window. He allowed the faucet to run for a few seconds before filling his glass. "What have you been reading lately?"

"I just started *Lolita*."

"Ah yes, 'light of my life, fire of my loins.'" He paused, waiting for a reaction, and when I gave none, he continued, "The entire book reads like a beautiful melody. You're going to love it."

"Cool." I brought my glass to my mouth and took a sip, then I licked the excess moisture from my lips.

"I've never seen your book collection." He was standing too close to me, leaning against the counter. My body tensed in an attempt to draw it away from him. He glanced at the door. "Why don't you show me what you have, and I can lend you some stuff that I think you'd like?"

Excited by the opportunity to move, I quickly replied, "They're upstairs in my room."

"Lead the way." He half-bowed and gestured toward the door, which made me chuckle.

"Thank you, my liege."

My English teacher followed me up the stairs, down to the end of the hall and into my bedroom. It was immaculate, as it always was, everything in its proper place; a perfect palace of symmetry.

"I knew you were a neat freak," my English teacher teased. "I could just tell by your handwriting."

"It helps keep my mind calm," I explained, and pointed at the wall. "There they are." My father had built me that bookcase when I was eleven. Once it was mounted on the wall, I had carefully arranged my books by size and colour.

My English teacher brought himself close to the bookcase and, tilting his head to the side, walked slowly forward, reading each spine. He fingered a copy of something by Irvine Welsh and delicately pulled it from its place, leaving a hole behind. "You're allowed to read this? He's absolutely filthy."

"Yeah, my parents don't really monitor what I read." I sat on the bed and crossed my legs.

My English teacher opened the book to a random page and began reading out loud as he moved toward me, sitting so close that our outer thighs were pressed together.

As he read, I noticed his hard-on through his wool trousers. Without looking up from the book, he took my hand and guided it onto his lap. Lifting his hips, he pressed himself into my palm. I felt my face flush.

"Do you want to see how hard you make me?"

I didn't know what to say, so I just nodded.

Standing, he undid his belt, button, and zipper, letting his pants flop to the floor. His erection sprung free. "Get on your knees."

I did as I was told.

He edged forward. "Open your mouth."

Parting my lips, he jammed himself deep inside my throat and I gagged, my eyes filling with tears. I peered up at him, but his eyes were closed, his hands on the black of my head, his fingers entangled in my hair, controlling me. My gaze drifted to the bookshelf, and I started counting the spines.

I had reached sixty-five by the time the front door opened.

Pulling myself free from him, I scrambled to my feet, wiping my eyes and mouth with the back of my sleeve.

"Hello?" my father called.

"Hi," I answered as my English teacher yanked his pants back on. "We're upstairs."

My English teacher shot to the other side of the room, frantically adjusting his pants to hide his erection, and snatched the bright orange book once again. He braced himself against the mantle with my snow globe collection.

My father was in the doorway. "What're you guys doing up here?"

I stared at my father, attempting to communicate what had happened with a secret Morse code of blinks—one I knew only someone I was made of would be able to understand.

"Just telling Grace here what she should be reading next." My English teacher ran his fingers through his hair.

My father glanced at me, then at my teacher. "Anyone ever tell you you're supposed to leave your job behind when you walk out that door?"

"You know me." My English teacher smirked.

The pain was what woke me that night. Razor-sharp serrations cutting through. I pulled myself into a seated position and clenched my swollen belly as a series of guttural moans escaped me. It felt as if I had swallowed a bag of scorched knives and was trying to digest them. I was being torn apart from the inside.

Jack was asleep next to me. I staggered out of bed, trembling and light-headed, and stumbled to the bathroom. Beads of sweat clung to my forehead and upper lip. I could taste the salt as I fell against the door, landing on my hands and knees on the cold tile floor; one hand shot to my stomach instinctively. I crawled to the toilet and pressed my back against the cool porcelain. Spreading my legs, I saw red. My white underwear was covered in blood. It was pouring out of me. Thick and bright. I'd never seen blood like it before, and I knew it was too much.

"Jack," I shrieked. "Jack."

He ran into the bathroom.

"What's wrong?"

"I don't know."

His eyes were fixed between my legs. The blood was now collecting below me on the bathroom tiling, a glistening circle of syrupy red.

He just stood there, frozen, staring.

"Call a fucking ambulance!" I screamed.

I stood outside my father's locked office door, braiding the stiff, auburn hair on the mask that hung in the centre of the frame. The mask had always frightened me when I passed by it in the nighttime on my way to the bathroom. Its face was red and contorted, like an angry, ancient spirit.

I listened as the keyboard clicked beneath my father's fingers, and hesitated. I knew I wasn't supposed to bother him when he was writing, but it was well past noon and Annabelle and I were hungry. My mother had disappeared again.

I knocked gently, three times.

No response.

I knocked again, this time louder.

The clicking stopped. My father answered with irritation, "Yes?"

"Father, will you make us lunch?" I called, pressing my ear to the door.

I heard papers shuffle and the wheels of my father's chair rolling along the hardwood floor. The door swung open and I stumbled. My father caught me as I fell into him. His face was stern. "Grace, you know the rule: when my office door is locked, do not bother me."

"Sorry." I pulled away.

"You are big enough to make lunch for yourself and Anna. Go see what's in the kitchen." He shut the door.

I crawled on my hands and knees down the hallway, pretending I was a cat. Annabelle was waiting around the corner, sitting on the floor, surrounded by piles of books. "What'd he say?"

"He got mad. But don't worry, I'll take care of you."

The paramedics lifted me from the bathroom floor onto the gurney, carried me out of the house, and slid me into the back of the ambulance. I tried to stay awake as Jack squeezed my hand, whispering my name. His voice seemed far away. Everything hurt.

The next thing I remember is the lights, yellow-white and blindly harsh. More voices; new voices. Surgical masks and pink scrubs. The wheels of the gurney on the concrete floor. Something was wrong—I knew something was wrong—but no one was telling me anything. The nurses, both male, attempted to comfort me through the wretched screaming. I heard the doctor say to Jack: "If we have to make a choice, we'll save her."

I felt a shift inside me, downward—scraping, tearing, flesh, fluid. Something wasn't right. I couldn't feel my baby moving anymore.

The operating room. More nurses flittering around. The shine of stirrups. The chipped nail polish on my toes.

The doctor approached. "Okay, Grace, the head is almost out, but we've lost the heartbeat."

"What?" I struggled to stand but the nurses held me in place. "What do you mean you lost the heartbeat?"

"The baby needs to be delivered now." The doctor pulled blue latex gloves onto his large, hairy hands.

A female nurse appeared at my side, taking my hand. A mask covered her face, a surgical cap on her head. Her only available feature was dark blue eyes.

Jack was a silent blur in the corner.

The doctor shoved his hands inside of me. The pain was crushing. I recoiled. "No," I screamed. "Get off of me."

"I need you to cooperate, Grace. Stay still and push." The doctor motioned to the male nurses, who grabbed me and held me in place. Struggling and thrashing, I tried to break free from their clutches.

"Jack," I cried. "Get them off. Help."

Jack just stood there.

I grabbed for the silver tray, knocking it. Metal clanking. The tools hit the floor.

"Push, Grace. Push."

Sweat poured from my forehead, running into my eyes, mixing with tears. My vision blurred—all I could see was a bright light and outlines of people. My body trembling and contracting. I squeezed the female nurse's hand, wailing.

"One more big push."

I howled. "Jaaaaaackkkkkkkkkk."

The pressure released and I collapsed with exhaustion. The room was quiet; everyone stayed in place. I turned my head and my gaze met the female nurse's, her blue eyes moist. I heard the door close, and Jack was gone.

The doctor approached, removing his mask. "I'm so sorry, Grace."

Weakly, I propped myself upright, catching sight of my still baby across the room, swaddled in a blue blanket. I disintegrated. My mouth opened wide, but no noise came out.

The female nurse leaned forward and wiped my forehead with a cloth. "There's nothing we could have done."

The doctor placed my dead son on my bare chest. I eased back the swaddling and wedged my finger inside his tiny clenched fist. He was perfect. White-blond hair, pink skin, little smushed nose, closed eyes. I kissed his head and lingered, inhaling deeply. He didn't smell the way newborns do. He didn't smell like anything.

My inhalations became sharp and sporadic. Something was beeping as my neck muscles gave out and my head lolled. Three shadowy, masculine shapes stood at the edge of my bed, reaching in, melding into a singular figure, its face slowly coming into focus. "Who let them in?" I whispered.

"Who?" the nurse asked, looking around the room.

"Them. Get them out of here." I pointed, shaking. "Leave me alone." I clutched my son in my arms as they tried to take him from me. They pulled until they'd snatched him, and his tiny hand, still wrapped around my finger, let go.

I'd never been much of a sleeper. My mother told me even as a newborn I never slept. I didn't spend my time awake unhappy or tearful, I was simply too curious. Mesmerized, unable to stop watching the world, I stared up at it with dark indigo eyes. As I was not yet able to control the muscles in my neck, my mother would place me on the sofa, propped up against a pillow, while she vacuumed the swirly grey carpet. I would trace her movements using only my eyes.

When my parents wanted me to sleep, they would strap me into my car seat next to William and drive around for hours, hoping I would drift off, even if just for a few moments. This often didn't work, and I would simply gaze out the window, enraptured by the world moving past me.

William would ask to lie down with me, insisting he could help me fall asleep. After my father had spent some time lying on his back, balancing me on his swaying knees, rocking me from side to side, he would place me next to my brother. We looked like two porcelain dolls in matching pajamas with our chubby, flushed cheeks pressed together. And then, miraculously, we'd drift off to sleep in our parents' bed.

I couldn't sleep. It was my fault. I knew it was my fault. Jack knew. The doctors knew. The nurses knew. My parents knew. They all hated me. That was why I was alone in my hospital room. They didn't want anything to do with me. I'd killed my baby.

I had spent the morning listening to baby trolleys wheeling past my room. Unable to turn my head, my eyes remained fixed on the fog that was collecting outside, clinging to the concrete of the parking lot below. I wasn't surprised that Jack had disappeared. I wasn't surprised that my father and my mother hadn't shown up. I lay glued to that hospital bed, staring out the window, unable to cry.

A nurse entered my room. "You know, you're lucky," she said, lifting the brown clipboard hanging at the bottom of my bed, bringing it close to her nose. "You're so young, you have plenty of time to have more babies."

My eyes followed the woman's motions.

"The doctor has cleared you to leave." She dropped the clipboard and it hit the plastic baseboard with a clack. "We called William, your emergency contact. He's waiting outside."

I sat up, and as the nurse left the room, William entered. His morose expression shattered what was left of me. Neither of us said a word as he helped me out of bed and into the black wheelchair he had been given. Grabbing my bag, he wheeled me down the long hallway of the maternity ward. The space was filled with the sounds of babies crying and cooing, families laughing together, oohing and aahing over the newest additions to their clans.

William hit the call button for the elevator. The doors dinged open, and once inside, he situated me between two other women in wheelchairs, both with newborns swaddled in their arms, my own arms empty.

I often practiced smiling in the mirror. Bringing my face close to its reflection, I would pull the corners of my mouth upward, a dimple forming only on the left side. I'd smile with my mouth closed, keeping my lips tightly pressed together. I'd hold it until my mouth began to twitch, staring into my own eyes, and then I would let the smile fall.

Then I would fake a laugh, pretending someone had said something funny. First, just a casual laugh with a slight tilt of the head. Then I would work myself up to a louder, more hysterical laughter. After a few minutes, the laughter sounded psychotic. At this point, I began to wonder who I was. My face would become that of the black-haired woman from the lake I had seen that night as a teenager, with her chapped lips and blueish skin, or my mother or father, swirling and contorted, red with agitation. I could no longer see myself; the thought that it was me behind those eyes became too much to comprehend. Frightened, I would break the stare and cover the mirror with a bedsheet.

I was told you can trick your brain into thinking you're happy if you force yourself to smile. Activating those muscles in your face stimulates your amygdala, increasing levels of dopamine and serotonin. They say if you fake-laugh for long enough, it will become real.

I was beyond trickery.

My insomnia was at its worst. I hadn't slept for more than ten minutes in weeks. I was a carbon copy of myself, only the faded imprint of pressure remained on paper-thin skin. Locked in the past, time had become hollow, and everything seemed to exist at a distance. Unreachable, unattainable, unimportant.

I didn't care when the towels weren't folded the right way anymore. I didn't care when Jack left his dirty socks lying on the living room floor for days. I didn't care that the kitchen sink was piled with dishes caked in gunk. I didn't care if I ate or starved or slept or drank water or washed my hair or hands. I didn't have the strength to pretend.

Sipping a cup of coffee over the kitchen sink, I watched Jack through the window. The vines from the hanging plant had dried and were beginning to turn an orange-brown. I reached out and pinched a leaf between my thumb and forefinger, plucking it from its stem. Crumbling it to dust, I let it fall onto the counter.

Jack was digging a hole beneath the lilac tree. He was struggling to break the earth with the plastic toy shovel we had bought for the baby. I lifted my mug to my mouth and tipped it, letting the liquid linger on my tongue. It tasted particularly bitter, and I knew Jack had made it that way on purpose.

I hated him. His stupid crooked teeth and messy hair. His ripped shirts and jeans, stained with paint. His unclean fingernails and unclipped toenails. The thought of him ever touching me again made me sick.

He was clutching a white, plush bunny in his free hand. I remembered the day we bought that bunny. I was restless—I hadn't had a drink or done drugs in months—so we walked downtown on an unseasonably chilly spring day. I was bundled in Jack's mahogany scarf, cranky because I was constantly sick, and the air, rife with pollen, was making my eyes watery and itchy. "Let's just go in here,"

I said, motioning to the store ahead, rubbing my eyes with the end of his scarf.

The shop was filled with beautiful household items. Handmade soaps that smelled of lavender and eucalyptus were piled on silver cupcake trays. Fluffy white towels and housecoats hung on hangers near vintage bathroom vanities with basins and washbowls. I stepped between the delicate items, careful not to bump into anything with my new belly.

Jack grabbed a stuffed rabbit with floppy ears and an embroidered pink nose from a crib as we passed by. He held the bunny by the back of the neck, bobbing its head from side to side, and directed a voice from the edge of his mouth like a ventriloquist. "Hey, sweetheart, you have any plans for later?"

I bit the sides of my cheeks, trying not to laugh.

"How about taking me home?" he continued, nodding the bunny's head up and down.

I allowed myself to smile as I reached up to touch the rabbit's ears. They were as soft as cashmere.

"Alright," I said, giving in. "But you have to buy me dinner first."

Relieved that he had cheered me up, Jack leaned in and kissed me on the cheek before heading for the cash register.

I carried the bunny all the way home by its paw, just like I had carried my own stuffed toys when I was a little girl. Halting on the corner, I pulled a loose strand of red hair off of the rabbit.

Presently, Jack beckoned for me to join him in the yard. His lips were moving, but I couldn't hear him through the glass. I cupped my ear, shook my head, and mouthed, "I can't hear you, you moron."

Placing my cup down, I rounded the kitchen table, exiting through the back door. I let the screen door slam loudly, which Jack hated, but this time it prompted no reaction from him.

I met him by the hole under the tree. All I could smell were lilacs and the dampness of the dirt.

"Should we say something?" I asked.

"What is there to say?" Jack dropped the bunny into the hole, picked up the child-sized shovel and started to bury it. The image caused me to tense up, the soft white soiled by the moist brown earth.

Jack fell to his knees, sobbing. He wrapped his arms around my legs and buried his face in the space between my thighs. He wailed mournfully, peering up at me with wet eyes. "Our boy," he whispered once he'd caught his breath. "What are we going to do without our boy?"

I couldn't look at him. I stared at the soil, noticing something pinkish-grey squirming around. I strained to see what it was, and realized it was two parts of a worm that had been sliced in half by Jack's shovelling. Both ends of it continued to writhe.

I thought of the grief that was eating me up inside; like maggots consuming rotten flesh, it was burrowing its way into my heart, tearing my ventricles apart. Then I pictured my baby decomposing in the ground.

Unlike the worm, I didn't think I had the heart to survive the split.

It was half past noon, and I was already a fifth of whiskey deep. Wearing my white nightdress, I stood in the living room staring out into the street. It was still and empty; most people had left for work hours ago. Swaying, I lifted the bottle to my lips, tossing my head back to get the last few drops from the bottom.

A blur of movement caught my eye. I tried to focus as a man stopped in front of our house to peek in the window before hustling along. I recognized him as the old, lanky man from the park. The bottle slipped from my hand, fell to the floor, and shattered. I ran to the door and flung it open.

"Hey," I shouted as the man hobbled down the street.

He kept walking, eyes forward.

"You. Stop." I careened down the sidewalk barefoot after him. "Why're you following me?"

I ran full speed toward him. The lanky man rounded a corner, and just as I rounded it after him, I collided with another man. He caught me by the arms as I tried to regain my footing.

"I'm so sorry," he said, clutching me firmly. My eyes refused to focus; he was foggy and lineless. I squinted him into view, making out a pair of black-rimmed glasses.

"Grace?"

"James?" I straightened up, trying to speak without slurring my words. I hadn't seen him since I'd left home.

"Are you okay?" His eyes widened with concern as they moved to my bare feet. He was still holding me and I wanted to collapse into his arms.

"Yeah. Fine." I smiled, exposing my teeth, feeling the tenseness of a headache coming on. "Cat got out. I was...chasing her."

James's face softened. "Do you want me to help you find her?"

"No." I glanced up and down the road. "She'll come back." I dipped forward, giggled, and began singing. "Cat came back the very next day. The cat came back, we thought she was a goner."

He was staring at my face. I wasn't wearing any lipstick; my lips felt dry and dehydrated. My hair was unbrushed, curly and untamed.

"My grandmother used to sing that." James nodded, seemingly amused. "How the hell are you? I haven't seen you in years."

"Yeah, been a while." I ran my fingers through my hair. "Good. Okay. Been better." I smoothed my nightgown. "Obviously."

He laughed. It sounded childlike and nostalgic, but it had deepened with age.

"Give me a hug." I stretched out my arms.

James enveloped me. His arms were hard and ridged with muscles, and he smelled of Burberry cologne. I inhaled him deeply, feeling myself lighten.

"Coffee?" I stepped backward, letting my arms drop. "I live..." I pointed up the street, then turned, pointing in the other direction. "...there." I stumbled, and he reached out and caught me again.

"Uh, you sure you're okay, Grace?"

"Fine." I brushed him off. "Didn't sleep much last night."

"Okay. Coffee sounds good." James let me go and we began shuffling along.

A car passed, honking as they sped by. I jumped, giving them the finger. I turned to James. "So, living in the city?"

"I am," he chuckled. "Been here almost a year now. People are so friendly."

"Just like home." I smiled as we reached the front door. In my haste, I had neglected to close it, and as we stepped inside and saw the mess of bloody footprints, I immediately remembered the broken glass on the floor. Bracing myself against the doorway, I balanced on one foot, and grabbing for the other, pulled my leg into a V to see the bottom. It was cut pretty badly. "Oh shit."

James stuck his head in. "Jesus, Grace, what happened?"

"Dropped a glass chasing the cat." I waved my hand dismissively. "Must have stepped on a piece."

"It looks like a fucking murder scene in here." His eyes moved to the gash on my foot. "Let's get you cleaned up."

Motioning for James to follow, we made our way down the hall and squeezed into my tiny bathroom. I had the spins and desperately needed a bump to straighten me out. Sitting on the edge of the tub, I tried to deep breathe as I ran the water, placing my hand beneath the faucet periodically to check the temperature.

James kneeled in front of me, and when the water was hot enough, he began to wash the blood from my foot.

"Bet you didn't think you'd be washing—" I was going sideways. I grabbed for the edge of the tub.

James's hands shot for my waist, pulling me back up. His hands lingered as he searched my eyes. "Good?"

"Mhm." I cupped my hand under the faucet and rubbed it on my face, then ran my fingers through my hair to smooth it out.

"Do you have any tweezers?" James was looking at my foot again. "I need to get the glass out."

"On the dresser."

James walked from the ensuite into my bedroom and I scrambled for my baggie of coke. I dumped a pile onto the back of my hand, raised it to my nose, and inhaled before stuffing it back into my bra. He returned as the drugs started to drip down the back of my throat.

"Okay, let's see." He closed the lid of the toilet and sat, reaching for my foot and placing it in his lap. "This isn't going to be pleasant."

"I can take it."

James began poking at the cut, digging the tweezers into the gash. He opened and closed them, trying to catch the glass. I wasn't feeling much pain, but was beginning to get turned on by James's composure as he dug in my open wound. I sniffled and wiped my nose with the back of my wrist, watching him intently. He clasped down and pulled, and I felt the glass sliding out.

"Got it." He extended the tweezers toward me, the piece of glass marbled with blood. "I need a Band-Aid."

I pointed to the medicine cabinet. "Right there."

He rifled through the cupboard. Grabbing the box and holding them toward me, he cocked his eyebrow. "Really Grace? Barbie Band-Aids?"

"Don't make fun." I grinned. "Barbie makes me feel better."

"Well, let's hope she does the trick again today." He crouched, grabbed my foot, and propped it onto his knee. He dried my foot with a towel, blew on it gently, and stuck the hot-pink and yellow bandage over the wound. "All done."

Our faces were close, too close. I was afraid he could smell the whiskey on my breath, so I kept my mouth shut tightly. I took a closer look at the Band-Aid. Barbie was jumping for joy as rainbows shot from her outstretched arms.

The front door slammed and I jerked away.

"Grace?" Jack called. "What the fuck happened in here?"

"Oh no," I muttered.

"Who's that?" James asked.

"My boyfriend."

I hopped up from the tub and limped down the hall. James followed behind. "Hey," I called, moving toward Jack. "Sorry, dropped a glass. Cut myself. I'll clean it up."

"Jesus, Grace, are you okay?" Jack was staring at me as I hobbled to the kitchen to get the broom. He was quickly beside me and grabbed it from my hand. "Let me do that."

For a moment, I forgot James was there. Then I realized he was standing behind me.

"Hey, I'm James." He extended his hand to Jack before I had a chance to introduce them.

"Sorry. Jack, this is James. James, Jack. I ran into James outside." *Don't mention the cat,* I willed. *For the love of God, don't mention the cat.*

"How's it going, man?" Jack spoke in a voice that was deeper than usual.

"James is an old friend." I patted him on the shoulder, the effects of the coke starting to kick in. My speech was speeding up. "We grew up together. I haven't seen him in years. Since I left home, I guess. Right?"

Jack was standing very straight, with his shoulders pulled back. It was the same way he stood when someone critiqued his art. Or after someone decided not to buy one of his pieces.

"I invited him in for coffee." I tried to ease the tension. "Speaking of, I'll put the kettle on."

"You know what, I should actually get going." James was already making his way to the door. "I have to head back to work."

"Of course." I followed him to the door. "Thanks for, you know, cleaning me up." I lifted my foot, staggering.

James extended his hand again in an attempt to catch me, but I caught myself first. "No problem." He eyed Jack, who was hovering around the corner. "It was really nice seeing you. Maybe we can get together and catch up soon?"

"I'd like that. Bye, James." I watched as he walked down the steps, shutting the door slowly behind him.

I turned to face Jack.

"Real fucking nice, Grace. Drunk at noon. And some random fucking guy, too. You're certainly getting better at causing a scene."

I stared at the ground, swaying in an attempt to keep my balance.

Jack threw the broom at me. "Clean up your own fucking mess."

Dear Sunshine,

It's time.

All those secrets that we promised we'd never tell, it's time we do.

Love,
G

The first time I got drunk I was thirteen. I convinced Annabelle to help me steal booze from my mother's friend's house. Her fridge was always filled with alcohol, and I figured she wouldn't miss a few bottles of beer.

I stood in the doorway between the kitchen and the living room, eyeing the adults while they chatted, as Annabelle transported the beers, one at a time, from the fridge into my purse. She gave me a thumbs up, and I interrupted my father mid-sentence: "Anna and I are going to the park," I announced, grabbing my bag and heading for the front door.

"Okay," my mother called. "Don't be too late."

Annabelle and I walked along the rocky shoreline, over shards of multicoloured beach glass, worn-down pebbles, creature-shaped seaweed formations, and fish bones. I leaned forward, allowing the tips of my fingers to graze the water's surface. It was frigidly cold and numbed my fingertips, causing them to throb. The ocean was always cold here, even in the summertime, but I didn't hold it against the water, loving it just as much as if it were hospitable. I splashed Annabelle and she giggled, bending and splashing me back. I licked my salty lips and smiled.

We continued down the road, waving at each passing car before crossing the bridge over the stream, ducking through the gazebo, and arriving at the park.

Hannah ran to greet us, falling into me in a sloppy embrace. She was already drunk. A group of boys were sitting at a yellow picnic table nearby, rolling a joint.

Hannah and I walked arm in arm to the swing set as Annabelle trailed behind. I plopped down on the swing, pulling a beer from my purse and unscrewing the top. "Do you want one?" I held the bottle toward Annabelle.

"Okay." Surprised, she stepped forward, taking the bottle from my hand. I opened another for myself.

James approached, passing me a lit joint. I took a hit as he began pushing me on the swing. "What are you doing bringing Annabelle around?" he muttered quietly so she wouldn't overhear. "She's too young."

"That's funny." I turned back, tossing my hair over my shoulder. "I don't remember you being declared king of the park."

"Hey, I'm just looking out for her. Someone's got to."

"Fuck you, James." I leapt from the moving swing and headed for the group of guys. "Come on, Anna," I called.

It was beginning to get dark; the sun had left its lingering post over the headlands and I was pretty drunk. Not cute-teenage-girl-stumbling-and-giggling drunk, but the drunk of a well-seasoned drinker. It felt right to me, this state of controlled chaos. I could tell Annabelle was feeling it too, but she was less in control.

Headlights appeared at the entrance of the park, and I assumed it was someone getting dropped off. I took a swig from my bottle just as I heard my mother sharply calling, "Grace?"

"Oh shit." I quickly stashed my beer under the table and made my way to the car.

"Are you drinking?" she demanded, her eyebrows raised.

"No."

"Get in the fucking car." Her head was hoisted out the open window. "Where's your sister?"

"There." I pointed to the monkey bars; Annabelle was lying beneath them in the grass. "I'll get her."

When I reached my sister, I saw that her eyes were closed. Her hair was draped over her face, covering her pale skin like a bedsheet. I knelt and nudged her. "Anna?"

She didn't move.

Panicked, I began to shake her by the shoulders. I could see that she was breathing—her chest was moving up and down slightly—but her eyes remained closed. James appeared, kneeling at my side. "Did someone give her booze?" I hissed at him.

"I think she was doing shots," he said, planting his hands on the ground to keep from swaying. "With the boys."

"What the fuck?" I pulled my sister to a seated position and began tapping her on the cheek gently "Anna, please wake up."

I heard the car door slam, and saw my mother headed toward me. "What's going on?" Her voice came out strained and clipped.

"I don't know." My breath was short and I felt my heart pound. "I can't wake her up."

My mother, now moving quickly, knelt and placed her index and middle finger on Annabelle's wrist. "Jesus Christ, Grace. Was she drinking?"

"She had a beer." Tears were beginning to stream down my face. "I didn't think it was a big deal."

"She's just a child, Grace." My mother scooped Annabelle up in her arms. "What the fuck is wrong with you?"

I followed as my mother carried her to the car, opened the back door, and strapped her in. Annabelle's head flopped to the side and hit the window. I was now sobbing uncontrollably.

"Quit crying and get in the car," my mother screamed. "Now."

My mother started the engine and I climbed into the passenger seat. I buckled my seat belt and turned, straining to grab Annabelle's hand. "Is she okay?"

"I don't know," my mother snapped, reversing onto the main road. "We'll see when we get to the hospital."

With my arm outstretched, I stroked the back of Annabelle's soft hand with my thumb, feeling the thump in my stomach every time her head bounced off the window. The sporadic motions and smell of gasoline were making me dizzy. My mouth tasted yeasty and stale, and the world around me was starting to spin. I needed some air but I was terrified to roll the window down.

My mother clutched the steering wheel, periodically eyeing Annabelle through the rear-view mirror. The engine revved as she pushed in on the accelerator, guiding her hand to the gearshift. "Let's just hope you didn't kill another one of your sisters."

The high beams lit the straight road ahead. The pavement was black and glossy like the skin of a wet serpent. There was no one else on the road. The street lamps flashed by as my mother geared up again.

"What do you mean?" I shouted, dropping Annabelle's hand and grabbing for the dashboard.

My mother shifted her gaze from the road, peering over at me. Illuminated houses snapped by as though they were being inconsistently captured with a flashbulb camera. She looked wild in the forefront, her dark hair flying upward as wind shot in through her open window. Her blue eyes had darkened—wicked and vindictive—and for a moment, I didn't recognize her at all. I thought she was going to kill us.

"You killed Sophia."

My stomach churned, and acidic liquid shot up my throat. I covered my mouth with my hand and "What?" came out like a breath.

My mother continued to stare at me. Her bottom teeth were pushed forward into an underbite. Her chin quivered. She wasn't watching the road. I swallowed the vomit in my mouth as her words came out even and pointed. "You rolled her over and she suffocated. It's your fault. Why do you have to take everything from me?"

"Did you hear?" Jack called from the living room.

"Hear what?" I asked, perched against the kitchen island.

"They're tearing down the old hospital."

I heard the newspaper crumple as he folded it, his mug hitting the coffee table.

"No, I didn't."

"Weren't you born there?"

My gaze drifted out the window where the snow was falling, collecting on the tree outside our house. "I was."

"We should check it out." Jack made his way into the kitchen. "You know, when they rip it down."

I was suddenly very aware of my impermanence. I couldn't help but acknowledge the symbolism attached to the destruction of my birthplace.

"I don't think so." I moved to the living room, picking up the newspaper to find the article. My eyes were met with a photograph of the hospital: tall and majestic, in its prime.

Jack was standing behind me. "What's wrong? I thought you loved destruction."

"Yeah." I dropped the paper onto the oxblood sofa. "Not of the self."

His eyes darted to the cigarette-burn scar on my forearm. "That's not what I heard."

"Fuck you, Jack."

"Come on, I'm just joking," he scoffed. "What happened to your sense of humour?"

"I guess it died with our baby."

Jack had disappeared again. I knew he was off somewhere drinking. This time, I sensed something wasn't right. It was a feeling that had been building for weeks. I tried calling him. No response.

I paced the apartment, trying to reason with myself. He'd probably just lost his phone again. He'd be home any minute.

I drank glasses of vodka mixed with Orange Crush. I counted and colour-coordinated the bookshelf between railing lines of coke I'd cut up with a razor blade. I hovered the blade near my wrist and considered digging it in—how good it would feel to get some relief—before placing it back on the shelf. I had promised Jack I wouldn't do that anymore. I dragged the oxblood sofa a little to the left, and when that didn't feel quite right, I dragged it a little to the right. I tried calling Jack again. It went straight to voicemail.

The feeling was darkening. I found myself grabbing his keys and walking to his car, figuring I'd drive to some of his regular places. I made a mental checklist: the bar, his studio, the deck, the path he usually took when he walked home. The feeling was in my guts, churning, creeping its way onto my chest. It sat there as I drove, trying to suffocate me. I reminded myself to breathe.

I texted one of Jack's friends to see if they knew where he had gone. He said Jack had left the bar hours ago. I circled the streets downtown, hoping I would find him stumbling along. I was calling him frantically, one eye on the road, one eye on my phone.

Reluctantly, I decided there was nothing I could do but go home and wait for him. I turned the car around, my palms forming sweaty prints on the steering wheel.

Parking the car, I noticed the light was on above our door. It was possible that someone walking by had set off the motion sensor, as our house was right on the street. I hated this fact, but Jack always said it placed us right in the world without ever having to leave our living room. But it was also possible that Jack was home. I increased my pace, reaching for the door.

Once inside, I tossed my keys on the entryway table. "Jack?"

No response.

I removed my shoes and jacket, calling again: "Jack?"

"I'm in the kitchen."

I moved toward his voice.

Jack was sitting at the kitchen table, two tumblers filled with whiskey in front of him. He was massaging the back of his head with the outstretched tips of his fingers.

"Where the fuck were you? I've been calling and looking everywhere for you."

"Sit down, Grace." He motioned to the chair next to him, then edged the tumbler in my direction. "We need to talk."

I perched on the edge of the chair.

"Grace, I don't know how to tell you this, so I'm just going to say it." Jack paused, interlacing his fingers and placing them on the table in front of him. "I've been seeing someone else."

It happened quick, like I had been stabbed in the stomach. Sharp and blinding. And then everything went fuzzy. "What?" The word barely came out.

He spoke more slowly this time, but his words were the same. "I've been seeing someone else."

All the blood drained from my body. My face muscles collapsed. I felt as if they were being sucked to the floor. "Who?"

"Does that really matter?" He looked tired, all sleepy-eyed and glossy.

"It fucking matters to me," I shouted. "Who is it?"

"Jessica, okay?" Jack slammed his fists down on the table. "It's Jessica."

Teeth. Brown eyes. Fingers in his hair.

"Jessica?" I shot from my chair, immediately on my feet. "Fucking Jessica? Seriously?"

He nodded, taking a long gulp from his glass.

"How long?"

"How long what?" Jack remained seated, staring into his glass.

"Don't play dumb—how long has this been going on?"

"Almost a year," he mumbled.

"A year?" I turned around and hit the fridge with my fist. My entire body was burning. "A fucking year?"

"Grace—"

"What do you mean, 'seeing'?"

"We've been spending time together, and I have feelings for her."

"Feelings?" I swallowed. My mouth had no saliva in it. "Feelings? What the fuck does that even mean?"

"I'm so sorry, Grace." He stroked his tumbler before he spoke again. "I think you know how bad things have been, though."

My hands instinctively went to my empty belly. "Wait. Let me get this straight—you were cheating on me with Jessica while I was *pregnant*?"

He looked down at his drink. "Yes."

"What the fuck is wrong with you?"

"I don't know," he admitted. "But I'm not happy, and I haven't been happy."

"How could you do this to me? You're pathetic," I snarled, standing over him. "You are a pathetic excuse for a man."

He stood to face me, his eyes filled with pain. "I never wanted to hurt you. You're just always going through something, and it's never been a good time." He couldn't maintain eye contact. "And then you got pregnant. I didn't know what to do."

"How about not sticking your dick in someone else? There's a fucking start."

Jack sighed.

"You are a coward. I fucking hate you." I pulled my arms back and shoved him as hard as I could. He stumbled backward, his arms helicoptering before catching himself on the kitchen counter. I shoved him again, over and over, toward the back door, screaming, "I want you to leave. Right now. Get the fuck out of this house. I don't ever want to see you again."

He didn't fight back. He tried to pin my arms down, but I kept flailing. I slapped at him, making contact with his head and chest and arms and face. My palms were stinging and he was red all over. I spit and cursed and shoved him again and again until I was panting and depleted, crumpling to the floor in a discarded heap.

I pointed at the door, shaking. "Go. You're just like your fucking father."

Jack buckled, his eyes searching my face as though he were looking for some semblance of recognition. I held his gaze, my face twisted with hatred.

Turning, he began to walk away from me. I was gasping for air, my chest heaving. "Jack, wait."

He stopped, his back to me.

I scrambled to my feet, scurrying to where he stood. I clutched his face. "Don't go, please."

He braced himself against the doorway, his eyes cast down. "Grace."

"We can work through this. Please, Jack. I need you."

"Grace, sweetheart."

"Please."

"I hate Hannah," I announced at the dinner table one night.

My father looked up from his plate, startled. "Never say *hate.* You don't hate anything. That's a very strong word."

"But I do. I hate her," I whined. "She told everyone at school we were poor."

"Grace, we're not poor." He pierced a piece of meat with his fork and brought it to his mouth. "And you don't hate her."

"I do," I screamed. "And I hate you." I shoved my plate with both hands and it hit the floor, shattering.

My father kept his eyes on me the entire time. "That's it, go to your room."

Hate became my new favourite word. I said it all the time at school, to my friends, to my siblings. *I hate that, I hate her, I hate him, I hate it.* I felt like it had more meaning because I wasn't allowed to say it. It was an act of rebellion. At seven years old, I didn't yet know the power of hatred.

I hated Jessica. I hated her face. I hated her teeth and her skin. I hated the freckles on her chest. I hated her red hair and her stupid brown eyes. I hated her voice. I hated that she was successful and had money. I hated that she was helping Jack. I hated that I let her touch him in front of me without saying anything.

Jack had loved me once and now he didn't. And it was all her fault.

As I sat there, blaming Jessica, I wished my father was there to tell me I didn't hate her, that hate was too strong a word, and that everything was going to be all right.

Haunted by what Jack had done, I was always angry, and so was he. He blamed me for killing the baby; I blamed him for abandoning me. He wanted to leave; I guilted him into staying. I told him I'd ruin him. I'd tell everyone *everything*. I'd do whatever was necessary to destroy his reputation and burgeoning career. He knew how resolute I could be when I put my mind to something, and I'm sure he was afraid.

I was afraid, too. Those days, I felt possessed and indomitable. If I'd been honest with myself—if my mind had been clearer—I would have known I didn't even want him to stay. I just didn't want him to want to leave. I wanted him to be miserable just like me. It wasn't fair for him to move on while I suffered. And so we stayed together, torturing one another in familiar discomfort. The trust was gone, we both knew it, and without trust there would be no reconciliation.

Jack would tell me he was going to the studio, but spend his days at the bar. I knew he hadn't been painting. There were no longer any signs of art in our lives. No paint or charcoal present on his skin; his usual smell of oil paint and turpentine had been replaced with booze and weed. I couldn't remember the last time I'd written anything. Our old dynamic—that unbounded, mirror-like ardour—was gone. We were no longer interested in the cyclicality of inspiration and creation.

One evening, I was sitting in the dark living room, sipping my fourth glass of whiskey and smoking a cigarette, letting the ash carelessly fall to the floor. The curtains were still open, and I watched as fluffy flakes of snow floated, almost in stillness, kindled beneath the street lamps.

The door flew open and Jack stumbled through. His curls were covered in a thin layer of snow. He removed his black, down-filled jacket and tossed it on the sofa.

"Where were you?" I asked as calmly as I could.

"The bar."

"I was calling you. Why didn't you pick up?"

"My phone was on silent."

I took a puff of my cigarette and blew the smoke in his direction. "Were you with her?"

He removed his gloves and used them to brush the snow from his hair.

"Were you with her?" I repeated.

Jack just stared at me, irked and unblinking. He couldn't even lie to me anymore.

Clutching my tumbler, I drew back and hurled it in his direction, narrowly missing his head as he ducked. The glass hit the wall and shattered behind him.

Jack's eyes shot from the mess of glass on the floor to me and back again. "What the fuck is wrong with you? Why do you want to be broken? What the fuck is wrong with you?"

Calmly, I stood and made my way toward him. His face softened in relief for a moment, as though he thought I would apologize. Maybe I would console him. Maybe I would let him hold me and tell him it was all going to be okay. We'd get through this; we always got through everything, together. Instead, I stopped in front of his easel by the window. His latest piece had been sitting there, untouched, for months. I picked up a tube of black paint, squeezing it slowly onto the canvas. Using my index finger, I smeared the letters: F-U-C-K Y-O-U.

My father was unchanging. He was neat, calculated, and controlled. Like a compressed spring, coiled and ready to launch. My mother drove him crazy—she always had—and that's what he had liked about her. She was a volcano, messy and artful, leaving burnt chaos in her wake. She was uncontrollable.

In unconscious juxtaposition to my father, my mother longed for continual change. She was always rearranging the furniture in the living room—moving the paisley chair under the window, switching the lamps from one side of the sofa to the other—whereas my father preferred that everything remain in its designated place.

After my parents thought we were asleep, they would rendezvous in the kitchen to discuss my mother's behaviour. This was a biweekly check-in, designed to diminish her position both as a mother and as a wife.

Sitting alone at the top of the stairwell, my feet dangling through the wooden railing, I would listen to my father's report.

"You can't even get out of the fucking bed," he'd shout with strained control. "What's wrong with you?"

My mother would remain silent; she knew it was a rhetorical question.

Through these one-sided conversations, I learned how communication worked. You simply listened as someone explained to you all the ways in which you weren't good enough. You didn't defend yourself, you didn't have an opinion. You simply accepted the abuse, because that was what you deserved.

I thought people belonged to other people. I had no concept of individuality, or doing things simply for the sake of being happy. I thought a woman's purpose was to serve her family, and keep her mouth shut.

I always hated the nighttime. The darkness, the uncertainty. It was all too overwhelming. While others slept, I moved around, waiting for day to break so I could see clearly again.

My own patterns were an unfortunate concoction of my parents. I had messily braided care into control. I was a walking, talking contradiction, wanting to be both managed and unmanageable. My father couldn't accept this polarity, and after I left home, he simply stopped taking my calls.

"Are you happy?" I asked Jack one night, after dark.

"Yeah, I'm fine."

"Jack, look at me." I searched his eyes. "Answer the question. Tell me the truth."

He hesitated before answering. "No, Grace, I'm not fucking happy. And neither are you."

I ran my finger along the rim of my wineglass without saying a word.

"Right?" Jack's head jutted forward, the way it did whenever he thought he was making a clever point. His eyebrows raised, the four wrinkles in his forehead deepened. "Don't make me the bad guy here. You're just as unhappy as I am."

My saliva thickened, as if I had just chugged a glass of milk. I cleared my throat. I couldn't bring myself to say it. I wanted so desperately to communicate my feelings to him, for my tongue to form words that I meant. But in the face of confrontation, I always went mute. The more I wanted to speak, the more silent I became.

"You can't even say it, can you?" He edged closer.

I averted my eyes, staring at the rim of clot-like residue on the inside of my glass. I began to count backwards from one hundred.

"Why even bring it up if you don't want to talk?"

Ninety-three.

"Why can't you ever just fucking answer me?"

Eighty-eight.

"You start this shit, and then you get all silent, and I'm left looking like the asshole yelling at someone who can't even respond. You act like a victim when you've manipulated me into this situation."

Seventy-six.

"Say something, for fuck sakes."

"Shut up," I snapped. "Shut the fuck up. I can't keep living like this."

"There she is." Jack wound his arm back, like he was about to toss a baseball, and released, pointing his index finger in my direction. "Finally."

"Stop being so condescending, you fucking monster." I shot up, planting both palms flat on the kitchen table in front of me. "You don't care about me. You've never cared about me. "

"You know, you're so preoccupied with the fact that I no longer worship you, it's driving you insane." He was beginning to calm, his anger alleviated slightly by the fact that I was now participating. "It's not even about me. You don't even want me. You just want someone. Anyone. It wouldn't matter who the fuck it was. So long as someone paid attention to you twenty-four-fucking-seven."

"What about you, huh?" I shrieked, jabbing my finger at him. "The minute I became a real person, that's when you gave up. When I stopped being some fucking perfectly manicured fantasy, made up of lipstick and high heels that you could tie up and fuck whenever you wanted. The minute I had needs, the minute things got hard, that's when you changed your mind."

"Needs, Grace? Seriously?" He threw his hands in the air as he paced in small circles. "As if it was so easy living with you. You are the neediest goddamn person in the entire world. I couldn't even go out with my friends without you losing your mind."

"Fuck you. You have no right to tell me the way I feel is wrong. That the things I need are wrong." The words were flying out of me as if they had been imprisoned in me for decades. I allowed the volume to rise without any restraint. "Oh, and by the way, that's because you were out fucking someone else. You think I didn't know? All this time, you really think I didn't know? Do you really think I'm that stupid?"

Jack sighed. "No, Grace. I know you're a lot brighter than you pretend to be. All the stuff you keep in, all the things you don't say. I know you can't ignore it anymore." He dropped into the chair and lowered his face into his hands. "So please, can we just admit that it's over? Why are we prolonging this? "

"You're right." I turned and laid my cup in the sink. "It's over, Jack."

When I was seven years old, I was strolling through the woods behind my house with Hannah. We had been learning about different kinds of trees in science class, and I was pointing out the various species as we walked, the light seeping through in uneven, rectangular patches.

"That's a black spruce," I announced proudly. "And that's a speckled alder."

Hannah wasn't nearly as bright as me. She struggled in school, particularly with math and science, so I often helped her with her homework. We'd sit at my kitchen table almost every day after class, studying together. I never had any difficulty learning, and I felt instinctively protective of Hannah, as if it were my responsibility to make sure she did well.

"Hannah, are you paying attention?" I asked.

Suddenly, she crumpled, falling to the forest floor.

Lying on her back, her long, golden-blond hair sprawled across the bramble, she raised her forearm and placed it over her eyes like a blindfold. Her faded blue T-shirt rode up, revealing a small section of her pale stomach, just below the belly button. Her voice came softly. "Does your Daddy love you?"

I plopped down next to her, gazing up at the canopy of trees. "I think so."

Hannah removed her arm from her eyes, turning to look at me. I examined her face. The peppering of freckles along her cheeks and the bridge of her nose were particularly pronounced from their exposure to the sun. Her bottom lip trembled as fat tears began streaming down her cheeks, blurring the collection of freckles and landing on the grass beneath us.

"Hannah," I edged toward her, scraping my elbows on the ground. "What's wrong?"

She stared up at the sky. "Sometimes, after Mommy goes to bed..." Her chest rose, and she gulped for air. Between sobs, she managed to squeak, "Daddy comes into my room and lies down with me." She swallowed and whispered, "He touches me."

I wrapped my arms around her, resting my chin on the crown of her head. Her face pressed into my chest, I continued to name the types of trees visible from our vantage point on the forest floor until she cried herself to sleep.

Jack and I notified our landlord that we'd be moving out at the end of the month. I had decided to stay with William until I figured out what to do next. I didn't tell Jack where I was going; I wanted him to wonder and, with any luck, worry. He didn't tell me where he was going either, but I knew.

We packed our things into boxes in silence, speaking only when absolutely necessary.

"Do you want this?" Jack pointed to the burgundy fringed lamp we'd purchased at a yard sale on one of our road trips. I thought it resembled a lamp from a boudoir. I used to pretend we lived in a speakeasy, cheekily whispering in Jack's ear about the cocktail specials before hiking up my skirt to flash him my garter belt.

I shook my head. I didn't want anything that would remind me of him or our life together. Hoping to rid myself of every possession, every memory, every scrap of evidence that I had ever known him, I kept only the bare essentials. Everything else went into the garbage.

On the day of the walk-through with our landlord, I met Jack outside the house. He seemed so different from that night we had met almost six years before. He was older, there was no doubt about that. No longer in his early twenties, his face had lost its youthful plumpness. His eyes seemed a darker green, almost ocean-blue, with high cheekbones protruding below. I tried to picture the last meal we'd had. We used to love to cook together. Playfully, he'd spank me with a spatula, and we'd end up fucking on the kitchen floor.

"Finally moving on, folks?" our landlord called as he approached.

I shielded my eyes from the sun with my right hand, faking a smile. "Yeah."

The landlord tugged at the rim of his baseball cap, the beak angled over his forehead. "Let's get inside and have a look."

We wandered through the house, in and out of each empty room, the destruction and chaos invisible to the landlord's eye. I'd spent a few days plastering holes in the Gyproc and scrubbing the floors, spraying everything with bleach to rid it of the smell of cigarette smoke and dope. The landlord examined the area for damage and cleanliness as I remembered everything that had happened between these walls. I kept trying to catch Jack's eye, but he wouldn't look at me.

"Everything seems good here." The landlord dug in the pocket of his jeans and removed an envelope. "Here's your damage deposit."

I accepted the cash, having been the one who'd paid it long before Jack moved in.

"Keys?" The landlord extended his open palm.

Jack and I placed our keys in his hand, our fingers brushing against one another. I felt a pull in my lungs. Everything was suddenly real, and I was brutally aware that I may have just touched Jack for the last time.

"Alright, you're free to go." The landlord moved aside, allowing me to leave through the front door.

Stepping onto the curb, my eyes landed on the pile of black garbage bags balanced around a telephone pole. There were ten or more, filled with everything I had collected over the last six years of my life.

Jack exited the house and turned, heading for his car. I watched his back, hearing the garbage truck in the distance coming toward us.

I tried to open my eyes but they were sealed shut, caked in sleep. I rubbed them until I was able to pry them open. It was completely dark in my room. The curtains were drawn, as they always were. Rolling onto my side, I reached for my phone, but it wasn't there.

I rose from my bed like someone who was learning to walk for the first time. My hands were shaking, my body was vibrating. I needed a cigarette.

"Don't look in the mirror," I muttered to myself, approaching my vanity.

I fumbled in the drawer until I found my cigarettes. Placing one between my teeth and biting down on the filter, I lit a match. The flash of the flame lit my face in a red-orange glow.

My face was swollen and puffy. Blood was smeared beneath my nose. I picked the dried blood from my upper lip and it flaked, collecting under my fingernail. I slowly inhaled, then exhaled a cloud of smoke through my nose, feeling the pain.

How fucking poetic. I stared at my reflection. *How fucking pathetic.*

The nameless guy lying in my bed stirred, shoving the blankets to free one of his arms. He held it out in my direction without moving his face from the pillow. "Hey, can I have a draw of that?"

Pretending I didn't hear him, I walked out of the bedroom, leaving the door open behind me. I wanted him to go. I wanted to be alone. I pulled on a jacket and headed out the front door, knowing that by the time I returned, he would be gone.

As I walked, the afternoon light stung my eyes. My head was throbbing. I thought about sex, and how my perception of it had always been skewed. The moment I entered puberty, boys began treating me like an object—and I accepted it, using myself as a bargaining chip. I used sex as a means of manipulation. Men were so easily manipulated. I knew how to accentuate aspects of my appearance to make men want me. I wore red lipstick; it made them think of my mouth. My mouth on their mouth. My mouth on their cock. I wore clothes that clung tightly around my hourglass-shaped body. They wanted to know what was underneath. I slept with people I didn't want to sleep with just to feel wanted, to know that I was desirable.

I tried to count them. The people since Jack. There was the girl from the punk bar with the pierced tongue. William's childhood friend who made me promise not to tell anyone. The married man who took his wedding ring off when he fingered me. The radio host with the hair plugs. The guy who wanted me to put my finger in his ass—which I did—and then cried after he came. I was always drunk when I went home with them. I always closed my eyes when we were fucking. It was all hazy.

I felt dirty leaving their houses, like I had betrayed Jack. He used to hate when other men looked at me. I loved being his possession, thriving under his jealous control. I remembered the day he told me how calculated I was, noticing for the first time that I wore white when I was guilty, red when I wanted him to fuck me, and yellow when he was feeling morose. I revelled in the fact that someone finally knew me so well, that he had figured me out. Exposed and excited, I denied his accusations, claiming it was only coincidence.

I lit another cigarette as I walked, and the voices began their lullaby.

Pretty little princess. Pretty little doll. Isn't she perfect? Stand up tall. Don't touch that. Close your legs. Be a good girl. Do as I say. Don't pout. Don't eat that. Give us a smile. What do you have to be sad about? Put on some makeup. That's too much makeup. Cover up. Get naked. Stop that silly crying. Don't talk back. You're overreacting. It didn't happen like that. Nobody likes a dramatic girl. I'm just trying to help. It must have been deserved. Fix your hair. Don't lie like that. Pretty little fuckdoll. Stupid little brat. Get out of bed. You've been in there for days. Shut the fuck up and spread your legs.

It had been four months since Jack and I broke up. I had resumed my university studies and landed a job writing copy for a small advertising agency.

Pulling up outside the office, I shut off the car and attempted to move my legs, but they were tingling like they'd fallen asleep. Using my arms to lift my legs, I placed one foot outside the car at a time. As they hit the sidewalk I gasped, laboriously trying to fill my lungs with oxygen. Short, shallow breaths choked me. I shook my arms and legs, counting to a sixty, slowly. Then I counted backwards from sixty, focusing entirely on my breathing.

When I felt my head clear, I drove to Dr. Brace's office and made my way inside. "I don't think the drugs are working."

"Why do you think that?" Dr. Brace asked, running his fingers along his moustache.

I glanced out the window; raindrops beaded and slid down the sill. "It's making me feel..." I couldn't think of the right word.

Dr. Brace's eyebrows were raised in anticipation.

"Disconnected."

He pursed his lips, nodding. "How so?"

At that moment, I felt as if I were floating above myself, just another framed artifact on his wall. "I can't focus."

"Okay, well let's try another antidepressant." Dr. Brace pulled out his prescription pad, scribbled something down, tore off the sheet, and extended it to me.

Later that day, when I picked up my medication, the pharmacist told me the side effects can include nervousness, restlessness, fatigue and insomnia, and I laughed out loud without meaning to.

The effects of the new medication were similar to that of an ecstasy high mixed with a tranquilizer. I watched the world through the thick-rimmed base of a crystal tumbler, somehow seeing things happening behind me while staring straight ahead. My movements were groggy and slow, uncalculated yet hyper-focused. By the time the light-imbued currents were transmitted from my retinas to my brain, so many other things had transpired it was like existing in the past.

The nights were the hardest. I'd lay awake for hours, replaying, with razor precision, those final conversations with Jack.

One evening, after finally falling asleep, I shot upright in a panic. I rolled out of bed, landing on all fours. I crawled across the hardwood. Standing, shakily, I began walking toward the bathroom; it felt as though I was wading through honey. Slow, sticky, heavy. My limbs were fighting gravity.

When I reached the bathroom, I checked my reflection. My pupils were fully dilated. The blue of my irises had disappeared. The blackness had arrived, surrounded only by white.

I turned to the toilet and started dry heaving. Thin yellow bile trickled out, leaving a rancid taste in my mouth. I couldn't remember the last time I had eaten.

I staggered back to my bedroom and grabbed my phone, dialling the numbers slowly, as if hypnotized by the device's light.

"Grace?" Jack's voice was groggy.

"Jack, something terrible..." I stammered. "...is happening. Call an ambulance."

"What's the matter?"

I pressed my hand against my chest, feeling for a heartbeat. "I can't..." Rasping, I drew in breath. "I can't breathe."

"You're okay," he whispered. "It's just a panic attack."

"Please, Jack. Please, come over."

"Grace."

I heard a soft voice in the background on the other end of the phone. "Please," I moaned.

"Okay," he relented. "I'm on my way."

The time it took for Jack to arrive seemed endless. My entire body convulsed as sweat dripped from my forehead and my teeth chattered. I brought the backs of my cold hands to my cheeks in an attempt to soothe my uncontrollable jaw.

I heard the jingle of Jack's keys outside the window. The front door opened and shut.

Jack stood in the doorway of my bedroom. "What's going on?"

My entire body was trembling. "I'm...dying."

"You're not going to die." He folded his arms across his chest. "At least not today. You have any more blankets?"

"The closet," I muttered, my teeth clicking together.

Jack pulled a knitted quilt from the closet and tossed it carelessly on top of me.

I examined the purple bags under his eyes. "Will you lie with me?"

Jack sighed. "Grace."

"Please, Jack."

Reluctantly, he sat on the edge of the bed. "We can't keep doing this."

"I don't know what—" My voice broke.

"I know." Reaching forward, he stroked my hair. My body continued to shake as I leaned into his touch, straining my neck to press into his hand, feeling a small sense of relief. His warmth began to stabilize my shuddering body.

Jack stared past me, his fingers in my hair, his gaze locked onto the headboard. I desperately searched his face, trying to catch his eye, willing him to see how much pain I was in. Words weren't working. I needed him to see. But he wouldn't look.

My body had started to settle, and Jack broke the silence. "I have to go."

"Please don't."

"Grace, I can't stay." He blinked several times and pulled his hand away, using it to rub his eyes in small circles.

When he recoiled, I sensed the impending finality, and instantly turned on him. "Because you have to get back to her."

Jack lowered his gaze and didn't speak.

"Hm?" I sat up and shoved his shoulder.

"Yes."

"Jack, please. Please don't go. Please."

He started to stand and I grabbed for his shirt, clutching the fabric. "You're supposed to be with me. Not her. How can you not love me anymore? I'll do anything. Please."

"Don't do this, Grace." He tugged his shirt free. "I have to go."

I continued to scream. "Don't go, Jack. I love you. We can fix this. I'm sorry. I'm so sorry."

He lingered in the doorway, his back to me, then disappeared down the hall.

"I fucking hate you," I shrieked, kicking the blankets until everything was in a heap on the ground. "You're a useless fucking coward. How could you do this to me? I wish you were dead. How could you do this to me?"

I heard the door open and slam.

"Come back," I sobbed.

The next day, I called Dr. Brace. "I'm not taking that shit anymore," I snapped.

"I don't think that's a good idea," he advised. "The medication is just starting to work."

"Work?" I opened the garbage can and dumped the pills inside, watching as the blue cylinders landed onto a pile of wet coffee grounds. "It's not going to fix things. He's not coming back."

I came home from school one afternoon to find a mouse-sized white and grey kitten bundled in a forest-green towel, sleeping by the fireplace. My father had found him in the bramble outside our house. His eyes were sealed shut, his mouth was a pale pink slit, and his nose like a jellybean. His legs were not yet strong enough to support him, so he wiggled around on his belly, using his limbs to push himself forward.

"Where's his mother?" I asked, stroking his smooth little head.

"He was abandoned," my mother answered.

"Why would she abandon her baby?"

"Sometimes, the mother will leave behind one of the kittens," she explained, "if it's sick or weaker than the rest of the litter. She does it to protect the other kittens."

My mother made a formula for the kitten, something supposedly similar to its mother's milk. It consisted of egg yolk, vitamin D drops, corn syrup, and Carnation milk. She held the kitten in her hand and parted his little pink lips with the tip of an eyedropper, gently squeezing the red rubber bulb to release the liquid into his mouth as he mewed sharply.

We named the kitten Bramble because of where my father had found him. I would think about Bramble all day at school, running home at the sound of the bell to find him napping or squirming about. I'd pick him up and clutch him below my chin, his hamster-like paws tickling my neck.

Then one day, Bramble died. My mother couldn't give me a reason why, other than he must have been sick. It didn't seem as if Bramble's sudden death was at all traumatic to my parents. My mother continued with her cleaning duties as my father scooped up the minuscule carcass and placed it inside a shoebox. He asked if I wanted to say goodbye, and kneeling, held the box open for me.

Sobbing, I tried to touch the kitten one last time, but the cold, lifeless body terrified me, and I screamed and shielded my swollen eyes.

Carrying the box, my father left through the back door. I peeked out the window, catching him just as he dropped it into the trashcan on the corner.

Dear Sunshine,

Say you found a magic lamp, and after rubbing it with the soft tips of your fingers, a genie appeared, offering you three wishes. Absolutely anything you could ever dream of. What would you wish for?

I would wish:

1) *You had never left me.*

2) *You had never left me.*

3) *You had never left me.*

Love,
G

Driving to work one particularly foggy and drizzly morning, I noticed three crows perched on the power lines as I passed the pharmacy. *What's that rhyme again? One for sorrow, two for joy...*I lifted my index finger from the steering wheel and drew an X three times in the air, over each individual crow.

Arriving at my office, I parked the car and entered the building, repeating in my head: *Three for a what? Three for a what? Three for a what?*

"How was your weekend?" the receptionist asked as I walked by her desk.

"Oh fine, thanks." I stopped, tilting my head to the side. "How about you?"

"Great." She grinned. "Just great."

"Greeeaaat," I repeated, dragging the word on for slightly too long. It sounded sarcastic. *What the hell is wrong with me?*

Continuing down the hallway, past the closed doors and dark offices, the left side of my body seemed heavier than the right. I dragged it along, lopsided, attempting to appear natural. It was as if something was holding my hand, pulling me downward.

Three for a what?

I unlocked my door, sat at my desk, and checked my reflection in the black computer monitor. I smiled, making sure both corners of my mouth turned upward. They did. Then, opening my mouth unnecessarily wide, I repeated, "the sssk-hiiiigh is bl-ooo in Ssssii-inn-cinnati, the sssk-hiiiigh is bl-ooo in Ssssiiinn-cinnati."

Deciding I wasn't having a stroke, I jerked my computer mouse from left to right to find the icon on my screen and opened my inbox. Jack's name appeared at the top. My chest tightened.

I lifted my hand from the mouse and began making small circles with my wrist before moving each finger, one at a time: *pinky, ring finger, middle finger, index finger, thumb.* My limbs were still working.

I clicked the email, looking away at first, my fingers trembling over the keyboard.

Raising my eyes to the screen, I read each word carefully.

Grace,

I wanted to tell you first before you heard it from anyone else. Jessica and I are getting married.

I hope you are well,
Jack

I was sure that I was disappearing, fading, each fragment of my body semiopaque. I checked my hand, touching the arm of the chair to make sure I was still made up of solid matter, that it didn't pass through me. I staggered from my office down the hallway, hitting each closed door with my fist as I passed.

"Grace, are you okay?" the receptionist asked as I rounded the corner, craning her neck to peer at me. "You don't look so good."

Translucent holes were shining through my hands. I braced myself on her desk and began muttering, "It's my fault. It's my fault. It's all my fault."

"What's your fault?" she asked, her eyebrows knotted.

"I killed him. He's getting married. I killed us." The holes in my hands were getting bigger. I could see the wood of her desk through them.

"Grace, what are you talking about?"

Watching her mouth move, I heard the words, but couldn't make sense of them. Shaking my head, my body wavered. I heard a soft cry and followed the sound with my eyes. Standing in the corner was a little boy with curly black hair and fat, freckled cheeks. He was sobbing, rubbing his eyes with the flats of his fists, repeating "Mother. Mother. Mother. Mother. Mother."

I leaned forward to comfort him, and then the darkness came.

I was confined by something. Strapped down. The smell of illness and antiseptic. The white ceiling burned my irises. I blinked my eyes.

I was in a hospital bed. A small window to my left with no curtains. A faded red chair next to me. Absolutely nothing else in the room.

A tall man with thinning hair and a strong jawline entered the room carrying a glass of water and a file folder. He leaned over the bed, peering down at me.

"Hi Grace, I'm Dr. Hurley," he said softly. "Do you know where you are?"

My throat was dry and itchy. I shook my head.

"You're at the psychiatric hospital," he explained. "You had an episode of psychosis." His eyes were so darkly brown, I could almost see my reflection in them. "I spoke with your doctor; she says you have a bit of a history of mental illness and insomnia. Is that correct?"

I cleared my throat. "I suppose." Lifting my head, I looked down at myself. My hands, chest, and legs were strapped to the bed.

"We had to confine you." Dr. Hurley leaned down and began unstrapping me. "For your own safety."

I sat up as he passed me the glass of water. Sipping it cautiously, I examined his face. He must have been in his forties.

"Do you have any kids?"

The doctor's face scrunched in confusion. "I'm sorry?"

"Do you have any kids? Children?"

He pushed my file into his chest and crossed his arms over it. "No, I do not."

"Oh." I stared out the window. All I could see was blue. "Do my parents know where I am?"

"We called your brother when you arrived. I'm not sure if he was in contact with your parents or not."

Dr. Hurley was silent for a couple of minutes, thumbing through the pages of my ever-thickening file. "So, based on your records, and your most recent episode, I'm recommending you stay here for a little while." He shut the file, glancing up at me. "I think the quiet will do you good."

"It's quiet time," my father would announce from the driver's seat of the car.

Sometimes, he'd turn the radio up loudly, Nine Inch Nails blared from the speakers as Annabelle and I held our hands over our ears, exchanging terrified looks.

Other times we would all sit in complete silence, hearing only the muffled noises of our old station wagon. No one dared utter a word. The risk of getting yelled at was even higher if you spoke during quiet time.

It takes great restraint to stay silent as a child, and I assume discipline is what my father thought he was teaching us. Or perhaps he just wanted some peace.

During those moments, my mind would flood with questions about how the world worked. Questions I wished I could ask him. *Where does the sun go in the nighttime? Why do the waves go out sometimes and other times come in? Why do people die? Where's Mother? What's that? Who's that? Where are we going? When will we get there?*

After some time, my father would turn around and say "It's over," and the noise resumed again. But everything felt different. I chose my words more carefully and acted with restraint. The imparted lesson was that quietness was synonymous with goodness. And good was all I ever wanted to be.

As I aged, it became easier to keep quiet. I learned to exist within my own realm, to answer my own questions. Perpetually silenced, my voice was less pronounced. I spoke more softly, behaved more submissively. I did as I was told, and cared more for others than I did myself. I had no idea who I was, so I pretended to be whoever others wanted me to be.

At some point, quiet time stopped being finite.

Coming out of solitary confinement, I was transferred to the hospital's main ward.

I spent my first morning lying in bed, facing the wall. There were two other beds in the room, but the occupants were in art therapy. I was sure I didn't belong here, and didn't want to participate. The doctors quickly made it clear that if I stayed in bed all day, I wouldn't be getting out any time soon, so I got up.

I soon realized that the psychiatric ward thrived on a rigid schedule. Like a child, you were expected to wake up when you were called, eat when you were given food, engage in group activities, and go to bed when the lights were turned out.

Tessa was one of the women staying in my room. She was schizophrenic, but she was so heavily medicated most of the time she just sat in a chair staring at the wall. The nurses helped her to the cafeteria and, after a few failed attempts of trying to mash food into her mouth, helped her back to her chair. In the brief moments between her episodes of catatonia, she would throw tantrums, ripping off her hospital gown, and curse, naked, at the nurses and other patients.

One day, after a breakfast of muted-coloured mush, I was walking up and down the hallway, which served as my sole pleasure. I loved moving without making any sound, the way I could almost float, undetected, the concrete floors and slippers snuffing my existence. There was no consequence to movement—unlike back home, where you couldn't take a step without everyone knowing what room you were in, the floors creaking, betraying you.

On my seventh lap, the unattended Tessa spotted me, her large brown-black eyes locking onto my feet. She bolted after me. Her breathing was strained and her nose produced a whistle like that of a boiling kettle.

"Hey," Tessa called. "Hey, you. Stop."

I paused, against my better judgment, and turned to face her.

"Where do you think you're going?" she demanded, pinning me against the wall.

"I'm going for a walk," I explained, trying to remain calm.

She leaned in close. "I know you have my baby." Her eyes were dark and unreflecting. "Give me back my baby," she screamed, her saliva flying at my face, landing on my cheek.

I wiped my face without saying anything.

"Give him back."

Within seconds, the nurses were running down the hall and pulling Tessa away from me. She continued to scream as they dragged her into a room nearby.

"I know you have my baby," she shrieked. "Give me my baby."

I sprinted down the hallway, my slippers flopping loose, slapping against the concrete floors with each stride. Panting, I slammed the door behind me and peeked out through the triangular wire mesh in the window.

All the noise reverberated inside me as I climbed back into bed and pulled the covers over my head.

I spent two weeks in the hospital.

My mother would come and visit, staring at me as if she no longer knew who I was. "Are you sleeping?" she asked, fidgeting in her chair.

Across the common room, a man started thrashing and shrieking. The nurses ran to him, leading him out.

I rolled my eyes. "Would you be able to sleep in a place like this?"

We sat in silence for a few moments. Patients shuffled around behind us like paranoid slugs, not really in the world at all.

Staring at my mother's shiny, dark hair, I was overcome with the memory of brushing it as a little girl. I'd run the comb through it, over and over, until she decided it was time for me to go to bed. I had the urge to touch it, and reached forward. "Mother?"

"Yes, doll?"

"Can I brush your hair?"

The edges of her lips dropped.

Dr. Hurley approached us, addressing my mother before she could respond. "Can I speak with you in private?"

"Sure." She followed him out of sight.

I sat deeper in my chair, pressing my head further into the cushion. The pressure in my neck intensified as I pushed, harder and harder. I could no longer differentiate the ghosts from the people. Everything was so bizarre, so far from reality, that there was no distinction.

After a few moments, Dr. Hurley appeared. "Grace, will you join us?"

I peeled myself off the chair, cringing at the sound of my bare legs slowly separating from the vinyl seat.

As we walked across the hall, we passed a young patient who was sitting on the ground, nonsensically singing to herself. I ran my fingers along the top of her head, and Dr. Hurley reminded me, "No touching."

Entering his office, the doctor shut the door behind me as I took a seat in the chair next to my mother.

"So, your mother and I talked, and we think it's best you go home," Dr. Hurley announced as he sat down behind his desk.

"Isn't that wonderful news?" My mother smiled nervously, intertwining her hands in her lap.

"Mhm. Wonderful."

"We feel that you're no longer a threat to yourself, and we believe you will have a better chance of recovering at home, where you're comfortable."

"Okay." I blinked. I felt nothing.

"We're releasing you into the care of your mother, so you'll need to stay with her." Dr. Hurley looked from my face to hers.

I eyed her.

"Well." He joined his palms together, his elbows resting on the desk. "If we're all in agreement, we can get started on the paperwork."

I forced a smile, closed my eyes, and nodded excessively.

As a child, it was impossible to separate me from my mother. I was obsessed with her. She was all that I knew, as mothers are when you are born to them. I loved to watch her. Every movement she made seemed miraculous. I didn't know her feet were on the ground. I thought she floated. I clung to every word that passed from her lips as if they were tangible, believing I could do no wrong if only I held on tightly enough.

When I was small, we had a turntable in the living room, and I would regard her as she selected a record from the shelf. Tipping the cardboard case upside down, the disc would slide into her open hand, and then carefully she'd place it onto the machine. She pressed a button, it clicked, and the needle would lift and then lower onto the vinyl, like magic. It would begin its melody of scratching before the instruments kicked in.

William, Annabelle, and I would dance with her. Bouncing up and down, bending our knees, swaying from side to side, our mouths wide open in carefree delight. My mother would take our hands, one kid at a time, and twirl us around. We would jump in time with the music, spinning in circles, running around, our toes sinking into the plush carpet with each leap.

I don't remember when we stopped dancing. I don't remember when the music shut off. I don't remember when I noticed her feet hitting the ground, or when her words stopped meaning so much. I don't remember when that house became a place of sadness instead of joy. When the memories became too painful to bear. I just know that the woman who I was obsessed with, who I spent every moment thinking about, staring at, clinging to, she became something unbelievable for a child: my mother became mortal.

I stared at my reflection. Below my right eye, at the tip of my cheekbone, was a small circular scar, as if the skin had been dented.

When I was six, I woke to find that a collection of itchy red dots had formed on my stomach. My mother took me to the doctor's office.

"Hop up." The doctor patted the examination table, the fresh paper crinkling under his hand. I stepped onto the stool and plopped down, lifting my shirt to show him the marks on my belly.

"That's chicken pox all right," the doctor pronounced, turning to look at my mother. "I'm going to prescribe her an antiviral."

We stopped by the pharmacy on our way home. "Two spoonfuls of this a day and she should be better in no time," said the pharmacist, handing my mother a white paper bag.

When we arrived home, my mother told me to get in bed. I was miserable. The itching was unbearable, and the pox were starting to spread.

"It's really important not to scratch, doll," she explained as she pulled my winter mittens onto my hands. "You'll get chicken pox scars."

"But I'm so itchy," I whined.

"I know." She poured thick, white liquid from the medicine bottle onto a spoon. "Open up, this will help."

I opened my mouth and accepted the spoon, swallowing the substance. It was vile, slightly sweet with a hint of artificial banana flavouring. I immediately threw up into the bucket she'd placed beside my bed.

"I need you to try and keep this down," my mother pleaded, filling the spoon with another dose.

I retched, but managed to not vomit this time.

"Good girl." She smoothed my hair. "Try and have a nap. Your fever will break soon." She pulled the covers to my chin.

I was trembling, but my skin felt like it was on fire. Closing my eyes, I soon drifted into a lucid sleep. I remember feverish dreams filled with vibrant colours and make-believe creatures.

I woke in a pool of sweat with my father sitting next to me.

"Where's Mother?" I asked.

Ignoring my question, he pressed the back of his hand to my forehead. "You're burning up." He took the thermometer from its case and placed it under my tongue.

I waited until it beeped.

"104." He looked panicked. "I need to call the doctor."

When he returned, he began peeling the blankets off me. "I have to get you into the bath." He scooped me up, carrying me to the washroom in his arms.

While the bath was filling, he ran to the kitchen. I stood there, listening as the water thrashed against the enamel.

My father returned, knelt by the tub, and dumped a bag of ice in. There was a crackling noise as it hit. He undressed me and I stood there, naked and shivering, trying not to scratch.

"Okay, doll, get in the tub."

I swung one foot over the side of the tub and let my toes touch the water. "Father," I squealed, "it's too cold."

"I know. I need you to get in though. Your fever isn't breaking. This will help."

I shook my head. "I can't."

"Grace, get in the tub."

"No."

He scooped me up, forcing me into the water.

"No," I screamed at the top of my lungs, waving my arms. "Father, stop. Help."

William came running into the bathroom, his little face knotted. "What's going on?"

My father held me in place. "William, go back to bed."

"What're you doing? What's wrong with Gracie?"

"I told you to go to bed," my father shouted.

William hesitated, tugging at the edges of his pajama shirt; his concerned eyes locked onto mine momentarily before he turned and retreated.

Completely immersed in the frigid water, I was silenced; only a sharp exhalation came out. My stomach drew closer to my spine, my shoulders tensed, and my father let go.

Submerged there, sweating, shivering, panting, and crying, I looked at my father, resting on the toilet with his head in his hands. Some ice cubes bobbed on the surface, others began sinking to the bottom. I lifted a fingernail to my face and scratched, hard, along my cheekbone.

"Where's Mother?" I shrieked, angry that she wasn't here to stop him from doing this to me.

"She's gone, Grace," he shouted back, quietly repeating it a second time. "She's gone."

When Hannah's father was dying, I had no idea what to say to comfort her. He was a horrible man, a vicious drunk who had abused her and her mother. His face was bumpy and scarred, and whenever I went to Hannah's house and saw him, I felt an uneasiness that I didn't understand.

He spent months in the hospital, withering away. His body was riddled with cancer. Despite the horrors he'd put his family through, they were there for him as he died. When I asked Hannah why, she said, "He's still my father."

It was the bond of blood; I could see that so clearly with Hannah. People can physically and emotionally destroy those they are supposed to love, and the victims continue to hold them dear because of the perception that in death, we owe them forgiveness.

After weeks in the hospital, Hannah's father finally went into cardiac arrest, and the doctors recommended he not be resuscitated.

I went to the funeral with Hannah. Her mother was dressed in black, and I watched carefully for her reaction. She didn't shed a tear. She didn't carry his blood in her veins. Hannah wept and I held her hand, passing her a tissue from my purse.

As mourners spoke fondly of the man he was, I realized that when you die you are absolved of all your transgressions. You become immortal. Your flaws and sins no longer exist. People remember you how they want to remember you—only the light, never the darkness.

I wanted that so desperately for myself.

Dear Sunshine,

Why did you stop kissing me goodnight?

Love,
G

I didn't want her to find me like that. Or maybe I did.

I had climbed into bed, wearing a white dress that I'd bought from a vintage store uptown. It resembled the christening gown I'd seen in my parents' closet as a child, laid flat in something that wasn't much larger than a shoebox. It was slightly yellowed and wrinkled, lined with lace, and smelled of mildew and incense.

Later, I dug through the drawers in our kitchen, searching for photographs of the day I was baptized. After separating the pictures with licked fingers for what felt like hours, I triumphantly placed three glossy prints, side by side, on the counter.

The first was of William wearing the gown, blond hair shining with moisture, in the arms of my smiling parents near the altar. The second was of Annabelle, all brown eyes, mouth exaggeratedly wide and ruddy faced as my mother held her close to her chest in what I can only imagine was an attempt to soothe the screaming darling. The third was of me, looking serene in a way that was oddly chilling. My parents, for some reason, were not in the photo, and I was being held over the baptism bowl by a priest who poured a stream of water onto my golden head.

I searched my face, desperate for some sort of familiarity. My infant pugged nose, my ocean-blue, saucer-shaped eyes, my tightly clenched fingers that formed a tiny ball. But no matter how long I stared, I couldn't recognize her. I saw nothing of myself.

I didn't write a note. I didn't need to blame anyone or leave my family with something to analyze and agonize over. I didn't want to write.

I lifted the blade with my right hand and pressed it against my left wrist. With one swift movement, I dragged it straight down along the green line, opening the vein.

Blood poured down my arms, drenching my white dress and bedsheets. A wince escaped my mouth as my chest heaved. I began to tremble. A feeling of warmth rushed over my body, beginning in my arms and making its way down to my feet. Then the smell came, like rusted iron.

Lying there, I watched the blood pouring out of me like honey. I'd always loved the colour red. I thought of my mother, what she had told me that day in the grass, and wondered if my eyes were seeing the truth.

Then a moment of terror seized me.

I don't want to die.

It typically takes forty-five minutes to bleed to death from wrist lacerations.

I don't want to die. I just don't want to be myself anymore.

Too much time.

It will be over soon.

Another memory came flooding back.

My father used to take us to church every Sunday, while my mother stayed home in bed. The cathedral was old, the architecture aggressively Romanesque. There was a grotto adjacent to the building with the Virgin Mary, adorned in robes, at the centre.

When mass was finished, we exited the church, shaking the priest's hand as we always did.

"Bless you, my child," he said, squatting down to touch my face.

Sprinting across the road, bound for our parked car, one of my sandals came loose and dropped in the middle of the street. I stopped and bent to retrieve it, oblivious to the minivan that was barrelling toward me.

I heard my father's hysterical cries in the distance: "Grace—move."

I was frozen in place.

Turning my head, I watched as my father ran for me, but it was too late. The car was inches from me.

The driver slammed on the brakes, and I felt a gust of wind that immediately gave me goosebumps.

My father was by my side. He scooped me up in one arm, yelling at the driver and pounding the hood with his fist. "Watch where you're going, you fucking idiot."

He carried me safely back across the road, laid me down, and kneeled in front of me, squeezing my upper arms so tightly they left a white imprint for a moment afterwards.

"Never, ever run into the road like that," he yelled. I watched his face transform from rage to fear to relief. He started crying and hugged me close, holding me in an embrace as families poured out of the church and traffic resumed unaffectedly.

When I was a little girl, I would pray every night before I went to sleep, as I had been taught to do. Kneeling by my bed with my sister, we asked God to bless our friends and family.

Oh Angel of God
My guardian dear
To Whom His love
Commits me here
Ever this day
Be at my side
To light and guard
To rule and guide
Amen.

As I got older, the ceremonial praying stopped. I didn't think I still believed in God, but whenever I was afraid, I found myself praying silently in my head, over and over.

I no longer knelt at the side of my bed for God; that position was now reserved for the men who told me what to do. With eyes closed and intertwined fingers, I would beg for mercy.

When someone tries to end their life, they become like a butterfly who has been handled excessively. The powder on their wings has been absorbed by the oil on their captor's fingers, rendering them incapable of flight. Suddenly, their beauty cannot be trusted and must be contained. They are poked and prodded, examined and dissected. Finally, a needle is stuck through their thorax and, with their wings spread wide, they are put on display.

I hadn't died, but I had killed something inside myself that day. The darkness wasn't so dark anymore. The pull of weight I had felt, the ghosts that were holding my hand, dragging me down, subsided ever so slightly.

I was in the hospital for a few weeks. People came to visit me—friends I hadn't seen in years, family members I didn't even know existed. Everyone loves a suicide attempt. It's just morbid enough to draw a crowd. People want their ticket to the freakshow; they want to see the scars and look into the eyes of someone who almost made it to the other side.

William was at the hospital the entire time. He would reluctantly go home to shower every few days, but mostly he would sit in the squeaky vinyl chair, making jokes and playing games with me, his head dipping periodically as he drifted in and out of consciousness.

One day as I flipped through a magazine, bored out of my mind, Annabelle walked through the door. Her dark hair was cut into a short bob, her pale skin glowing like a cup of cream. I dropped the magazine, believing, for a moment, she was an apparition.

William sat upright in his chair, his eyes wide, a controlled smile spread across his face. "Well, well, well," he announced. "The prodigal child returns."

Annabelle burst into tears and laughter at the same time. Falling into me, she wrapped herself in my arms. William piled on top of us, holding us together with outstretched hands.

When we finally pulled away and they climbed off the bed, I held Annabelle's face, feeling the tiniest shard of hope that, with the three parts of me reunited, together we'd be able to make sense of it all.

Every fall, the wood truck would arrive. The big, ugly, dirty wood truck. I'd listen as it pulled into the driveway, disturbing the gravel with its unusually large tires. I'd run to the kitchen window, pull back the lace curtains, and watch it drive across the lawn. It would beep, reversing alongside the barn, and the back of the truck would lift with a piercing gush, as though all the air in its tires was escaping at once. There was a rumble when the logs began to fall and as they bounced off one another, the sound produced was like an instrument that had been hollowed out.

I hated the wood truck. It always left tire marks across the lawn, flattening the grass and destroying my childhood oasis. I asked my father why it had to come every year.

"Wood is essential," he replied. "It provides us with heat for the winter."

We had electricity—it wasn't as if we needed to keep a fire—but for my parents, it was part of the idyllic country life they'd aways imagined, the romanticized fantasy that couldn't have been further from the truth.

William, Annabelle, and I would have to help my father prepare the wood. The logs arrived as full, limbless trees freshly cut from the forest. My father would yank the pull-cord several times before it caught, while the three of us sat nearby, the smell of gasoline wafting through the breeze. He'd balance the uncut logs on the misshapen sawhorse he had built from wood of years past. Wood chips and sparks shot up as the chainsaw met the fresh log.

I thought it was a horrible sight, these logs having to hold their brothers still as my father massacred them. To me, it was like cannibalism.

My father paused, shouting over the noise of the chainsaw for us to come help, his red-and-black flannel jacket covered in wood shavings.

We would begin to stack the wood. The first stacks were left outdoors in neat, triangular piles, like the great pyramids of Egypt, in order for it to dry. After a few days, we would transfer those piles into the barn for storage, pressing the logs against a wall until we could no longer reach the top.

As wood was needed for the fire, we would re-stack it a final time inside the porch. To a child, this seemed an unnecessarily complicated ritual, and so, every year, I would cry and try to get out of helping.

William, as the only boy, had the task of chopping the wood for kindling. I would study him as he laid the thicker pieces of wood upright on the chopping block, raising the axe over his head with both arms, and thrust it down, the wood splitting perfectly in two.

One day, I was stacking wood in the barn when I heard William's scream. I ran outside to find him clutching his right hand, a hatchet in the other.

"My finger," he groaned. "I cut off my finger."

I ran indoors, calling hysterically for my mother and father, but neither were there.

Filling a bag with ice, I grabbed a towel then dialled 911, telling them to send an ambulance.

When I went back to William, he was sitting on the ground with blood droplets on the grass below him. He wasn't crying. His eyes were vacant, his mouth slightly agape.

I knelt next to him and wrapped his finger tightly with the towel. "Where is it?"

William opened his hand and, there in his palm, bloody and pink with a clean, bitten-down nail, was the tip of his pinky. He had cut it from the middle joint.

I grabbed his finger, disturbed by how little I felt looking at the severed joint, and placed it in the baggie. Rubbing his hair, I shushed him soothingly. "It's going to be okay," I repeated like a prayer. "The ambulance is on the way."

By the time we got to the hospital, it was too late. They were unable to reattach William's finger, so they stitched it up. It wasn't a huge loss, they said, you don't use your pinky for anything.

Looking at William, stoic and strong, a little boy who was unfairly, prematurely made to be a man, I became furious with my parents. Why weren't they taking care of us? Why were we taking care of ourselves? What else would we have to lose for them to pay attention?

I stood by my hospital bed, dressed for the first time in weeks, wearing the clothes that William had brought for me. I had laughed when I initially opened the bag, pulling out my black T-shirt embroidered with the word *anti-social.*

I packed my few possessions and waited as William signed the paperwork. The nurse had opened the blinds of the window that morning, and as I peered at the outside world, I felt the slightest tinge of significance.

"Hey." William was standing in the doorway. He smiled when he saw the shirt.

"You may be the only person darker than me in the entire universe," I joked, gesturing to the embroidered words.

"I think it's a pretty close tie." He looked so small. Skinny and pale. I felt sorry for everything I had put my him through.

"I'm ready," I announced, attempting to pick up the bag, forgetting about the stitches. I tried to hide the wince, but William was already there, tossing my bag over his shoulder.

He grabbed my hand and squeezed it gently. "Let's go."

With that caring touch, I was immediately brought back to childhood days spent at the pond by my house. My parents never taught me to swim, so I would just stay in the shallows. The floor was rocky and hurt the bottom of my feet as I stepped, bobbing with the movement of the water.

William sat on the shore reading as the water reflected the sun's sparkle in a line that led directly toward him. I watched as he turned the page and took a bite from a peach. He and I were the only ones there. It was late in the afternoon and all the other kids had gone home for dinner.

Turning away from the shore, I glided from rock to rock, dragging my feet, hopping and counting. *One, two, three, four, five, six—*

The ground dropped, and I was completely underwater. Standing there, holding my breath, the world drowned out as I was swallowed by the lake. I felt strangely calm knowing that any minute, William would be there. I opened my eyes and let my head fall back to the sky. They stung as I absorbed the sight of blurring blues above me.

I heard a dull splash, and within seconds William grabbed me and pulled me to the surface. I thirstily gasped for air, coughing and spitting out mouthfuls of water.

Dragging me by the arm, he manically paddled to the shore. As I kept perfectly still, he was careful to keep my head above water.

William pushed me onto dry land. Panting, he shook me. "Gracie, you okay?"

I nodded, staring up at him. His wetted blond hair looked brown, and his curls were flattened against his head. Hugging me, he pulled my head into his chest, and I could feel his heartbeat between the heaves.

"Don't ever do anything that stupid—" His voice broke.

It was the only time I ever saw him cry.

After the incident, I began seeing Trevor in that tiny beige room with the coffee pot. The doctors agreed to release me from the hospital so long as I went to see him twice a week.

Trevor was a social worker who specialized in addictions and suicide. Before his transition into therapy, he had worked with the police as a suicide negotiator, convincing people not to take their own lives. He was good in a crisis.

Trevor was in his forties. His face was chubby beneath black stubble, and his eyes were soft with rings of hazel and green. His voice soothed me in a way that made me feel like a child. Not the child I had been, but the child I knew was inside of me. A child who was able to trust, to depend on people, and to be vulnerable.

"You've been through a lot of trauma, Grace," Trevor said decidedly, after I had given him the condensed version of my life: my childhood, my parents, my siblings, my work, my drug use, my hospital stays, the ghosts, Jack and the people in between, and our baby boy. Not the rehearsed version or the one I told to feel better. My monologue had been edited. I shared the truth, as close as I could get to it.

"Yeah." I nodded, smiling through the discomfort. "I guess you could say that."

"Have you ever heard of kintsukuroi?" Trevor asked, his hands resting on his knees.

"No."

"It's this amazing Japanese art form." Glancing out the window, he watched a group of kids run by, squealing with delight, seemingly in a game of tag. A smile spread across his face, lost for a moment. He pulled his eyes away, continuing slowly, "Right. Kintsukuroi. So they repair vases that have been broken. They piece them back together, bit by bit, and use gold to fill in the cracks."

I listened as the cries of the children grew gentler and gentler, until they disappeared entirely.

Trevor grinned. "More beautiful for having been broken, they say."

I didn't realize I was crying until I tasted the salt of tears on my tongue.

"Well, first things first, you need to get sober," he explained, leaning forward to hand me a piece of paper and a tissue. "I would recommend you start attending meetings."

Taking both, I glanced at the paper's heading: *Narcotics Anonymous.*

I didn't want to be that butterfly anymore. I no longer wanted to be on display, my beauty merely a convenience for strangers who wished to admire it. "Okay," I said, wiping my eyes with the tissue.

"Good. And Grace, you're a writer." Trevor held my gaze. "That's an incredible gift. You need to use it."

I felt the familiar tinge of shame. I hadn't written in years. "How would I do that?"

"Well, I think a great exercise would be for you to write about your experiences and emotions. Write about everything you've been through. Write about your childhood, and your parents. Just write it all down."

"But I was never any good."

"How can you say you were never any good? How can you even measure that?" He gestured as he spoke as though his hands were an extension of his mouth. "Tell me this, Grace, why were you writing?"

I had never considered this, so I thought for a moment. "I think when I was little, I had all these stories in my head. All kinds of questions and observations. I didn't know what else to do with them." I ran my fingers along my lips; catching myself, I returned my hands to my lap. "Then I stopped, for a long time. I started again to help deal with my mother leaving."

Trevor nodded, inviting me to continue.

"I think I kept writing because Jack liked it. It was part of how he saw me, or wanted to see me. The idyllic version of me."

"Do you think you were writing for Jack, or for yourself?"

I hoisted myself up in my chair, my skin tingling. All this time, it had been for someone else. First, my parents, then Jack. The words

I let out, the words I kept in. In my performance of being who they wanted, I had sacrificed myself. "It was for other people."

Trevor's head bobbed. "It's sounds to me like it wasn't working because it wasn't for you. You need to write for you, like when you were a child. Just write, without judgment, as if no one is going to read it. Do it for you."

"And they lived happily ever after." My father closed *The Little Mermaid.* It was my favourite bedtime story, and the one he read me most nights before I went to sleep. I had preferred the Grimms' version, but after having a recurring nightmare of my tongue being cut out by a witch, my father switched to the adaptation with Ariel and Prince Eric.

"Father?" I asked as he reached to shut off my lamp.

"Yes, Grace?"

"Do people really live happily ever after?" I grabbed at the edges of my covers, feeling the indentations of its seams.

My father ran his hands along his forehead, messing his thick eyebrows, wiry hairs sticking out in every direction. He exhaled. "I'm not sure. I think people want to be happy, and they can be happy most of the time. But I don't think anyone is happy all of the time."

I reflected for a moment. "But why not?"

"Because if you were happy all of the time, you wouldn't appreciate it. You need balance and duality in life. If we didn't feel sadness, happiness would mean nothing."

Staring at him, I furrowed my little brow.

He petted my head. "Imagine if it was light all the time. The sun was shining. It was bright and beautiful every single day. If it never got dark, how would you sleep? If it never rained, how would you know that the sun was beautiful?"

I thought about how the rain and darkness made me feel. I liked the days when we stayed inside because it was too wet and muddy to play outside. Mother would let me put my hands in the clay, moulding misshapen mugs and vases before she'd dip them in glaze and fire them in the kiln. "I want to write stories about people who are happy, even when it rains." I decided.

My father sighed. "You don't want to be a writer, Grace."

"Yes I do," I declared, sitting upright. "I want to be just like you."

He rubbed around his mouth, the stubble on his face making a scratchy noise. "Come with me, I want to show you something." My father pulled the blankets off and led me downstairs, reaching in his pocket for a key before unlocking his office door. I had hardly ever been inside. Father's office was off-limits.

The room was painted a deep mahogany. The entire space was lined with bookshelves filled with hundreds of books. There were piles of books on a table next to a striped sofa. Books on the floor, books on his desk, and books next to his computer. There was a typewriter in the corner surrounded by scribbled-up pages of paper, and even more books.

He began to dig in his filing cabinet as I stood there, shivering in my nightgown.

When he turned around, he was holding a thick file folder. He placed it on his desk and motioned for me to come look.

"These are all rejection letters," my father said as he thumbed through the enormous stack. "For every story I have published, there are about fifty rejection letters that come first. If you want to write, you can't just write about being happy. Because no one is just happy. No one is just anything."

I watched as he flipped, page after page, laying them flat on the desk.

I stopped wanting to be a writer after that night.

"Tell me the first time you felt anxious."

I was reclined in a La-Z-Boy chair by the fireplace, covered to my neck in blankets. My legs were angled so that the heels of my boots laid flat on the leg rest. My eyes were closed, my face soft, intentionally relaxed. My arms were folded beneath the blankets.

The hypnotherapist, Julie, sat cross-legged in a chair alongside, clipboard and pen in hand. Her proximity was meant to provide a sense of security as I entered the subconscious world, but it only made me feel more claustrophobic.

"Don't think too much, just tell me the first thing that comes to your mind," Julie continued. "Where are you: inside or outside?"

"Inside," I replied as a memory flooded in.

"Okay, good." Her voice was soothing, singsong-ish. There was a youthfulness to it that made me think of her as less of an authority figure and more of a friend. "What can you see?"

"I'm at my elementary school." I recognized the coat hangers and cubbies, the children's colouring pages taped to the wall. "Standing outside my grade one classroom."

"Are you alone?" Julie asked.

"Yes." I could see that the halls were empty. I stared down the corridor, bookbag in hand, desperately scanning, waiting for my parents to appear. "I'm waiting for someone to pick me up."

"Okay, good." Julie's chair creaked as she shifted. "I want you to relax even deeper. Sink into the chair. Breathe."

I nodded, my eyes remained closed. I inhaled loudly, and as I exhaled, I attempted to further relax my body, sinking deeper into the chair.

"Think about a time, before that, when you felt anxious. No wrong answers here, whatever comes into your head, just say it," Julie continued. "Where are you? Inside or outside?"

"Inside, again." I felt as if I were in the space between waking and sleeping. The heaviness of someone who had just woken up from a nightmare, fighting to stay awake so you wouldn't drift back into that same bad dream.

"How old are you?"

I could hear the clock ticking on the wall. Muffled yelling. The crackling of the fire. Oil spitting. I was no longer sure of what was happening in my head and what was happening in the room. "Three-ish."

"Who are you with?"

I turned my head, and William was standing there with his cascading blond curls. He was perfectly still, staring straight ahead. "My brother, William. We're under the kitchen table."

"Where are you?"

"My grandparents' house." I followed William's eyes with my own. My grandparents and my father were screaming at one another, but I couldn't hear what they were saying. Their faces were contorted, their arms flailing as their mouths moved, nothing coming out.

"What do you see?"

My grandfather turned and snatched a butcher's knife off the counter. He held it out at my father. Threatening. I looked back at William, who had moved closer, wrapping his arms around me and trying to cover my eyes. Then the police. "The police are arresting Grandfather."

"Do you know why?"

"No." The officers were pinning him to the dishwasher, his hands behind his back. Handcuffs. A silver flask peeked out of his pants pocket. A fallen cigarette burning a hole in the linoleum tile. "I can't hear anything."

"Okay. I want you to go deeper now, Grace." Julie sounded far away. I tried to reach out and touch her but my hand was too heavy to lift. Her words were clipped, not all there. "Think...back...a time... even younger...afraid."

I was in water. Fully enveloped. I could see nothing, but I felt the pulsating ripple of the tide. A rhythmic dum-dum, dum-dum, dum-dum. It was outside of me, but it was a part of me. It shook me. It shook everything.

"Innsssi—d—e—ooo—rr—ouut—sss—ide?"

I was in complete darkness. I heard my mother's muffled voice. I felt her hand, separated by something. I could feel her. Then, suddenly, I was terrified. She was terrified. I could feel her. Panicked and small and young and trapped and not yet ready, I could feel everything she was.

Sobriety works in stages. First, there is a period of hopefulness. The goal of getting better is within reach. It's almost tangible, this prospect of a fresh beginning.

After a couple of days, the hopefulness lifts and despair rolls in, thick and cumbersome. It brings a great deal of pain, searing physical pain, as your body plunges into withdrawal, but also emotional agony.

No longer numb like when you were using, you are forced to feel it all, every sense heightened to the point of insanity by your brain's attempts to level up. You want that drink, you want that line, you want that pill, and you'll do anything for it. You'll lie to yourself: *Maybe I don't actually have a problem.* You'll get angry: *This isn't fair. Why do I have to deal with this? It's not my fault. Why can't I just have a drink?* You'll bargain: *This will be the last time. Just one more time. Then I'll stop.* You'll feel sorry for yourself, pitying the lonely creature you've become. You'll ask yourself where all your friends have gone. You'll tell yourself they never liked you: *Why would anyone like you? You're a pathetic excuse for a human being.* You'll do anything to avoid facing yourself, to avoid seeing what has led you here in the first place.

And you'll break.

I got clean so many times I stopped keeping track. At first, I would celebrate the milestones: thirty days, sixty days, ninety days. But I always relapsed. Then I would cycle through it all again. Guilt. Pain. Sobriety. Hope. More pain. Clarity. Relapse. Whenever I decided to sober up, it came at a cost—friendships, relationships, the places you can go, the things that seemed safe. You lose a version of yourself, the version you think people like.

I drank to escape myself. It allowed me a break from my own thoughts; the constant droning of voices telling me I wasn't good enough, the never-ending counting. A break from the extreme swinging of emotional highs and lows that seemed unwarranted. It was the only time I didn't have to be perfect.

I realized that I'd hated myself, but when I drank I hated myself a little less. That version of me was funny, honest, open. People listened when she spoke. They laughed. They wanted her. How could I live with myself if I couldn't be her?

In the weeks that followed, a degree of separation evolved between me and reality. There was a heaviness. My head felt too large to carry. The city was closing in on me.

I spent my days walking the streets. The houses appeared to droop in the humid air, sinking close to the sidewalk, eager to reach equilibrium and rest on my shoulders. Whenever someone spoke to me, it took a few seconds for the sound waves to reach my ears. It took even longer for the words to register. The synapses in my brain were relearning how to fire.

On a sunny Sunday afternoon, I was driving around the city aimlessly, when I found myself in front of a familiar two-storey blue house sitting lonely on a corner. Stopping the car, I climbed out, and allowed my nails to drag along the clapboard as I headed for the front door. I hesitated momentarily before rapping on the glass three times.

A fiftysomething man, short and round, quickly answered the door.

"Hi, I'm Grace," I fumbled. "This is probably very strange and inappropriate, but I have to ask."

The man watched me intently, his hand on the doorknob.

"I used to live here, years ago, with my ex. We lost our baby while we lived here, and I buried one of his toys in the backyard."

His face softened.

"I was wondering if I could have a look. Feel free to say no. I just had to try."

The stranger smiled, the apples of his cheeks plump. "Absolutely. You do what you have to do."

"Thank you so much. You're very kind."

I walked around the outside of the house and into the open backyard. The grass was vividly green and freshly manicured. A barbecue was placed near a table, sheltered by an open violet umbrella and two chairs. The lilac tree was in full bloom, and it smelled heady and beautiful. I knew exactly where the bunny was; we had buried it beneath that very tree.

I knelt, and whispered to the earth.

Grabbing handfuls of grass, I ripped them clean from the ground one after another until I felt the moisture and coldness of dirt. I sank my fingers in and dug with my bare hands. Leaning closer, I dug faster, the dirt jammed under my fingernails as the soiled whiteness of the bunny became visible. Pulling him by the ear from his resting place, I cradled him, rocking him back and forth, loose soil falling into my lap.

Fat, hot tears streamed down my face while my body heaved with great, uneven breaths.

On my knees, I remembered the way I had kneeled on the cold floor with my elbows on my bed, reciting my prayers when I was a little girl. I remembered the way Jack had left me waiting for him, tied up on my knees in our bedroom. I remembered the way silent tears had fallen as I wished my teacher would stop, his hand on the back of my head.

Sobbing and clutching that rabbit, I allowed myself to feel the pain, all that I had repressed, and with it, I felt the possibility of forgiveness.

I arrived at Trevor's office, carrying a wrapped canvas. Peeking my head into the open doorway, I extended the parcel. "I have a present for you."

Trevor was sitting in the armchair in anticipation of my arrival. He raised his eyes and smiled. "That's very thoughtful of you, Grace." He waved me in.

I handed him the gift, watching as he began to peel back the wrapping. The shades of red—mahogany, crimson, brick, currant, candy apple, and garnet—slowly being revealed.

"Wow." He held the painting at a distance, admiring it. "This is one of Jack's, isn't it?"

I nodded.

Trevor stood; placing Jack's painting against the wall, he took down one of his framed degrees and laid it on his desk. "I've been a fan of his work for years."

"Really?"

"Really. I wasn't sure it was the same Jack." Bending, he picked up the painting and hung it on the naked nail. He stepped back, studying the piece, tilting his head slightly in recognition. "Thank you so much."

"You're welcome."

"I also have something for you." He began shuffling through the papers on his desk. He handed me a brown envelope. "Here we go."

Weeks ago, we had requested a copy of my complete medical history. It had finally arrived.

I ripped the seal of the envelope, allowing the pages to slide out.

My mental health records began when I was eighteen years old, when I was referred to Dr. Brace for anxiety and depression.

Quiet, soft-spoken female was scrawled in blue, scratchy handwriting across the top of the sheet. Dr. Brace's first impression of me.

My record contained referrals to psychologists, psychiatrists, social workers, emergency room visits to the mental hospital, and addictions counselling. They labelled me with generalized anxiety disorder, panic disorder, social anxiety disorder, obsessive compulsive disorder, depression, borderline personality disorder, and as an addict.

I scanned the commentary on the documents:

Client is prone to extreme highs and lows.
Intense bouts of anger.
Seductively dressed eighteen-year-old.
Breaks things frequently.
Insomniac.
Unstable.
Frequent visits to the emergency room.
Self-harm.
Suicide intent.
Fearful of self.
No longer a threat to herself or others.

I read each page carefully; twenty-two pages of my past self. I lingered, remembering who she was, what she had done, and seeing, finally, how she had been perceived.

After a long period of silent reading, I lifted my gaze to Trevor.

"How do you feel?" he asked.

I felt as if I were reading about someone else's life. Most of these experiences I could barely remember. I glanced up at the painting, the only colour in the room. "I feel lighter."

Dear Sunshine,

I wanted to write to you one last time to tell you I've changed. In spite of you, thanks to you, I've grown. Without you, without all the sorrow, the joy, the rituals, the silver and gold. Without the secrets, the lies, the silence, and the wrenching heartbreak, I wouldn't be living consciously.

And now I know, I'm not innocent. I'm not a victim of you or of circumstance or chance. I wasn't born into anything I didn't have a responsibility to. I had a choice, and I accept the consequences.

But you know what? I made it, and I'm fine. I guess what I'm trying to say is, I don't blame you anymore.

I know, I'm just as surprised as you.

Love,
G

After the hospital and the medication, after the flashbacks stopped and the darkness didn't visit so often, after the ghosts had finally disappeared, and the stitches came out, I decided I needed to deliver the letters. The letters I had been writing for years.

I packaged them carefully into a brown envelope, stamped them with a red wax seal, and looped the parcel in twine. Clutching the envelope, I stepped out into the summer heat, deciding to take the long route through the park.

Walking the gravel path through the grass, people threw Frisbees back and forth, kicked hacky sacks, and tossed footballs around me. A group had gathered to watch as a man balanced on a slackline fastened between two crooked trees. Others laid nearby in hammocks, lifting their heads only slightly to take small sips from their bottles of beer, liquid spilling lazily on the ground.

My heart fluttered as my eyes landed on Jack sitting in the grass, reading beneath a tree. His hair was shorter, his unmoving curls coiled in place, and he was wearing tortoiseshell glasses. I chewed the inside of my cheeks, examining his white shirt. It was clean, glaringly so, without any paint or charcoal stains. I felt a tug inside me, like my skin was being tightened around my bones.

Jack glanced up from his novel but didn't see me, and as he lowered his gaze, turning the page, his gold wedding ring caught the reflection of the sun. It didn't hurt so bad.

"Heads up," someone called from a distance. I ducked, avoiding a soccer ball to the head. I moved after it, bent and took the ball in my arms, holding it for a second before tossing it back to its owner. The ball landed, and with it, two crows that had been disturbed by the commotion flew off.

I stared as they silently glided into the air, flying in circles, one alongside the other, dancing a sky-bound waltz.

Two for joy.

Continuing on through the park and down the road, I noted the colours of each house that I passed, giving them names—mosaic green, butterscotch yellow, lilac lady purple, gingerbread brown, newborn pink—until I arrived at a small grey bungalow. Scanning the horizon, I watched as the sun's light shimmered and shook through the trees and realized, as I passed the free-standing mailbox labelled *J. Orianna*, I was no longer counting.

I made my way down the narrow pathway. Reaching the house, I stopped to peer inside the curtainless window. The kitchen table was set with Blue Willow china dishes, as though the inhabitants were about to sit and have dinner, but there was no one in the kitchen. There was no smell of food cooking, or sign that the oven was turned on. It resembled one of the museums I had loved to visit as a child—the spaces that weren't meant for living, but merely a display of the past. The ones that felt nothing like home.

I approached the door, touching the brass knocker and rapping it against the wood.

I waited.

The door opened, just wide enough for my mother's slight frame to slip through. Her feet were bare, and I glanced at her naked toenails on the threshold, buckling against the silver as she inched forward.

Lifting my gaze, I met her eyes, the same eyes she had given me, and handed her the letters, without saying a word.

Acknowledgements

Thank you to my family and friends for their love and support as I lived and floundered, working to create this book.

Thank you to the team of remarkable women who stood with me: my editor, Whitney Moran, and my agents, Carolyn Forde and Chelene Knight.

Thank you to Lisa Moore, Joel Thomas Hynes, and Barry Callaghan for their early encouragement of my work, without which I may not have dared to complete this project.

Thank you to the Canada Council for the Arts and the Newfoundland and Labrador Arts Council for funding that contributed to this project.